GORGEOUS

RENALDO CHRISTOPHER

For the *Gorgeous* day ones.

Joshua, Tyler, Nikki, Julie, Kate, Anthony, Larissa, William, Carletta, Michael, Wahlida, Inga, Rashid, Maurice, Alicia, Clifton and Renzo.

GORGEOUS

RENALDO CHRISTOPHER

"And beauty is a form of genius — is higher, indeed, than genius, as it needs no explanation. It is of the great facts of the world, like sunlight, or spring-time, or the reflection in dark waters of that silver shell we call the moon. It cannot be questioned. It has its divine right of sovereignty. It makes princes of those who have it. You smile? Ah! when you have lost it you won't smile..."

OSCAR WILDE

one.

ON HIS SECOND TO last day in San Rafael, Todd Mosley was finally met with proof of his suspension, but the child wouldn't know it as that. All Mateo knew was *La Roca,* who shadowed the seasoned therapists at the clinic, never mentioned any kind of fame. But here Todd was in an ad snatched from a magazine, suspended several feet off the ground as he and another model soared above a net, not reaching for a volleyball but a twenty ounce bottle of neon green water promising hydration and the stamina of a superhero.

Mateo held the page up to Todd with wide, hopeful eyes. "Ese eres tu en la foto?" *Is this you in the photo?*

Mateo had advanced in the six weeks Todd worked with him and now processed and even welcomed the sensation of affectionate touch. He lightly mussed the boy's hair. "Si."

"Por qué estás aquí?"

Todd spoke slowly. "Estoy aquí para . . . ayudarle a sentirse mejor." *I'm here to help you feel better.*

"Eres famoso?"

Todd smiled warmly. "No."

"You should be more confident with your Spanish by now," Mateo observed in the clearest conversational English Todd ever got from him.

Todd chuckled. "You've been hustling me this entire time, huh?"

"You're the hustler, Roca." Mateo squinted his eyes. "I saw

you in another picture, like this."

"I used to take a lot of pictures a long time ago."

Mateo accepted the answer without further interrogation, and when he left with his mother Todd regretted Mateo wouldn't know it was his last day until after he was gone. Mateo would likely have more questions then and it was best Todd wasn't around to answer them. For a child like Mateo, being in magazines didn't square with humble volunteer work. Todd didn't have the language, in Spanish *or* English, to explain the pain associated with those images and why, even today, he was still suspended.

He boarded his flight the next day, tan and bearded, legs covered in hellified mosquito bites. He'd lost some muscle weight since he didn't have the same access to equipment. His hair grew dense, curly and sunkissed. He hadn't shaved his entire time there. He thought he appeared more rugged, even biblical. *Less pretty,* he thought one of the few times he checked his reflection.

La Roca. A cute nickname given by Mateo but picked up by the licensed staff. It followed him for most of his stay. The teasing was innocent and slightly flirtatious across all orientations. His six-foot-three, two hundred and forty-five pound physique with broad shoulders and powerful traps, towered over them. Todd made every effort to be disarming, to put them all—especially the kids—at ease.

There was no such relief for the passengers who flanked his middle seat, where he apologized for existing at his mass. A tight ride for everyone with barely any sleep for Todd. As the plane took off, he regretted apologizing.

TWO MONTHS EARLIER IN a chic Downtown Los Angeles office, Todd was the patient.

"Your guilt over your father's crimes is holding you hostage," Dr. Walker said. "You're a people-pleaser. You shrink yourself so others can feel comfortable. I know I've said this before but—"

"I know. I need to talk to him." Instead of falling back into the cushions and staring at the ceiling, Todd leaned forward, hands clasped. "What could he have to say to me? Why should I bother?"

Dr. Walker crossed her legs at the ankle. "I'm not saying he's responsible for what happened to you, but our parents can pass things onto us we don't understand, things we don't realize came from them. Something in your relationship with him changed once you became an adult and you tried to replace it with—"

"Don't say his name—"

"Other men. You need to find out what changed or you'll be in this state of suspension for the rest of your life."

"I can't just sit across from him and talk about my feelings while he's serving a sentence," Todd explained. "He's a street dude. And I'm grown now. It was different when I was small."

"Listen, Todd, I don't want to keep saying the same thing while collecting a check. That's not fair to you. You've been coming regularly and, while that makes me proud, the point of this is to progress."

"And you need to see other people."

She casually leaned back. "I am in demand and you're nice to look at but, professionally, I need to know this is working. You last visited him ten years ago, after your mother passed. He was indifferent then. Maybe he was in pain and didn't want to break down in front of you. But that was a long time ago. How do you know he hasn't changed?"

"I guess I don't."

"Look him in the eye. Tell him what happened to you."

Todd sat at his laptop an hour later, ready to book a flight to Washington, DC until a familiar dread returned. The man who adored Todd when he was little completely turned once Todd became an adult. *Indifference* barely scratched the surface.

Todd decided to procrastinate, but what was procrastination without a purpose?

THE FIRST TIME TODD mentioned Dr. Walker's suggestion to return to DC, William Kendall shrugged it off. "You're always welcome to stay with me if you ever come home, but you don't wanna go to that prison again, do you?" Todd dropped it and proceeded with therapy until the doctor's advice sank in.

William answered the call as Todd settled into the back of an Uber. "You've been threatening to come to DC for months and then I didn't hear from you. What changed?"

"I stopped off in Costa Rica for six weeks, volunteered in a clinic. I just landed at Dulles."

"*Stopped off* in Costa Rica on the way to *DC?* You make it sound like a day trip to Philly."

"Does your concierge still have a key for me?"

"It's been sitting down there forever, but I was expecting you a lot sooner."

"So what you're saying is, the invitation didn't expire?"

William sighed. "You're my only open door policy. Have you eaten?"

"Yes but we both know that barely means anything."

"I have reservations and you're free to join. How are you dressed right now?"

"Sandals and cargo shorts."

"Jesus, and you probably smell like the plane. How many bags you got?"

"One roller and a backpack. If it's too fancy I can—"

"I'll send you the address."

"Perfect."

"So Costa Rica, huh? What brought that on?"

"I can't wait to see you so we can catch up."

An hour later found Todd at Prime, a cigar bar and steakhouse along the U Street corridor. Masculine and modern, rich mahogany shelves lined with expensive bottles, a bluesy soundtrack—the kind of place where William Kendall could easily blow a few hundred on himself in one evening. Even with the traffic, Todd managed to beat him and rolled his bags to the bar, settling two stools down from another solo guest.

He was medium height, lean and brown with a thick beard, his hair faded on the sides with a curved part. Dapper in brown glen plaid suit pants, an open matching vest and a crisp white shirt. A camera and an English driver's cap weren't far from his drink. He offered a brief nod with warm, friendly eyes.

Todd's mouth went dry but he supposed it was only right he introduced himself. "Are you here for William?"

"I am." The guy leaned in, offered his hand and smiled. "I'm Linc, man."

They shook. "Todd."

Linc's eyes fell to the bag. And the sandals. "What brings you to DC?"

"That obvious, huh?"

"I don't wanna say you don't look like you're from here," Linc grinned. His voice was clear with a grimy street cadence in spite of his refined appearance. Todd found it immediately sexy.

"If you did you'd be wrong. I'm a native."

"Oh, a native!" Linc laughed. He waved the bartender over and ordered two ryes on a big rock before taking the stool next to Todd. "So where are you now?"

"LA but I've been out of the country."

"That's dope." Linc regarded him for a bit. "Have I seen you somewhere before?"

Todd's pictures still circulated the Internet one way or another, often divorced from their original context, fronted on fake dating profiles and unauthorized, spammy advertisements. People recognized him for any number of reasons and today was no different, in spite of having not shaved in weeks. "You probably have." His eyes drifted to Linc's camera. *He's a photographer. He's observant. And hot.* He breathed him in. *Some woody notes, caramel, amber.* "I might have some pictures floating around."

"So you're a model? Underwear?"

Todd laughed louder than he intended. "Yes, and protein bars and sports drinks and training gear. It was a brief time in my life and it's over." His drink arrived and Todd gulped down half of it. Alcohol always made it easier. He knew where this was going and wanted Linc to stop asking questions, but didn't necessarily want to stop talking to him.

"Maybe on the next one we can toast," Linc said.

"I'm sorry, I really needed this. Thank you."

"All good. No judgment." Linc took a sip. "How long have you known William?"

"About ten years."

"Funny."

"Oh?"

"Ten years? He never mentioned you."

two.

Before Todd could respond, William Kendall arrived, tall and tailored. His platinum Patek Philippe watch glistened prominently when he reached out to hug Todd. "How was your flight?"

"First leg was kind of tight. Otherwise, uneventful."

William offered a knowing grin. "I see you've met Linc." He wasn't alone. "Todd, this is Julian." Julian, if Todd had to guess, was no more than five-foot-six. Shaved head, dimples, muscles like boulders. They shook hands and the four of them were escorted to their table.

Over the next hour, Todd learned Julian Keys was a personal trainer and in the past month opened Definitions, a sprawling gym Downtown. It was state of the art with plenty of buzz, DC's success story of the moment. The energy between Julian and Linc was chilly. Anytime Julian cracked a joke Linc shot Todd a look to see if he bought it. Todd figured Julian to be shallow but harmless.

"Where do you train?" Julian asked between bites of New York strip.

"Me? I don't like commercial gyms. I mostly train at home," Todd told him. "I built a power rack for the garage."

"You're a big dude. How much weight can it take?"

"About four hundred, maybe more."

"And you built it with *wood?*"

"Not unheard of."

"You certified?"

"Yes."

"You should come work for me."

William cut in. "Julian, knock it off. He's visiting. He has business to take care of."

"What kind of business?"

"Family stuff," Todd answered before William had the chance. "I can check it out, though. It sounds great." His eyes caught Linc's for a moment and he distracted himself with his food. He didn't feel like eating but knew he needed to get it down. He regretted not going straight to William's condo. William's hand brushed against Todd's back.

"You should be in magazines," Julian went on, leaning in. "Oh shit, you *have* been. I *knew* I recognized you! How long you plan on being here? A week? A month?"

"I'm not sure yet—"

"My man, I *need* you to do an ad for Definitions."

Todd managed a smile. "I don't do that anymore."

"What? Take pictures? Why?"

"Julian—" William began through clenched teeth.

"You must be rejecting dudes left and right—"

William again: *"Julian."*

"—and I *know* they get mad and claim we're all shallow 'cause they get rejected by people who look like you, 'cause they sure as shit ain't hittin' up average dudes, am I right?"

"Todd's had a long flight," William said. "He's tired. He probably hasn't slept in a comfortable bed in weeks—"

"My bed was quite comfortable," Todd interjected before Julian went on.

"Sean tried to rope me into a conversation the other day. 'If I was less attractive, would you be with me?'"

"If he had any *melanin* would you be with him?" Linc asked with slits for eyes. He hadn't spoken a word to Julian directly all night, even though they sat right next to each other.

Julian continued without a flinch. "And then I was like, why are you even worried about this? He keeps starting arguments with me, but this time it was about *how the community is so shallow.*" Julian rolled his eyes. "First of all, he's in a relationship so why does he care about single people's problems? Secondly, he's on TV. He looks like a GQ cover hisdamnself so he ain't exactly helping."

"What did you tell him?" William asked. "If he was less attractive, if he wasn't Sean Lively of *Live With Lively* and didn't have perfect teeth, hair and could make a backup on 295 sound like sex, would you even be there?"

Julian scoffed. "Of *course* not, but that doesn't make me shallow."

William took a sip of his Macallan. "Not that alone."

"I can't be the only one at this table with standards. We're all self-made, reasonably attractive and we *own* shit. Why should I worry about somebody getting in their feelings because *I* know what I want and have the means to get it? It's not my job to give everybody a chance. Do you want someone who wants you back or someone who feels sorry for you?"

Todd considered his own lack of personal achievement at the table. Perhaps Julian, in his own superficial way, believed appearing in a national campaign for a sugary sports drink was about even with owning a gym or an interior design firm.

"Your standards are a little different from mine," Linc remarked, clinking glasses with William.

Julian responded without facing him. "Now if anyone's shallow, it's *you.*"

Linc chuckled. "You don't know me, dude."

"You have never slept with someone who doesn't look like a model. Stop playing."

"And again, you don't know *me,* dude."

Julian waved him off. "Take that bass out of your voice—"

"Oh, you about to show me how they do it in Brooklyn Heights, with your free ride to Howard and two-parent household? I'm shaking."

Julian's body tensed, veins popping from his neck. He took a breath and a sip of his drink. Linc was cool about the matter.

Todd was happy the attention had shifted away from him.

William, seizing the opportunity to change the subject, went on about his biggest project of the year and being profiled for a magazine and trying to win a Designer's Choice award or at least landing on Architectural Digest's AD100 List next year. Julian hung on his every word, chiming in as a fellow business owner. Linc was encouraging, and would occasionally glance at Todd, becoming more comfortable as the night wore on and those glances became sweet smiles.

Todd had never been so sure of an attraction. He knew men like Linc existed, even in LA, but rarely had he come across them via his own circle. Classic, erudite and confident, raised on Gil Scott-Heron, the Native Tongue collective and vintage Black fashion lookbooks. Todd figured it was all carefully crafted personal imaging that allowed Linc to breeze through social events with his camera to grab or influence the perfect shot but still sincere, effortless.

William's eyes drifted towards the ceiling. "You hear that? It's so obnoxious." Nancy Wilson had given way to Sarah Vaughan in the dining room but a distinct EDM bassline throbbed upstairs. "Why does every goddamn establishment in DC have to turn into *that?*"

"You sound old and cranky," Julian quipped. "They need to make money like everyone else."

"They have a great menu, atmosphere and the best whiskey selection in DC. They've gotten greedy."

Although Todd and William were on separate coasts for most of their friendship, Todd came to view William as a man of pragmatism and sophistication. William maintained a practiced, detail-oriented elegance that appreciated fine, conventionally masculine things—the sweetness of a fresh cigar, the smoky aroma of a good scotch, the calm of his favorite, dimly lit steakhouse—all of which he believed were under direct threat by shrill, millennial turn-ups.

"Part of living here is dealing with a confluence of cultures and competing rhythms in the smallest spaces," Linc offered.

"It's hit or miss, but in this case I can barely hear it."

William checked his watch. "It's time to get out of here anyway." He gestured for the server. "I'm tired. You have a gig—"

"I think we should go up and check it out," Julian said. "We don't need to be up there all night."

"You don't wanna go home?" William asked.

The implication of William's tone stunned Julilan only for a second. "I wanna hear some music. I haven't been out in ages. I just want a *hint* of a party. Is anything wrong with that?"

William slid his black American Express card into the bill slip and handed it over, not bothering to check the total. "Whatever."

"What are you doing?" Linc demanded.

"Paying the bill."

"This was your treat?"

"Is this going to be a problem?"

"The rest of us got money, man."

"I appreciate it, William," Julian cut in.

"Every single time," Linc mumbled. William either didn't hear or simply ignored him. There was no animus once he pocketed his card or when they hugged.

Linc invited William and Todd to join him at his gig. A friend was singing at a spot down the street. They both declined and Linc made himself scarce. Julian reminded Todd he'd promised to come check out the gym and expected him this week, then disappeared upstairs.

Todd slung his backpack over his shoulder and William took the roller bag on the way out. It was mild, mid-sixties and without a hint of the oppressive humidity the city would see come spring's end. As they walked up Eighteenth towards William's parked BMW 7 Series Sedan, Todd considered the six sexless weeks he spent in San Rafael. If there were any opportunities to hook up with someone he was completely blind to them. It simply wasn't at the front of his mind. Now his body was alive with the prospect and he mildly regretted not following Linc to his gig.

THE QUIET OF WILLIAM'S zinc and glass condo overlooking Rock Creek Park.

It was spotless, expansive and photo-ready. Todd was afraid to put his bag down but dropped it anyway and fell into a plush white sofa. He was full of booze, prime rib and breathless anticipation for his next encounter with Linc. William went to the back, gathering amenities and preparing the guest room for Todd's visit. "You don't have to do any of this," Todd called out to him.

"You're right, I don't. Especially since you've known for at least six weeks you'd be in DC and didn't bother telling me."

Todd relaxed into the cool, buttery softness of the sofa. "I'm ready to move past that whenever you are."

"I won't let you forget it." William emerged in a pair of gray Puma lounge pants and a white tank top. His skin was deep brown and flawless, his muscles lean and defined, not carved merely from chocolate but what chocolate must have envied. He sat next to Todd. "You're going down to Petersburg to see Anthony?"

"Eventually," Todd told him. "That's definitely the plan but now that I'm here . . . maybe I can enjoy it?"

"I think that's a good idea. Stay as long as you want. You might wanna take Julian up on his offer so you aren't bored out of your mind."

"Coaching at his gym? No. I don't think I'll be here *that* long."

William shrugged. "You never know."

"I forced myself to engage and be personable when I was in San Rafael. But training in a gym, especially here, is a different thing altogether." *And there are mirrors everywhere.* "When I was down there I could be no one, well, for the most part." Todd briefly explained what happened with Mateo. "That would be happening to me every five minutes here. I can't handle the attention. Not yet."

"It will be tough wherever you go," William reminded him. "You've heard it often enough. You know how you look." He pinched Todd's hair. "This is new, though."

"You like?"

"I left a pair of clippers on your bed."

Todd laughed, then, "I appreciate this. I'm sorry for the lack of notice. But I needed to be here. DC is my home."

"Whatever you need, let me know. In fact, we can hit the organic market tomorrow and stock up on whatever you eat and, considering your current physique, that's gonna cost a smooth three hundred dollars—"

"I can buy my own food, William. I'm not a child. I was barely a child when you met me ..." Ten years ago in a bar still standing in spite of the city's many changes. Todd was eighteen then, able to finagle his way in due to his height and good looks, William thirty. He taught Todd how to shoot pool and guided Todd through a period he never thought he'd emerge from with any clarity. He was an older brother, a mentor, a solid, unshakeable male presence. "All I need is a bed," Todd told him. "And I promise, I won't overstay."

William stood and held out his arms, and when Todd followed he squeezed him tight. "I want you to be okay. I mean it." He pulled away, searching Todd's face to make sure it registered. Todd was physically strong and striking, but often shy and anxious, especially in groups. He had his reasons.

Now Todd was exhausted. He grabbed his bags and William led him to the guest room. After an indulgent shower he considered finally shaving, but he was much too tired and terrified of what he would see when he faced himself in the mirror.

three.

Gerel Lincoln realized long ago he indulged too much in male beauty. It was constant and distracting, fatal when it came to maintaining relationships and the source of nebulous gossip. His reputation was as much a part of his brand as the Nikon D800 hanging from his neck or the nickname he gave himself—Linc.

In a basement lounge seven blocks from Prime, his reputation likely inspired the song being covered on stage—"Who Is He (And What Is He To You)?" The singer was Melvin Blount, who channeled D'Angelo, Marvin Gaye and Prince most times. He sang about love and pain and sex and was playfully sexual. When he wasn't on a stool strumming his guitar as he did now, he swayed slender hips to the beat or hit a light body roll.

He left the stage amid applause, cheers and at least one marriage proposal. Linc met him at the end of the bar, blocking the potential for additional company. Mel ordered a drink and leaned back as Linc flipped the camera and previewed the images for him. They were tight in their little corner, accustomed to each other's heat.

Mel was satisfied with the photos. Linc's angles cast him as more powerful than his limited fame within their circle and the U Street scene would indicate. Mel's big, bushy hair was pulled back in a wild puff and appeared as a crown in the images, set against a misty light so it had an ethereal effect. Just over six feet and lanky with long, intricately tattooed arms. His thick wayfarers did nothing to temper his sex appeal since his eyes were mischievous and he had the carefree swagger of a rocker. In photographs shot by Linc, he appeared legendary.

Mel reached into his pocket, withdrawing a few hundreds. He jammed them into Linc's hand.

"What's this?"

"For doing your job tonight. And I owe you for weed."

"I don't want this," Linc told him. "You know I would've come regardless." He placed the bills on the bar defiantly.

Mel chuckled, swirling the brown liquid in his glass. "I'm glad you're here, but it's because you're the best at what you do. That's the *only* reason."

Linc leaned in, his lips at Mel's ear. Mel was amused with the proximity, a closeness to which Linc felt entitled. "Is this how you're punishing me now?"

"Why do you think you're being punished?"

Linc was incredulous. "Don't play. You know I'm trying to fix this. I'm doing everything you asked me to do—"

"All I asked you to do is take pictures. That's all I need you for."

Linc stuffed the bills into his pocket.

"You plan on backing up anytime soon?" Mel asked him with a slight grin. "We don't want people thinking we're together."

"We haven't told anyone that. I miss you. And I'm sorry—"

"I accepted your apology the last twenty times, Gerel." Mel placed his hands on Linc's shoulders, which probably didn't help matters. "You're free now. You can fuck whoever you want—"

"I never promised you monogamy."

"You're right. You didn't. I'm willing to take the L. But that's not exactly what this is about. This is about how you become *infatuated* with other people, long enough to get a nut and for them to fall for you. A side nigga or two wouldn't have bothered me as much if you didn't treat them like they mattered."

Mel's voice alternated between stern and playful. *Keep*

groveling, you will never have me again. He dangled the prospect of a reconciliation just out of reach, not with his words but his manner. No matter how close Linc got, Mel never exactly pushed him away.

Mel's jeans were snug and Linc was inebriated from the drinks at Prime. Liquor didn't impede his ability to get a perfect shot but it made him more persistent. He took Mel's hand, tenderly brushing his palm with his fingertips. "I don't understand how you're able to let go this easily. You know I can't see past you."

"You saw past me many times but I should've known what I was getting into." Mel said this softly, not as a lecture but it was unmistakably condescending. "I don't need you to change. I don't need you to do anything, In fact, I won't ask you to shoot any more shows. I seem to be confusing you."

This was how Mel defended himself, through humor and spite. Once sensitive and naive, heartbreak after heartbreak hardened him. But Linc always won him back, seducing him with tender declarations and the comforting promise of the best sex Mel would ever have. Mel fell for it and coped by becoming withdrawn and brooding. His music consumed him and he wrote his best material. People then referred to him as "emo" so he corrected course by dumping Linc for the final time and developing an impenetrable sarcastic grin.

Mel once wondered why Linc fought to keep him. He didn't believe he was as beautiful as the men who found themselves in front of Linc's camera and eventually in his bed. He soon came to understand Linc genuinely loved him—his creativity, his exuberance, his wicked intellect. They got high and talked about classic soul music and fucked all night. They had a pattern and a language Linc found hard to shake.

"I'm not confused," Linc told him. "But I know you're fucking with me. Maybe I deserve it."

"Like you said, you never promised me monogamy."

"I promised to love you the way you needed to be loved and then I didn't. You were also young; you weren't ready to be with someone like me. And I kept pulling you back in. That's why I'm sorry."

Mel relaxed a bit. "Are you gonna stop trying to pull me back in, now?"

"I guess I have no choice, right?" Linc backed up, raising both hands in defeat. He soon disappeared into the crowd and Mel exhaled, relieved he didn't allow his resolve to crumble but disappointed in how dangerously close he'd come.

four.

Julian struggled with the keys to his Petworth home. His boxer, Romulus, whined and scratched against the other side of the door in anticipation. "Okay, boy, I need a minute," he called to him. "Daddy's a little fucked up right now!" The keys slipped from his hand. "Fuck."

For Julian, the seconds were hours as he stood on his porch, staring at his keys on the concrete before Sean opened the door, holding Romulus back by his collar. "What are you doing?"

"I'm getting my keys." Julian pointed. "They fell."

Sean grabbed the keys and guided Julian to the sofa where he drunkenly played with the dog. "The keys have been falling for some time now. Did you have fun?"

"I don't know. What's fun these days?"

"I guess it depends on how much whiskey you can pound in a single night."

"We hit up Prime. William has a friend in town. Brad. No, *Chad.* I think his name is Todd. Four letters. He was a model but he's also licensed which means he can come work for me. And they left and I went up to the roof to listen to some music for a little bit."

"Yeah, it's pretty late." Sean calmly went to the kitchen.

"I know. Why are you wearing shoes inside?"

Sean returned with a bottled water and handed it to him. "You need to be sober for this."

"Or I can pass out and we'll address it—whatever *it* is—in

the a.m. But I might have an idea. It's the 'What are we?' conversation. Am I close?"

Sean chuckled. "More than sex, less than love. Private, but not entirely a secret. Just having fun, but for the last *thirteen months*. It's clear what *I* am—a live-in date. Or a dog walker."

"Okay..."

"I have a career where I have to be extremely clear in how I communicate. I can't be vague when I send a message, i.e., if you were staying with me in *my* home, instead of staying out all night to avoid you, I would just ask you to leave."

Julian noticed two duffle bags at the bottom of the staircase.

Sean sat across from him, more relaxed than Julian was used to. Sean didn't pivot to his news voice but was just as composed. Trimmed blond hair, strong chin, a smile as winning as it was damning. A sentient Ken Doll. "I thought I would ask why you gave up but you were never really in this with me. I've always been more invested in this, in *you*. The more I think about it, I'm not sure why."

"Two words: *Muscle worship.*" Julian swigged his water. If Sean wanted direct communication, he'd get it tonight.

"That was fun, but it turns out muscle worship does not a relationship make. At least you played the part in the beginning."

"Did I?"

"Whenever I wanted to talk about anything that mattered to me? You sure did. It was nice to be fooled, but I guess that's what we do."

"We?"

That damning smile again. "Now, Julian, you know exactly who I mean."

Julian nodded, snapped his fingers. "Right. Shallow gays."

"Easily distracted, biding our time and wasting someone else's until a better option comes along."

"And who would've thought Sean Lively of *Live With Lively* wasn't the best option?"

"It's good to finally hear you say it."

Julian rubbed the space between his eyes. "I'm not gonna let you do this."

"I'm definitely leaving."

"Oh, you can leave, but I'm not buying this spin. You've been picking fights all this time, finding things to complain about—things that weren't a problem until you realized all of your friends are married now. That's what this is about. But keep telling yourself *clarity* is your core principle."

"And with that, he's sober."

Julian realized this would be a marathon. He rose, swayed a little, and went for another water. Romulus followed. "So I'm vain," he declared from across the house. "I've heard it multiple times. I'm in the business of vanity. I'm what's wrong with the community, *etcetera, etcetera.* I'm so tired of this complaint. This is what you all want. You want us to have money and education and a fitness routine. You want us to go on a vacation at the drop of a dime, because money makes that easier. We need to be able to navigate different rooms, be easily consumable. *Perfect.* You're on TV. Your job is to be fake. You're a bigger example of what's wrong with this culture than I am."

"You're far from burdened," Sean told him. "You were raised by two doctors—scratch that—by two doctors who employed help. Free ride to Howard, engineering program. Lexus, freshman year. Investment capital from your father for a luxury gym with a minimum two hundred dollar monthly membership."

"I can't tell you how much I love being lectured for not being poor."

Sean rose as Julian reappeared with another bottle. "The lecture is because you pretend it's otherwise. You put up this front like you're . . ."

"From the hood?"

"Certainly not a Huxtable."

"Now we're getting to the root of it."

"Same trajectory, right? Pampered and privileged, but let me attend an HBCU to find myself—"

"Be very careful what you say next, Dartmouth."

"Julian, you're smart but you choose not to be. You can have a conversation that isn't about training splits and meal plans—"

"I know it doesn't matter as much as reporting the news, but those things matter to *me*. I'm a business owner and the healthiest person you know."

"And you act like a child."

"You're giving me a headache."

"Take an aspirin."

Julian didn't respond immediately. He didn't want it to escalate. It was already ugly and could get uglier if he gave into haste, if he didn't breathe properly when addressing the reasons for his rage. He considered what he could say out loud, then wondered why he put himself in a position to choose his words carefully in his own home. "I can't shake the feeling you're trying to humble me. And before you say what I think you're gonna say, *I know what it looks like.* I know how it *sounds*. People have been trying to humble me my entire life. It's the reason they bring up my lack of struggle as an insult. It's why I get nitpicked by men who look just like me, because we didn't always have the same experiences. And I get that. But it lands differently when it comes from men who look like you, who have more privileges than I ever will. Everyone thinks I need permission to be fly, to not be a below average motherfucker because that's the only way they can be comfortable around me. I'm here to tell you right now—fuck your comfort." Julian kicked off his shoes and rejoined Romulus on the sofa. "I'm sorry for being a bad boyfriend, but that's all you're getting out of me. If you want someone who got dirt under his nails, there's the door."

Sean reached into his pocket, detached the house key from its ring and placed it on a nearby end table. Romulus stirred as he grabbed his bags, leapt from the sofa and raced to paw him. "You don't ever have to be humble, Julian. For your own sake, you should start being honest with yourself. You're thirty-four now."

"And a *fine* thirty-four at that."

"The next six years will go by fast. If you want to be a forty-year-old baby, that's your choice, but don't expect someone else to be by your side when you get there."

five.

"IT ALWAYS AMAZES ME who America decides to canonize," Todd mused before an image of a doe-eyed, waifish model emerging from a pile of gummy worms. Todd, who had modeled for more utilitarian purposes, couldn't grasp the artistic concepts governing fashion, even as he explored the stark white Special Exhibitions hall in designer jeans the average American could not afford. Fashion as culture was a curiosity to him. "It's a beautiful photo, I guess they all are. But I don't get it."

"At the time a lot of this stuff would be considered groundbreaking," William offered. "There was no Instagram in the sixties, no Kardashian-Jenners. And any white man with a camera could qualify as a genius. But as an artist myself, I have to say it's well-composed." William wondered if he assumed the right posture then, if the promise he made to himself to shake off work for the next couple of months was palpable, even if it led to more networking at an after-hours retrospective for a long dead fashion photographer at the Portrait Gallery. He bought the tickets months ago at seventy-five apiece and promptly forgot about it until his assistant James reminded him. William opted to use them with Todd instead. "Linc might be better equipped to offer some perspective," he added.

"Linc's here?" Todd asked.

"He's working, taking pictures for a local blog. He's always at events like this."

"I didn't see him out there."

"I'm sure we'll bump into him eventually."

"Why didn't you say something earlier?"

"Why do you care?"

"It's strange you wouldn't mention it."

A flat chuckle. "You have *got* to be kidding me." William was prepared to nip this in the bud right away. He knew too much about Linc's proclivities and Todd had not completely recovered from his experiences in LA.

Todd cut his eyes at him and moved down the hall to a mounted flat screen playing a 1977 Barbara Walters interview with the photographer. The volume was low and Todd could barely hear it over the dj set bleeding into the hall, so he leaned in. William took his arm, pulling him away. "It's a bad idea."

"You didn't give me a chance to tell you what I think of him."

"I already know. I've seen people react to him. He's disarming. He engages you. He figures out the one thing that defines who you are, the most important thing in the world to you, and connects to it. It's magic." Todd tried to pull away but William held tight, his voice steady and low, seasoned with a hint of admiration for Linc and concern for Todd. "It's part of what he does. He's a photographer. People take off their clothes for him. They fall in love with him. He's fun and nice and has beautiful brown eyes but everyone he's ever been into has been temporary. All but one."

"And that's your friend?" Todd demanded. "Does he know what you think of him?"

"I'm not saying anything about Linc he wouldn't tell you himself, if asked."

Todd gulped his drink. "Well then maybe I should ask him."

William let him go. "I won't stop you. I'm just thinking of what you've been through. You didn't come here for this."

Todd gave him a final look and started for the courtyard. William went after him, delayed by ten minutes so he could lose him. He wanted Todd to get over his anxieties. He wanted him to meet and enjoy new people. He wanted him to be happy and satisfied for once. But he also wanted Linc to be on his best behavior.

Powered by brown liquor, Todd attempted to relax into the stylish crowd inside Kogod Courtyard. It was after nine and the night was clear and black against the glass canopy overhead. Strobes of pink, green and blue pulsated against the walls of the museum complex, casting the party in kaleidoscopic light as everyone chatted, danced and snapped photos for social media. The crowd had not yet peaked so it wasn't too dense, but the courtyard was so expansive Linc wasn't easy to find on Todd's initial survey. He eventually caught him chatting up a vendor, English driver's cap in place, pale denim shirt with sleeves rolled to his elbows, tucked into vintage jeans. His camera dangled from his neck and he was smiling and nodding, working his magic. Todd absently bit his lip, placing his now empty glass on a nearby surface.

Linc's eyes caught his and he smiled. Todd took one step before crashing into a girl carrying a tray of bourbon shots. They splashed against his white button-down before hitting the pavement. Todd stumbled back slightly, not from the impact but from the memory triggered by the sound of the shot glasses, which managed not to shatter.

The girl, who wasn't a server as much as a promoter for the bourbon brand, quickly apologized, but they both knew it was Todd's fault. Once he realized what happened, he bent down to gather the glasses and place them on her tray. "I'll pay for every last one," he offered, visibly chagrined.

She laughed. "They're free. No worries."

"There must be something I can do. I feel awful. I'm so, *so* sorry."

"It's okay, really," she assured him.

"I wasn't paying attention and I—"

"Relax." She was firm this time but worried. "But if I were

you, I'd ditch the shirt." She winked and was off.

He was still crouched on the ground with his hand to his chest, frozen by a two-year-old experience. He could nearly feel shards of glass piercing his face and arms. A hand was suddenly against his back, "Hey, buddy, are you okay?" Todd nodded and the hand disappeared. He took a few deep breaths to lessen the pounding in his chest and stood. With his heart rate back to normal he realized how soaked his shirt was. The only option was to take it off and tuck it in his jeans like a tail, which meant exposing more of himself than he intended tonight. The tank top underneath saved him from being completely indecent.

"Somehow I feel like this is my fault," Linc said, appearing before him. He had the same twinkle in his eye from a week ago.

Todd laughed nervously. "I guess I need to mind my surroundings."

A few passersby marvel at Todd's physique. His chest nearly stretched the cotton of his tank top threadbare. He'd finally hit the barber and his head was shaved close, not quite bald, and his beard neatly lined. "They probably think you're here to work," Linc told him. "A model on duty. A piece of living art. I know you said you quit, but I'm putting together a book and you'd be perfect for it."

"What's it about?"

"Black male beauty."

"And that's it? Eye candy?"

"It's definitely eye candy, on the surface. But not exploitative. Nothing worse than what you've done already." Linc leaned in. "I wouldn't have you posing in your underwear, it's not that kind of book."

"But maybe a tasteful palm leaf?" Todd quipped.

Linc chuckled. "We'll see. If you decide to do it, that is."

Todd considered it. He hadn't taken a professional photo since The Incident but Linc seemed perfectly capable of swaying him. "I'll have to take a look at your work."

"I'll tell you where to find it. But when in doubt, there's Instagram." He whipped out his phone and pulled up his profile, quickly thumbing through the gallery of street style and little-known landmarks. "Most of my work captures the character and texture of DC. As much as it can, considering all the changes."

"How long have you lived here?"

"Most of my life, and I've seen it through every stage."

Todd folded his arms across his chest, trying to relax with Linc although so many eyes were on him. "So how do you feel about this party? This exhibit?"

Linc shrugged. "They all blur together after a while, but I appreciate the culture. You need another drink?"

"I need another shirt."

"You look fine."

"I feel obnoxious, like I'm showboating or something, and that's not who I am."

"I can tell. It's fascinating, though. You've modeled but it's almost like you're a little shy."

"Modeling was never something I wanted to do. Long story."

"So being in front of a camera, being gawked at and objectified, isn't your thing? There's not even a hint of narcissism there?"

Todd laughed again, averting his eyes. "I've never demanded attention. It just shows up whether I like it or not. And it also doesn't help that I'm an enormous klutz."

"Clark Kent. Built like a superhero, but kind and humble. I'm sorry, sometimes I get ahead of myself, thinking I have people all figured out. You might be an asshole."

"I might be."

"But I'm rarely wrong. I'm actually still trying to figure William out, though. Look at him." Todd followed his gaze to spot William chatting at the bar. "He's polished, disciplined and always prepared. I've never seen him sweat. You only get like that once you complete basic training and I know he didn't serve. I'm thinking he's gone through some shit."

"He's your friend; aren't you close? Wouldn't you know?"

"I haven't known him *that* long. We hang out. We drink. We

bump into each other at events like this. But do I know his secrets? No."

"He seems to know a lot about you."

Linc winked. "I don't *have* any secrets."

WILLIAM FIRST MET TRAVIS DeWitt at an event not unlike this one, a trendy, artsy party near Dupont Circle four years earlier. William accompanied a female client who had intentions other than platonic socializing. When she realized William wasn't into women, they had a good laugh, and for the rest of the evening she proudly introduced him as the genius designer behind her salon and spa. After a while, William stepped out onto the balcony for a breath of fresh air, only to find Travis smoking. Aside from the occasional cigar, William was a former smoker and was visibly irritated at this. Travis, who was halfway drunk, pounced on him. "If it's a problem, you can go back inside."

William thought better than to match his tone. He was thirty-six then and guessed Travis was roughly ten years younger. William wasn't interested in a pissing match so he offered a tight smile and started back in. Travis reached for him and apologized, explaining his shitty mood had everything to do with a date standing him up. He promptly stomped out his cigarette, they chatted and William took him home.

They tried to date, but over five months William proved to be too into his work, too ambitious. He was always looking for the next client, for opportunities to increase The Kendall Design Group's profile in the region. Travis claimed to understand, but it yielded way too many arguments. He eventually phased himself out. Linc referred to them as "carcasses," men who quickly fooled themselves into thinking they would ever be as important as William's career, only to be cast aside after being picked over and used for their meat.

Presently, Travis waited on his drink order. Four years ago

Travis was thinner and rocked a fauxhawk. He was also trendy to a fault, often spending money on clothes he'd have no use for months later. He'd put on a little weight and his face was fuller now, shoulders broader. He'd let his hair grow evenly and it was thick and curly. He was completely oblivious to William.

"Travis?"

He turned to him and offered a once-over behind light, stylish frames. "The dead has arisen."

William laughed. "Do I deserve that?"

"I didn't peg you for the *where-my-hug-at* type."

"Can I have one anyway?"

Travis relented and William pulled him in, holding onto him a bit longer than he intended. "It's good to see you," William told him. "I mean it. You look great."

Travis took a sip of his drink. "And you look exactly the same, which is a good thing. You found something that works and stuck to it. I didn't mean that in a shady way at all. The word I'm looking for is 'timeless'."

"Appreciated. What are you drinking?"

"Macallan. The one thing I took away from our brief, harrowing time together was your exquisite taste in spirits. And *To Sir, with Love.*"

"I'll have one too." William gestured to the bartender. Then, to Travis, "It's been a while."

"Are we gonna do this thing where we pretend to have some fondness for each other and try to reconnect and go on a few dates but with totally modified expectations?"

That mouth again. Travis was snarky, sarcastic and often correct. There was a charm to it now, not as much insecurity behind it. "I couldn't not say hi," William told him. "And I'm genuinely interested in what you've been up to, what's changed. Etcetera."

"You are so fucking smooth, William. For one, I quit smoking and started to get fat so I panicked and got a gym membership. I was promoted to Assistant Sales Manager at my hotel so I'm making grown-up money now. I was briefly in a relationship but

I'm single again. What about you?"

"I decided to slow down and back away from work a little, invest in my personal life more."

Travis gasped. "You? Surely you're joshing me!"

"I'm here strictly in a social capacity. I left the business cards at home and everything."

"Who cares about a business card? You can still exchange numbers if you find the right potential client here."

"No one here is gonna be any client of mine. These millennials can't afford me."

Travis rolled his eyes. "Here you go."

"I mean, maybe *you* can, since you're making grown-up money now." William gave Travis's hand a playful squeeze.

"What are you doing?" Travis asked him, his smile fading.

"We're just talking."

"Don't bullshit me. Tell me right now what it is you want."

"If you're asking if I'm trying to take you home with me tonight, the answer is no. But maybe you were right the first time. Maybe I am trying to reconnect and go on a few dates with modified expectations. What's wrong with that?"

"How do I know you've changed? I just got out of a relationship and I'm in no rush to get back into one, but I'm not trying to waste my time either. And we both know what you do to me, William. If you asked me to come home with you tonight I'd probably say yes."

William pulled him away from the bar and to a marble bench outlining a patch of ficus and olive trees. "Every couple of weeks I drop by my mother's house with a bag of groceries. I bring her some gifts, things I know she needs but never asks for. I make sure her bills are paid and that she wants for nothing since she worked hard to provide for me. Each time I'm there she asks me why I haven't found somebody. She gets in my ass about my car and my condo and why I don't have anyone to share it with. 'You're almost forty-one, William. You need to go on a date, William. I don't care if it's with a man or a woman or a goddamn chinchilla, William.' That's what she says to me, like

I'm her spinster daughter who can't find a man. Let me take you out. Let me make up for how I screwed up back then."

Travis gazed out to the crowd. The music was louder. A circle of breakdancers had formed. The party was in full swing. "That's quite a story."

"It's not a story, Travis."

"Then kiss me. Out here. Right now."

"Seriously?"

"See, your problem is you need to loosen up. You can do it. No one's watching."

Deciding he had nothing to lose, he took Travis by the neck and kissed him. It was tender, lingering. When he pulled back Travis's eyes were still closed a second longer, anticipating more. "Do you believe me now?"

Travis took a breath to recover, then a healthy gulp of his Macallan. "Nope, not at all. We need to have sex. Right here." He laughed.

William squeezed his thigh. "You're crazy. I think I've missed it." He leaned in and kissed him once more, longer this time. He pulled away before he could lose himself in it and wiped the corner of Travis's mouth in a familiar way. It was almost loving. Travis quieted his doubts and luxuriated in it.

six.

Linc was swept into his duties as photographer-for-hire for the party's duration, occasionally flirting with Todd, who found himself alone since William had become occupied. He claimed a corner of the party and watched Linc work the crowd. There wasn't a soul he didn't know, as everyone he came into contact with received a hug or a dap. When he glanced across at Todd in between chatting up the crowd, it was like they shared a sexy secret.

Eventually they exchanged numbers. Once Todd made his way back to William's condo he couldn't keep his hands off himself. He imagined Linc was there with him, his body wrapped in Todd's legs, his eyes locked with Todd's as they fucked. Todd imagined the heat and scent of Linc's skin, how he tasted, how he came as Todd finally came. Unconcerned with William's warnings, Todd needed the heat and weight of another male body and wanted it to be Linc's. He just needed Linc to initiate it.

Men were intimidated by Todd, assuming his physique and editorial features rendered him potentially arrogant and cruel. The less presumptuous ones who got to know him soon realized he was harmless and took the lead. Todd had zero game.

As a kid, he found himself constantly fielding questions about what he "was" or where his "people" were from if they didn't make outright assumptions about his ethnicity, as well as obsessing over the texture and color of his hair. When he turned thirteen his growth spurt made him more awkward with limbs that hang off the bed. He tried to keep a low profile at school but became a target and got into fights. He begged his mother to transfer him, but she ushered him into sports, convinced isolating himself would only make his time at school less bearable, regardless of where he was enrolled. He was moderately good at basketball but worse at everything else. When he began lifting he corrected his posture and his chest and shoulders filled out. He was nearly two-hundred pounds by senior year and had grown into his face. His confidence improved and the kids befriended him. He did well until he learned his mother was terminally ill.

As an adult he found ways to manage or mask his anxieties without resorting to prescriptions. These days, most of his issues stemmed from having to explain his existence when he just wanted to live. Not to mention the memory of being propelled through a pane of glass.

Two days after the retrospective found him at Definitions and he was eager to grip a bar again. He had to admit, it was an impressive facility. The main floor was divided between strength equipment—mostly free weights and benches, a few machines—and a TRX zone. Two impossibly-muscled guys flipped tractor tires across green astro turf while a couple others carried loaded barbells overhead in the opposite direction. Cardio equipment on an extended landing overlooked the strongmen and athletes below. "I see exactly why the membership is so high," Todd remarked as Julian made his way across the floor to greet him. "This place is official."

"It is, isn't it?" Julian said proudly, sipping from a blender bottle. He wore a white stringer tank top with "Definitions" emblazoned across the front and black cropped sweatpants. "I wanted a place like the old gyms back in the day, where people could seriously lift and grunt and yell to get out that last rep. I'm creating superheroes." He gestured offhandedly to the cardio equipment above. "Ignore all that. You ready?"

"What, you got something planned for me?" Todd chuckled.

"I was gonna run you through a circuit to see how rusty you are."

"I just came to work out, not audition. I already told you I keep getting my certification renewed out of habit."

"Look, I know coaching isn't as high on the sports medicine totem pole as physical therapy, but—"

"That's not it, Julian. It's not a prestige thing for me. I wanna help people."

"As I recall, the people you wanna *help* typically make about 2.5 million per year. NBA players aren't exactly what I'd call in-need."

Todd sighed. "But they need treatment and recovery too, right? I know I can finish school and go right back down to San Rafael and do it for pennies or set up shop somewhere in Middle America and make about eighty grand a year. And I might do that. I just wanna be good enough to help whoever needs it."

"And live comfortably in the process."

"And not be judged for it."

"I would never! All I'm saying is, if you wanna feel benevolent, you can still do that by coaching. A confidence boost can have remarkable healing effects, for my clients *and* my business interests. Even if you decide against it, what I have in mind for you today isn't that grueling." Julian's grin was enough to confirm he would push Todd to the limit. The circuit consisted of five rounds of burpees, pull-up variations, box jumps, dips, mountain climbers, hanging leg raises and Romanian deadlifts. Julian was a snarky drill sergeant the entire time, alternating between detached affirmations and shouting at Todd to pick up the pace. By the end, Todd was drenched in sweat and a little irritated. Julian was astounded. "You are a goddamn machine."

Todd sat on a nearby bench, wiped his face with a towel and took a swig from his water bottle. He glared at Julian. "Thanks?"

"Where did that come from?"

Todd's chest heaved as he recovered his breath. "What do you mean?"

"Your focus. Your speed. You attacked that shit like an athlete in his prime; I've never seen anything like it. I tried to break you."

Todd shrugged. He was exhausted and didn't feel like explaining there was a time when all he could ever do was work out. "I guess you'll have to try harder next time."

After a shower he and Julian sat at a nearby cafe before plates of roasted fish and yams. Todd wondered if he could be friends with Julian, who was still shallow and cocky in some ways but not as obnoxious as the week before, and Todd noticed Julian was a lot smarter than he'd initially let on. He was curious why Linc despised him so much while William exercised the patience of Job.

"So what was that when we were at dinner? It looked like you and Linc were ready to come to blows."

Julian rolled his eyes. "He don't like me so I don't like him."

"You think that's a good enough reason?"

"Why would I like somebody who don't like me?"

"I would think the two of you could get along because—"

"We're both friends with William? You would *think,* huh? But he's on that fake-ass incense and oils godbody shit. The *minute* he found out I don't deal with Black dudes exclusively he started acting funny. As if who I date is any of his business."

"You date white men?"

"I date men, period." Julian leaned in. "If you don't mind me asking—"

"I'm Black. Mom is white. And I've only ever dated Black men."

"You were in LA for a decade and never fucked with a white dude?"

Todd laughed. "Honest to God. There were opportunities, of course, especially when I was modeling. Turned them all down. Sometimes it got ugly. A lot of them felt they were entitled to me or something. Weird."

"Of course they did! Plus you don't exactly come off like you *wouldn't* date a white dude. No offense."

"I get that a lot. It's okay. I guess I never had the desire."

"I can dig it. I think people should be with whoever they wanna be with. Too many feelings are wrapped up in who chooses who, you know what I mean? It drives me crazy, man. Linc has never flat-out said that was his issue, but I catch his little side comments."

Todd changed the subject. "I like your gym. I don't know if I like *you* right now because of that circuit, but I would consider spending some time there. Maybe as a temporary employee. But only on the condition you diversify your clientele."

"I don't know if I like where this is going."

"It was your idea. You said a confidence boost has healing effects. So that's what I wanna do. I wanna work with people who aren't already bodybuilders and athletes. I used to get pushed around a lot as a kid—"

Julian vigorously shook his head. "Nope. *Hell no.* I'm not letting a bunch of kids in my gym."

"Hear me out. Maybe not kids but regular people who aren't comfortable gyms but also need that confidence boost."

"For all that someone can carry their ass down the street to LA Fitness or, dear God, *Planet Fitness*. I'm not turning Definitions into some regular-ass commercial gym for a bunch of regular-ass people with regular-ass budgets."

Todd sighed and returned to his plate. "Fine."

They were silent as Julian watched Todd eat. Then, "Why are you so hellbent on being a nice guy?"

"Because not enough of us are."

"As long as you work with enough big dudes who are paying us a lot of money, you can do your Fitness Jesus thing in moderation. It seems like it's important to you and even though you might not like *me* right now, I like you. I think you're crazy, though." He offered his hand.

Todd smiled and shook it, realizing he'd committed to sticking around DC a lot longer than he intended. He knew all of the mirrors at Definitions could be a problem, but he felt stronger when he helped someone else. And he needed all the strength he could muster if he ever expected to face Anthony.

seven.

THE APRIL TEMPERATURE HAD climbed to seventy-two degrees so William's gray Burberry London suit jacket was draped over his arm and his shirt, cerulean and Italian cotton poplin, was open at the first two buttons. His eyes squinted from behind gunmetal Tom Ford aviator sunglasses as a wily squirrel skittered across his burgundy Oliver Sweeney oxfords. His thumbs moved across his phone at lightspeed: *Where are you?*

He scanned his surroundings, swatting at a cluster of gnats gathered in his face. He finally spotted Travis crossing D Street carrying a white and yellow paper bag, nearly colliding with a honking taxi, jovial in his work wear.

Travis spread his arms and they hugged. "I only got about forty-five minutes left. I had to get the chicken."

"There's a Bojangles in Union Station now?" William asked him, impressed although he had zero desire to eat it.

"I know, right? And today is such a nice day. This is definitely chicken-in-the-park weather."

William managed a forgiving smile. "I'm not super hungry right now."

"Are you sure?"

"I'm more of a Popeyes man."

They made their way to a bench and William stared at it for a moment. "Having trouble figuring out how it works?" Travis asked him.

"This isn't quite what I was expecting when you said meet for lunch."

Travis sat and dug into the bag. "William, this is perfect weather. I'm tired of sitting inside all day. And why are you wearing a suit? I thought you weren't working this week."

"I said I wasn't accepting new clients, not that I would be on vacation. And I always wear a suit," William answered tightly.

"Got it. You wanna have a seat now? I'm sure if you get any bird shit or derelict piss on your fancy suit you can have it dry-cleaned."

William sat next to him, removed his sunglasses and offered a perfunctory smile. "How's your day so far, Travis?"

Travis shrugged and took a bite of his biscuit. "Work is work. I've gotten pretty good at smiling in everyone's face all day. You have to be such a whore in sales. I was hoping when I saw *you* today I'd have a *legitimate* reason to smile, but you're acting kinda funny right now." Travis gestured around William's face. "Your energy is way off. Like you don't wanna see me."

"Of course I wanna see you, I just wasn't expecting to be sitting in a park with you by Union Station, which is very busy this time of day and crawling with tourists and, you know, people on their lunch break, and there's flies buzzing around and . . . Before you say it again, I get it—*It's a nice day.* Maybe I wanted to sit and talk in a place that was *enclosed.*"

"With tablecloths and a wine list."

"Travis—"

"*William,* this is how the rest of us live. Everything happening around you right now is *The World.* Some of us have enough money and time to sit in the park with our chicken or our ham and cheese sandwiches on our lunch breaks. Some of us even enjoy it and think it provides peace of mind. Have you been living in a fortress?"

"I didn't mean to offend you."

Travis wiped his hands on a napkin and draped his arm across the back of the bench. "Why can't you relax? Even your apologies sound too polished."

"I'm not sure what you want me to do—"

"I want you to act the way you acted when you fucked me."

William's eyes darted around and upon confirming no one was in earshot he managed a laugh. "What are you talking about?"

"You're nasty and a little mean and you don't have any manners. You're a completely different person. You don't give one damn in the bedroom. Outside of the bedroom? You give way too many."

"Well—" William adjusted his tie, pulled at his lapels a bit—"most people are less inhibited at home and reserved in public. I'm a professional. I'm the face of my firm. How I look to the world means everything to my success."

"I'm not asking you to ravage me on this bench. That would be hot but I'm no longer in my twenties so that's not what I'm asking. *This* time. I want you to be a person and not a product when you're with me. Isn't that why you stopped taking on new clients in the first place? To free yourself?" Travis reached into the bag and withdrew a chicken wing. "You know you want it. C'mon, lemme feed it to you."

William laughed again. He was charmed by Travis, to be sure, but he still had no intention of taking a bite. "What if I said you don't have to brandish a chicken wing to get me to agree with you? You're right. I need to relax more. I've been trying. I just need you to go easy on me. Be patient."

Travis shook his head. "Nah. I tried that the last time."

"Okay, then. This weekend I have an event—*social*—a birthday party for a woman who's like a second mother. They have a house in Tenleytown and their parties are filled with interesting people with a lot of money, the best liquor and food. I've usually gone alone—*alone* meaning I bring my assistant since I'm in business mode. But never a date. Never someone who might be special."

"Are you saying I'm special?" Travis gushed.

"I think you're delightful and they would love to get to know you. Will you be my date?"

eight.

THE PARTIES HELD BY Langley and Monica Baptiste were major networking events. Among the blend of expensive fragrances including his own Tobacco Vanille by Tom Ford, William was certain he smelled money. These were the parties where deals were made and super-partnerships were seeded. William could walk away with at least five new clients.

As Roy Ayers played from a cleverly hidden sound system, cater-waiters ghosted through the crowd with trays of champagne and cocktails. William grabbed two glasses and handed one to Travis. They'd slipped in only moments ago, not bothering to announce themselves. William first wanted Travis to observe the scene before they were pulled into the inner sanctum. He pointed out the major players.

"You see that huge guy there by the bar? The one who looks like a cross between Rocky Johnson and Ron O'Neal?"

"I have no idea who those people are," Travis said.

William rolled his eyes. "Either way, that's Langley Baptiste. He's a partner at Sweeney, Rothchild and Baptiste, one of the largest law firms in DC. Langley is the one who initially invested in the Kendall Design Group." He guided Travis's eyes to the glass doors leading out to the deck. "The woman who looks like Diahann Carroll—I *know* you know who that is—is his wife, Monica, and it's *her* birthday. She's well-connected, responsible for my firm's first round of clients. Next to her is their daughter Nicole. She's in commercial real estate and the reason my firm expanded on K Street."

"Tell me again how you know them."

"I've been friends with Langley's son, Sidney, since forever. We met when we were both seventeen and working at Up Against the Wall." William chuckled. "That was a *long* time ago."

"And where's he?"

"In New York. He's an entertainment lawyer. His clients are mostly rappers which, to me, sounds like a perpetual migraine."

"But I bet when he comes home he has the best stories," Travis mused, sipping his champagne. "So what you're telling me is you owe your success to this entire family?"

William nodded. "Absolutely. I wouldn't be a fraction of the man I am without them."

No sooner had he said this than he caught the eye of Cintra Mason-Baptiste—tall, slender and deep mahogany brown with a close, nearly bald cut. Cintra was strikingly feline, the kind of intimidating, cutting-edge beauty modeling agents mortgaged their souls to sign. But she wasn't a model. She was a gallery curator, part-time installation artist and ten-year wife of one Sidney Baptiste.

William's mouth went dry. If Cintra was here, Sidney wasn't far behind.

Tonight she was in snug, washed-out gray Diesel denim, tall sandals and a white drape halter tank. Her jewelry was silver and dangly and William identified Prada cologne when she hugged him. Cintra often opted for mens fragrances.

"Look at you," she marvelled, pulling back from their embrace. "I feel like I haven't seen you forever, William."

"I had no idea you were in DC," he said, not meaning to sound so inconvenienced. He quickly recovered. "You look amazing as usual. Cintra, I want you to meet Travis DeWitt."

Travis reached out to shake her hand but she hugged him. "I'm sorry, babe, I'm a hugger and you're adorable."

"It's cool," Travis choked, startled by the gesture.

To William's relief, Cintra didn't bother asking what their relationship was, although he could sense Travis eagerly anticipating a designation. "How long have you two been here? Have you eaten? Did you wish Monica a Happy Birthday?"

"We just got here," William told her.

"And what are you doing? Lurking?"

William was firm yet gentle as he repeated himself. "Cintra, we *just* got here."

She offered a dramatic sigh and linked arms with the two of them, escorting them into the thick of the party. "You in here acting simple like there aren't people who wanna see you!"

Travis soon realized that designation would be long coming. As they exchanged introductions with Monica's guests it became clear his personal relationship to William mattered little. His professional title was what they all wanted, and what a modest, unexciting role it was compared to everyone here. *Assistant Sales Manager for the Chambers Hotel Group.* A few of them along the way misheard (any attention they paid him was fragmented, at best) and thought he sold entire properties.

If only, he thought, swallowing his second glass of champagne. It all went by so fast. The hugs, the light brushes of cheek-to-cheek contact. Cintra was doting, proud to have a new friend in Travis, and held his hand tightly as the other guests fawned over William. There William was, in his sharp Boateng suit no doubt personally tailored by Ozwald himself, breezing through small talk about his firm and deals and, to Travis, complicated matters one could only grasp once their salary crossed seven figures. During these exchanges, there was barely a follow-up acknowledgement of Travis. He found himself on the margins, afraid he would lose William in the crush of the crowd.

And he did. Travis broke from his thoughts long enough to realize Cintra's hand had disengaged from his and William was nowhere to be found.

"WE HAVEN'T TOLD A lot of people we're in DC. It's only been a couple of weeks. But I'm glad you're here. I have a project for you and I want you to please say yes," Cintra told William after pulling him off to the side.

"So you're not just here for the party?"

She smiled. It was sheepish. There was a story. "We kind of moved to DC."

"Kind of?"

"We bought a house here. And Sidney is at the firm now."

"The firm?"

"Yes. His father's firm."

William's heart dropped to his toes.

"Did you know reciprocity meant he didn't have to pass another bar?" she went on, grabbing a Cosmopolitan from a passing tray. "He just *slid right in.*"

"Are you telling me the two of you left Manhattan and are now living and working in DC?"

"Well, *he's* working and I'm on a break. I need to focus on my art, you know? But back to the project. Sidney and I were talking and we want you to do the house."

"Right. The house."

"It's so beautiful. A Queen Anne-style rowhouse. And it's *huge.* It faces Lincoln Park with a brick path that leads out to a brick sidewalk. I love the character of Capitol Hill, especially in the Fall." Her voice was melodic, seductive, as if she was selling the property herself. "We were able to snatch it up fast. Didn't even hit the market. I can't wait for you to get your hands on it."

She wasn't giving him adequate time to absorb the information, but this was her way. Cintra shared inconvenient news like a charming anecdote. *I know I'm fucking up your life right now and completely ignored the part where you said you weren't accepting new clients BUT HOW CUTE IS THIS?*

"Cintra, I would love to come and take a look at the house but I gotta ask you, why did you leave New York?"

She tilted her head and took his hand, pulling him away from their corner and down a hall. "C'mon. I think I saw the two of them head into Langley's office."

Baptiste men were tall, broad-shouldered and athletic with strong noses, full lips and hooded bedroom eyes. Langley, especially, took up a lot of space, with his voice full of bass and imposing gut. He and his son were well-groomed with fresh cuts and tailored suits, every hair and thread immaculately trimmed and placed.

Sidney reached out to shake William's hand once he and Cintra made their way into Langley's study, and the handshake quickly evolved into a tight hug recalling summers celebrated in the Hamptons. Stolen moments in the middle of the night while the family slept. The many firsts shared between them . . .

To the family they were like brothers.

"It's good to see you, man!" Sidney exclaimed with his infectious smile. "Where have you been?"

Cintra sat on the edge of Langley's desk. "William's been hiding from us," she said with a teasing lilt to her voice.

"Keeping major clients happy," William jumped in, before it could become a full scale ambush.

Langley draped an arm around William's shoulders. "This is a man about his business. He's focused. Determined." He gestured to his own son with his glass of gin. "Pay attention."

It was a familiar refrain. Sidney loved the law, but not as much as his father did. He loved basketball more, and at forty longed for it the same way he did as a teenager. William wondered if Sidney left New York at Langley's behest instead of making the choice for himself. "I got this," Sidney said, confident as ever. "I'm gonna make you a lot of money. Once you represent a rapper, you can do anything."

"I know that's right," Cintra laughed, shaking her head.

"You *stay* in Boateng." Sidney remarked to William. "I ain't mad, though. This dude has been out-dressing me for the last twenty years!"

William found himself gazing at Sidney's lips, absently responding, "Longer," remembering the magic of his mouth, seduced by the youthful cadence of his voice. Even at a polished, well-accomplished forty, Sidney Baptiste was the same knucklehead rapping along to Ice Cube's "It Was A Good Day" as he nearly burned bologna for thin, greasy sandwiches after school.

"Oh here *you* go!" Sidney laughed. "I stand corrected, as usual."

Neither Langley or Cintra caught the edge in his voice, but William knew it was a dig at Langley's tendency to dangle William before Sidney as a beacon of structure and discipline. It made William bristle with guilt. Langley maintained a stubborn resentment for Sidney, offended he would ever choose basketball over following in his father's footsteps. Even though Sidney relented during his first year at Syracuse (to his chagrin he wasn't nearly as skilled or coordinated as the other student players), Langley was still sore. He wanted The Law to be Sidney's *first* choice, and choosing sports was like choosing another father. So Langley, more or less, chose another son.

He taught William how to appreciate fine cigars and spirits and the logic behind the cut of a man's suit. *A suit on a man is like lingerie on a woman. It's your most ideal presentation. The lapel enhances your chest and draws the eye from the shoulders to the waist. That's what women like—broad shoulders and a small waist. It makes you look powerful. You'll likely never look more powerful than you do in a suit.*

So William wore suits as often as he could, occasion or not. Langley looked him over every time they met, observing how much shirt cuff appeared at the end of the jacket sleeve, how well the pocket square complimented the shirt and tie—*The square should never be an exact match*—and if there was too much room in the shoulders. When he was satisfied, as he had been each time once William had a solid suiting budget, he offered a brief nod of approval. When Sidney applied this advice, no matter how impeccable he looked, Langley called him "a nigga in a suit." To Langley, his son didn't have quite the right posture or walk. He was too relaxed, too much like his rapper clients. He might as well have continued to pursue basketball.

One time William came right out and asked Sidney, "Do you

think your father respects you?" Sidney wouldn't, or couldn't, answer.

Now William quickly pushed the conversation elsewhere. "So when are the two of you thinking about moving into the new house?"

Sidney turned to Cintra. Shrugged. "No rush, right?"

"A month or two. The work shouldn't take long. William's a whiz." Cintra winked.

"I didn't agree to anything, yet." William knew he would but she needed to sweat.

"I have a bunch of ideas but we can discuss them over dinner. You're free next week, right?"

"Should be."

"Boom." She hopped off the desk and gave William another squeeze and a kiss on the cheek. "We'll see you then." To Langley, "Let's give these BFFs a chance to catch up."

Once Langley gave William's shoulder a final approving pat and disappeared with Cintra, Sidney took a seat at Langley's desk, propping his feet on top. They were surrounded by rows of identical law books and appointed leather furniture so the gesture was decidedly rebellious. "So who's your friend?" he asked right away.

"What the hell were you doing? Watching me instead of coming over to speak? That's Travis."

"Travis *who?*"

"You're awfully invested for someone who's happily married."

Sidney chuckled. "That's not where I was coming from. I just wasn't aware you decided to be . . . *out*. It could call our entire friendship into question. That's all."

"You have nothing to worry about," William countered. "You are, after all, *happily married.*"

"Is he nice?"

"He's wonderful. I can introduce you tonight."

"I would like that."

"So why are you here?"

Sidney tapped his fingers on the desk, his eyes rolling up to the ceiling, searching for the right answer. "It was time to slow down. The work was too glamorous, too scandalous. I needed to get out of there."

"Or was there too much temptation?" William countered.

Sidney's eyes narrowed. "I would never cheat on my wife."

"Is that the truth?"

"You think I'd lie to you? Of all people?"

"Anything is possible these days, Sidney."

Sidney brought his feet to the floor and stood, coming back over to William. "Why are you trying to fight me? You're not happy to see me?"

"You've been here for weeks and said nothing. Forgive me if I'm a little defensive. Why keep it secret?"

"It wasn't a secret, we just didn't tell *you*. Plus, I've been taking over some cases and she's doing her art thing. We knew we'd see everyone tonight, so what better time? What, you got a problem with me being in DC?"

William searched his face for a moment, then decided the doubts weren't worth his time. "It's great to have you back."

They hugged again and, before releasing him, Sidney whispered in William's ear, "Thank you for keeping it between us all this time."

nine.

MEL BLEW CLOUDS, MANAGED not to laugh himself into a choking fit and passed the blunt left.

Bree, Mel's occasional manager, took the pass. "He's already starting. Do you want to let the rest of us in on the joke, Mel?"

Upstairs a raucous Spades tournament unfolded against Stax classics and Southern Hip Hop. In the basement, four friends spread out on large, comfortable cushions. Only two knew why Mel was laughing and it wasn't from the quality of the herbs. Of the two, one had been silent all night.

Mel spread his arms like a cult leader before his acolytes. *"This is the joke."*

Linc, directly across from him and awaiting his turn, didn't take the bait.

"Chile," Bree said in her husky voice, "you're always talking in riddles. Anyway, the pictures from the show will be used in all marketing going forward. If that's okay with you, Linc. I'm not the one who paid for them so I don't wanna get into usage drama."

Mel's occasional photographer gave her a thumbs up.

Bree shot Omar a look.

"I wish I could've made the show," Omar offered. This was his third time expressing regret, along with his vow to never rely on the Megabus again. "But you looked good. You took the advice I gave you about going full Hendrix." Omar divided his time between New York and DC and was Mel's occasional stylist.

"Minus the perm."

"I'll never perm my hair."

"Never say never," Bree added. "It could make a big comeback. When something falls out of fashion all it takes is someone with any kind of influence to wait until the right moment to bring it back and—*boom*—trendsetter."

"Oh yes, that's all I want, to be influential. A trendsetter. You know what happens when you're influential? Everyone is in your business."

"And that's why you're afraid to be good," Bree scolded. "That's why you won't move to Atlanta or LA."

Omar: "Or New York."

"I want my music to be mine. I want my image, my life, to be mine."

"Writing and singing backup are always an option," Omar said. "But you're on that bullshit right now. Songwriters and doo-wop pop-pop background singers don't need their own photographers and stylists. You want the attention and the praise—"

"Without the cost," Bree finished. "I get it. Being supernaturally gifted is such a burden."

"Do you mind?" Linc asked.

"Oh yeah." She passed to him. "Good to finally hear from you, friend."

Linc nodded to Mel as he pulled: *Roll another.*

Mel obliged. "I'm fine with being DC famous for now."

"You're not DC famous—*yet,*" she countered. "That was your first showcase, your first time not doing backup. But it's not too early to be thinking about the long term, i.e., vocal clarity, i.e., other ways of doing *this.*"

Mel smiled as he wet a gutted wrapper. "I have other ways."

"I do amazing infusions," Omar added. "Butters, bourbons—"

"That shit is dangerous," Bree said. "So how do we figure this out? You want to put your *talent* in front of people but not *you.* We don't live in a time where that's possible, unless you're—"

"Janet," Omar said.

"It always comes back to Janet with Omar but he's right. It takes a while to get to that level. To do this job, you need to let people in."

"The reason I want to do this *job* is so I don't have to go into an office and be asked what I did over the weekend, or talk to my coworkers about my personal life. I shouldn't have to do that as an artist. The art should speak for itself."

"*Should* and *will* are two different things. If you come out the gate being weird and elusive it's gonna turn people off and, considering the kind of music you do, you're already at risk for people thinking you're weird."

"The kind of music I do is what we listen to all the time. We're listening to it *right now.*"

"Baby, I get that, but there's animus towards R&B these days. People hate artists who can actually sing."

"Especially if they're male," Omar added.

"Exactly. A man who can sing with a big-ass 'fro who talks in riddles looks pretentious."

"Or a fun time," Mel said.

"Or like he's putting up a smokescreen."

"I know where this is headed and I don't like it."

"It's headed to a point you're already circling—the reason you want to keep your private life separate from your output." Bree sighed and made a desperate bid for support. "Talk to him, Linc, or, you know, just *talk.*"

Linc passed to Omar. "What do you want me to say, that it's 2016 and it should be easy now? Mel isn't alternative, he's not Frank Ocean. His style is rooted in the Black soul tradition which, by extension, is deeply rooted in the Black church. He can be fashionable, he can be sassy, he can be fem. He can be all of those things and deny access to his personal life because that's what his target audience has accepted if not demanded for decades. *Be who you are, just don't say it out loud.* You really want him posting videos on Instagram kissing on some man?"

"No, and, if I did, it wouldn't be *some man,* it'd be *you,* unless that's in flux for the umpteeth time?"

Mel wagged his finger. "No no, there's no flux."

"So it's permanent? That's why both of you are acting funny?" Bree glared at Omar. "Did you know about this?"

"He don't tell me shit."

Bree was concerned when Mel was twenty-four, Linc thirty-one. A seven year age difference didn't mean much down the line but, to her, twenty-four was still tender. Too tender to be tethered to someone like Linc who was charming but reckless. But she got used to it, they all did. Mel and Linc broke up and reunited so often their friends stopped cataloguing the changes. The assumption was, whether or not they were *presently* together, they would end up together tomorrow. That was the rule.

Mel was hardened now, pushing thirty and cynical. His music was better. He was sexier, more confident. As Bree considered all of this, she realized for the first time Mel had triumphed. Her cheeks tingled from the intake.

Linc rose from the cushions and took the stairs. Bree followed.

HE DELAYED INTERROGATION BY pouring himself another rum and caught up with the tournament players. They all stopped mid-hand to sing along to The Staples Singers and when Bree stood before him—arms folded, demanding the details—he pulled her into a hand dance, his red cup so steady it barely quivered as he spun around. The song wasn't long enough for her to completely forget her mission. When it was over she shoved him into her kitchen and asked him "Are you okay?"

"I'm maintaining," he said with a lax grin.

"So this isn't a break?"

"We're done. You should be ecstatic."

"For him. Not so much for you."

"Nice."

"You put him through hell."

He nodded and sipped. "I think he's outgrown me. It hurts a little. No, it hurts a *lot.*"

"Is it your ego that hurts?"

"There's a heart in here, too," he assured her.

Bree took his drink and sipped enough to wet her rapidly drying mouth. "When did it happen?"

"Four, maybe five, months ago."

"And neither one of you said a word. So all this time you've been pretending to be together when y'all were around me?"

"What you saw was me trying to get him back."

"Tell me what happened."

His face fell but he recovered with another weak, weed and rum-infused grin, then a dismissive shrug. "He doesn't want me anymore."

"Okay. I get that. I wanna know what the *straw* was. What did you do? What did *he* do?" Linc reached for his cup but she held tight. "You're not gonna tell me? I'm drinking the rest of your shit."

"Cool. There's plenty."

"So you didn't fuck around on him this time? Something else happened. Something so fucked up he put his foot down and you can't even say what it is. Y'all kept this quiet for *five* months. *What happened, Linc?*"

Linc wished it was as simple as what Bree was used to hearing. The truth was so messy. So embarrassing.

"Did y'all fight?" she pressed. "Like, physically?"

"Of course not. It was just time. No inciting incident. I promise."

"You're probably lying. I'll ask him."

Linc was confident Mel wouldn't spill the full details since he didn't come out of it looking so pristine himself. "Ask him. Do whatever you want. Can I have my cup back?"

"No." She turned on her heel and went for the basement but Mel emerged at the top of the steps, followed by Omar. His eyes were glazed and his mouth was a fixed smirk.

"You tell her?" he asked Linc.

"She left me no choice."

Mel chuckled. "Good. Now everybody can move on."

"He didn't tell me shit!" Bree hollered. She stood between them, looking from one to the other and back. She was so tiny and furious the visual made Omar break into a fit of laughter, holding onto the kitchen counter for support. Mel soon joined and Linc fell into a nearby chair, doubling over, his entire body shaking. "I don't see what's funny!" she went on.

They laughed even louder at her distress. Mel cried and fanned himself. Once he pulled it together he draped an arm around her shoulders. "The details don't matter. But you'll be happy to know I watched him beg for the past five months and it was great. It's the most fun I've had in a long time. But he got the hint last week. Didn't you, Linc?"

"You don't need to do this," Linc said, voice barely above a growl. "You had your fun and I deserved it, now let's move on like you said."

"Are you sure? You ready to move on, finally?"

"You're showing off."

"Maybe a little."

Omar slowly backed out of the kitchen.

"I'm not gonna keep beating myself up for how you are now," Linc said carefully. "At some point, you being mean and nasty is *all you*. This has nothing to do with me. We were good a week ago at your show and have been good since. Now you're being petty. *I'm good*, Mel."

Mel was game. "Then I don't need to worry about you showing up to my gigs? I don't need to worry about bumping into you when I'm out?"

"Nope!"

"And I don't need to pretend to be your friend for the sake of everyone else?"

Linc bit his lip to keep from responding. He was angry enough to let slip what happened five months ago. What he told

Todd in Kogod Courtyard was a lie. Of course Linc had secrets, who didn't? And this one wasn't *so* bad when he considered it long enough but it was definitely *The Straw* and, beyond that, a little gross. It couldn't come out tonight, not with all these people in the house.

Todd. Thinking of him made Linc less angry. But it was time to go.

He hugged Bree, promising they would get together soon.

Mel watched with contempt as Linc exited without giving himself the satisfaction of a last word. He said his goodbyes to the players and it was a wrap. Once Linc left, the party was over.

ten.

Julian turned to Todd as Arena's surly, mountainous bouncer patted him down. "I haven't been patted down for a club in years." The line behind them groaned and a few impatient remarks were uttered under breath. "Seriously. You're patting *me* down. Who do I have to be worried about on the inside? Who's gonna protect *my* ass?" Julian glared at the bouncer before advancing to pay the cover.

Arena was a high profile Downtown club, the kind of spot from which radio personalities broadcast during peak nightlife hours on the weekend. It was straight but had a "gay sensibility" according to what Julian knew of its reputation, the perfect place to celebrate his new single status and Todd's employment at Definitions. Todd stood before the bouncer, his arms and legs spread as he was thoroughly inspected for weapons or drugs. He stifled a giggle when the bouncer's hands slid up his inner thigh. He'd taken advantage of William's stocked bar before leaving; without alcohol in his system from the start, club outings were intolerable.

They proceeded down a dark corridor rocked by the bass of "Controlla" and the lights became brighter, as if they were a champion boxer's entourage clearing the tunnel to the ring. The walls receded, and the walkway soon overlooked a wide sunken dance floor. Todd held onto the railing as a few girls in skintight dresses rushed past him to get to the bar. He didn't catch how they stopped for a moment to gawk at him; he was too captivated by the packed floor. It was festive, awash in purple and blue flashing lights, champagne and sweat.

"You like this Drake shit?" Julian asked, leaning against the railing to survey the bacchanal below. "Man, the clubs back home still not afraid to play *that real shit*—Gang Starr, Ghostface, Beatnuts—no matter how old it is. I guess a lot of spots here do too if you come early enough. Then the queens show up and they switch to Beyoncé and Rihanna."

"So you were one of those little thugged-out dudes holding up the wall? You wore a durag in the club didn't you?" Todd laughed. "I can see it!"

Julian joined in the laughter. "Yeah. I was definitely that, mean mug and all. I was so skinny back then." He shuddered, although his recollections of being younger in the club were fond—the humidity and closeness that came from a dense crowd, men packed into one room moving to the same beat, bumping into a new friend, stealing kisses in a drunken haze, sliding hands inside of pants to measure the potential. "Part of me misses it, though. But this is cool, too. I have *these* now." He flexed both biceps. "I have more options these days. Just make sure you keep a safe distance from me. I don't want your pretty ass stealing all my thunder. I'm kidding. But if I need you to skedaddle, I'll let you know. How about you let me walk in front so people see me first?"

Todd couldn't tell if he was serious.

Julian cackled, slapping him on the back. "C'mon, let's get a drink!"

They made their way to the bar, good looks and broad shoulders clearing a path. Instantly, Todd felt them all trying to figure out who he was. Tonight he wore a red buffalo plaid shirt unbuttoned with a gray tank underneath, slightly shredded jeans and dark brown chukkas. He looked ready to pull a tree from the ground with his bare hands.

Julian, in a thin v-neck sweater that clung to his torso and dark jeans, started them off with shots of Jameson. Highballs followed, which they took to an empty section of banquette along the perimeter. "They're all so skinny," Julian mused as the scene unfolded. "Everyone is dressing a lot better these days, I noticed, but these men are small. Put down the blunt and pick up a sweet potato!"

"Sadly, I don't think buff is in," Todd laughed over the music. "You gotta be skinny with a Philly beard and lots of tattoos. Which isn't so bad."

Julian's eyes narrowed. "Is that what you like?"

"I like different things. Most of the guys I've dated have been big, like you or me, but every now and then I go for a smaller guy."

Julian gestured to the dancefloor with his drink. "So if you had your pick . . . What are you looking for?"

Todd shrugged. "I don't think I'm looking for anything. I mean, there might be someone I'm interested in. He's not here, though."

"Motherfucking Linc," Julian spat. "I knew it. From the night you got here. *Why?*"

Todd laughed again. "Because he's sexy and interesting and he smells good. I don't know, I just like him!"

"You do know you can have anyone, right? Like, anyone in this entire city and you choose *Linc?*"

"I know you hate him but we hit it off."

"Did you tell William?"

"Yes. He already warned me."

"And you didn't listen?"

"No, because William talks to me like I'm a child."

"Everyone's a child to William. That man is old. But I agree with him."

"I didn't even tell you what he said!"

Julian shook his head. "You didn't have to, I already know! Linc has a reputation. He became a photographer so he can fuck a bunch of people!"

"And you're a personal trainer so the same argument could be made."

"We don't need to make that argument. I'm a

relationship-oriented person. He's not." Julian lifted his glass to his lips and realized he was already empty. "Oh wait, he was with that one dude but I think he cheated on him the entire time. Linc is a ho, which wouldn't be that big a deal if I liked his ass. I need another drink."

"I'll get them," Todd offered, only since he didn't want to spend the rest of the evening being lectured. For Todd, the matter was a simple one: He wanted Linc to fuck him. Sure, Linc's character and history were of interest to Todd, but his immediate goal was sex. Besides, everyone had a different baseline for what defined a "ho," and Julian's flimsy criteria hinged on who he liked and didn't like.

By the time Todd returned from the bar, Julian had attracted two young women who were squeezed on either side of him. They were both slender with big curls and appeared to be either Eritrean or Ethiopian. Todd couldn't hear as he approached but figured Julian was telling crass, inappropriate jokes. His caramel bald head, dimples and muscles worked in his favor and they were charmed by him.

"This is my boy Todd!" he announced, an amused glint in his eye as he took his drink. "He's a model an' shit."

Todd blushed. "I used to be. I'm not anymore."

"Y'all are fine!" one girl said. "Almost *too* fine."

"Are y'all together?" the other asked.

"*Us?* Nooooooooo," Julian scoffed.

"Look, we don't care if the two of you are gay. Just dance with us so we don't have to worry about these bums all night. Shit, they're all skinny and smell like weed."

"I. Said. The same. Thing!" Julian declared, slapping his knee to punctuate each word.

They soon found themselves on the floor, amid a crush of jiggling breasts and twerking asses. Travis Scott became Migos, which became Future, then Fetty Wap. Todd sang along with the crowd, easily falling into step when the Howard kids broke into the latest moves. Julian, for most of his part, was puzzled by the song selection but maintained enough of a rhythm to not draw attention to himself.

The dj, who spun from a platform overlooking the entire club, brought the current hits to a complete halt to make way for "Get Me Bodied" and Todd was eighteen again. Julian rolled his eyes and tried to leave the floor but Todd grabbed him. "You're not leaving on this song! Are you crazy?"

"I don't know why I thought I would go an entire night without hearing Beyoncé!"

With a goofy grin Todd did a body roll in front of Julian. The girls cackled. When Julian didn't respond Todd broke into The Snake which also yielded nothing from Julian, but the crowd around them was in hysterics. "Who hates Beyoncé?" Todd demanded of anyone within earshot, but it was only meant for Julian.

When Todd and the group gathered around him danced in unison to the instructions near the end of the track, a smile formed. By the time the dj transitioned into Missy's "Work It," Julian was laughing, big and loud. "You are so corny!" he told Todd. "Do you know that?"

"I'm well aware!" Todd responded.

"I need to take a piss, I'll be back!" Julian hollered over the music, and left Todd to his dance crew. Aside from an attendant, the men's bathroom was blessedly empty. Julian released a cathartic moan as he relieved himself, wondering how Todd managed to spend the entire night drinking and jumping around on the dancefloor without creating a puddle. *That dude really is Superman,* he thought.

He was in the middle of washing his hands when the door opened and his ex entered. Not Sean Lively, but an ex from much longer ago.

"I thought I saw you come in here," Dr. Blair Covington said with a grin.

The attendant handed Julian a paper towel and he absently dried his hands. "Shit."

"Nice to see you too."

"Did you follow me in here?"

"That's exactly what I did."

Smug son of a bitch. Blair always appeared once Julian broke up with someone else. He had his theories about why he couldn't maintain a relationship, none of which were material to Julian.

"There's nothing to see here. No hardened plaque, no gingivitis, no cavities. See? *They're done.*" He grinned wide, tossed the paper towel in the trash, slid the attendant a five and hurried out.

"I heard you were dating white boys now," Blair called after him.

Julian re-entered the bathroom and looked at the attendant. "Can I have five minutes with this fool?"

He guffawed. "Funny guy. I like you."

"What do I look like? Aladdin wishing for more wishes? You telling me it can't be done?" Julian demanded.

The attendant folded his arms and planted his feet. "Have your little fight. I'm not moving." Julian reached in his pocket but he stopped him. "You can flash all the money you want, *I'm not moving.*"

With a clenched jaw, Julian faced Blair, who looked better now than he did six years ago. He didn't know whether to be impressed or angry at this. Anyone who'd been with Julian walked away with a greater investment in their health and fitness, as well as an over-exercised patience. By now, Blair was forty-six and distinguished silver already formed at the temples of his close-cropped curly hair. His complexion was smooth, his goatee razor-precise. "It's none of your business who I date, Blair."

"No need to be so defensive. I just wanted to see if you were happy."

"No, your M.O. this entire time is to make sure I'm *not* happy."

Blair snapped his fingers as the name came to him. "Sean Lively, the one on the news, right?"

Julian turned to the attendant, who rolled his eyes and waved it off. He'd heard far more interesting gossip from and about people with names worth a lot more than Sean Lively from the *local* news.

"Because it interests you, that's over as of last week," Julian told Blair.

"How long that one last?"

Julian narrowed his eyes. "Less than two years."

"You made it past a year, that means you've been learning. Impressive. But let me guess the reason you broke up—"

"If I knock your teeth out, can you put them back in yourself or do you get another dentist to do it for you?"

"You treated the relationship like an extended date. Can't get too emotionally invested, since that means Julian must be held accountable once in a while. Wait, did you even *call it* a relationship? Or were the two of you *kickin' it?*"

"May I ask why your *old ass* is in this club?" Julian demanded. "Shouldn't you be on a Tom Joyner cruise or at a Sinbad comedy festival in Jamaica with the other Black, middle-aged divorcés? Why are you bothering me?"

"Because I care about you, Brat. Every time I see you I'm gonna ask if you're happy, whether you're with someone or not. How old are you now? Thirty-four? I want you to figure out how to be someone that *you* believe deserves to be happy, 'cause what you're doing now ain't it. You keep repeating the same cycle over and over. You still wanna be doing that shit when you get my age?"

"So you got it all figured out, huh? Where's your dude?"

"I don't have one because I don't want one and I don't need one. And I came to that conclusion because I figured my shit out. You should do the same, and stop wasting people's time."

"He's got a point," the attendant weighed in.

"And his point is trash," Julian shot back.

"I don't understand you so-called 'relationship-oriented' people," Blair went on. "What does that mean nowadays? It just means you have your shit together. I guess that makes you a catch? I'm a doctor and—"

"A *dentist.*"

"—and you don't see me out here flashing my credentials like keys to a Benz. You all get in relationships to say you've checked off all the boxes, that you've reached Peak Adult! Either be in love or be alone."

"Are you finished or are you done?"

"Oh, I'm done. In fact, lemme go pee since my old bladder is all agitated now. Enjoy the rest of your evening, *Brat.*"

Blair made his way to the urinals and Julian gave the bathroom attendant one final glare before leaving to hunt down Todd on the dance floor. It was time to get out of this place before another ex popped up. While he didn't find Todd, he did find their two new friends who explained Todd made a break for it. Julian whipped out his phone to check if Todd left any messages and sure enough—

Left to go see him. Will catch up later.

eleven.

TODD WAS STILL TIPSY when his Uber pulled into the lot, dead quiet amid a cluster of warehouses. "Sir, are you sure this is your destination?" his driver asked. He sounded not a little panicked, as if Todd lured him into some gritty, urban danger. Todd, unsure himself, checked the address Linc texted while he was still on the dance floor and scanned the lot until he spotted him, holding open a heavy metal door to one of the faceless structures. He thanked the driver and got out, lighter in his walk than usual. Linc was in a white tank top and red basketball shorts.

"This is where you live?" he asked. "My driver thought I was about to rob him."

"How much you think he had on him?"

Todd laughed and followed Linc up a brightly-lit stairwell. "It had the space I needed," Linc explained. "It's not scary during the day, I promise." He opened a door to an unfinished hall with concrete flooring and exposed brick walls. He went on about finding the perfect studio space and real estate and credit and gentrification and how, since he found what he wanted, he'd likely never leave DC. He unlocked another door and they entered an expansive, sparsely furnished loft. A backdrop with various lights and a reflector were stationed in a far corner opposite a kitchen area. An iron spiral staircase led up to a bedroom landing. *Bitches Brew* played faintly from a dock. "Is there anything I can do to change your mind about shooting you?"

"I'm thinking about it."

"What if I told you William's in it?"

"William? Why?"

"I mean, look, he's my boy and all but I can appreciate fine. William is *Morris Chestnut* fine. Don't tell me you never noticed."

Todd frowned. "I never *wanted* to notice. He's like my brother."

"Even if he *was* your brother you could admit he's a good-looking dude. There's nothing wrong with that. But to each his own."

"Is Julian in it?"

"Fuck no," Linc scoffed.

Todd laughed. "You two really can't stand each other. What happened?"

"Pssh! First of all, he wasn't meant to be there that night. That's William's friend. I was supposed to be having dinner with him since I had a gig down the street and for some reason, probably because you were coming, he invited Julian's ass. Everything he does is performative and he's *loud.*"

"He's a good-looking guy, though," Todd countered. "Isn't that what your book is about? Black male beauty, of all kinds?"

"Sure, if I was just putting out a book of pretty faces. But every man has a story and that's what I want to capture—the multitudes. If I thought Julian's no-neck-having-ass was remotely interested in being authentic in the time it took to shoot him, I'd have no problem asking him to be in it. I'm sure that makes me petty, huh?"

"A little."

"I'll be that. You want something to drink?"

"I should probably have some water, but I'm not ready to stop drinking."

"I opened a bottle of Malbec yesterday. We can finish that; you probably don't need anything hard right now."

Todd chuckled as he followed Linc to the kitchen and

watched him grab the bottle and two glasses, oblivious to his own entendre.

"I was about to roll when you texted me back. You smoke?"

"It's not my thing. But I don't mind if you do."

Linc handed him a glass. "Word. Cheers to finally getting you in my studio." He winked and took a sip. "So tell me your story."

Todd took a deep sip. "My story is very depressing."

"Depressing? It's part of who you are, how I feel about it doesn't matter. I just wanna know you. Your energy doesn't match the look. And I mean that in the best way. I've been around a lot of good-looking dudes in this city who expect everyone to genuflect when they walk into a room, and none of them have what you do. There's a tenderness in the eyes. If I ever had the privilege of shooting you, every photo could be from the neck up."

Todd leaned against the counter and smiled, his face reddened by the wine and his own anticipation. He wanted to tell Linc everything. "Thank you," he managed to respond. "Maybe I should start with the reason I'm here. I came to see my dad. He's in prison. I might have some unfinished business with him."

"What's he in for?"

"Drugs. He was kind of a big deal back in the day. Anyone who's lived in DC long enough knows his name—Anthony 'Ant' Mosley."

Linc gasped. "Your father is Ant Mosley? Damn, dude, I never would have guessed."

"The problem is, I carry around all this guilt about who he is and what he did and the fact I basically abandoned DC while it was still recovering from it but none of that recovery benefited the people who have always been here. I know it's not *my* fault but I feel like I chickened out, you know? I should have stayed."

"Why'd you leave?"

"It was William's idea I leave DC for school. He regretted not doing it himself."

"So what about your mom?"

Todd shifted uncomfortably. "See, the thing is, I met William back when I was about to lose her. I was a mess back then. She was dying. And I was a bad son. I would go out almost every night and drink, drinking was better than dealing with it. But what could I do about cancer? Once she was gone, I didn't go right to school like I wanted, I wasn't ready. So I took a year off, and during that time I became good friends with William and eventually he was like 'You don't need to stay in DC.' So I pulled myself together and moved to the West Coast." Todd decided it was best to end there. Explaining what happened while he was in LA was bound to destroy any chances of getting Linc out of those shorts.

"Losing a parent, man, that shit is rough. I'm sorry you had to go through it. And fuck cancer."

"Fuck cancer."

"It's good you've been talking to someone, though."

"You can tell I'm in therapy, huh?"

"Nothing wrong with it."

Todd finished his glass quicker than he intended. "I warned you it was depressing. I didn't want to kill the vibe."

"The vibe? When I texted you, I wasn't trying to get you over here for sex."

"Well, that's disappointing."

Linc looked him over, sizing him up for action. He almost reiterated how radiant he thought Todd was, but realized it would be overkill. He could have gone the rest of the night taking pictures without laying a finger on him. "You want sex?" he asked.

"I think I do."

"You think?"

"I *do.*"

LINC WONDERED HOW OFTEN Todd hooked up. Surely he had options but there was a pronounced modesty that didn't lend itself to hookups.

He drinks. Linc's eyes strayed to the empty wine glass on the counter. "Are you sure?"

Todd spoke so softly Linc almost didn't hear: "I need it."

Linc took his hand and led him up the staircase to his bed. Todd sat on the edge and Linc untied his shoes. "What are you doing?" Todd asked. Linc smiled at him, pulled off the shoes, then his socks. He moved on to Todd's belt, and as Todd lifted his waist for Linc to remove his jeans, he knew the answer. Linc was caring for him.

As a submissive man who was also large and muscular, Todd craved the weight of a lover with a similar build. Failing that, as Linc did with his fit but slight frame, Todd preferred other compensations. When he was down to snug briefs, Linc urged him back and kissed skin that blushed and tingled. Todd slid his hand between them and moaned, gratified upon discovering Linc overcompensated.

Linc braced himself for the disappointment that came with when trying to fuck someone new. If they weren't prepared for his size, they'd be reduced to "messing around" until he was ready to give up and go to sleep. Todd was game, but Linc also knew how frustrating it was to make the attempt with a man who only pretended to relax. As they tossed aside their remaining clothing, Linc made sure their encounter did not devolve into a series of letdowns if Todd couldn't take it. "Before we do this, I need to know for sure what you want because . . ."

"Are you asking if I'm a bottom?"

"I'm only making sure."

Todd laughed and squeezed him. "I'm a big boy. I know how to take it."

"Turn over, then."

Todd did. Linc devoured him, summoning sounds and words Todd didn't know were in him.

THE CLUB, THE DRINKS, Linc's stamina, a nap, a harder, more vocal round—they all blurred as Todd finally felt at home. His celibacy came to an end that night—that *morning*—not with a transient, desperate hookup but with a body he would have known had he remained in DC. In one night, Linc anchored him there. Half asleep, he reached for Todd, clutched his chest to make sure Todd hadn't disappeared. His tongue was in Todd's mouth again, his hand stroking him until Todd moaned for the final time and drifted off.

In the late morning, Todd showered in the adjacent bathroom, wiped the condensation from the mirror and faced his reflection. He grabbed the edges of the sink to steady himself as memories flooded back, clear as crystal—the glass breaking against his face, slamming against the wooden deck on the other side, the bloody gashes and bruises that never went away. He saw them now in the mirror. His skin was practically flawless and he knew they weren't there, but he counted each one—the long gash on his right cheek, the sores on his scraped chin, the slashes across his forehead. His nose crooked from being split open. Gashes on his forearms, crisscrossing with healthy veins protruding from his muscle.

He squeezed his eyes shut and took measured breaths, willing the memories away. When he faced himself again the wounds and scars were gone.

Linc sat at the bed's edge rolling a blunt when Todd returned, expertly and tightly, his tongue gliding across the wrapper to seal it. He withdrew a lighter to lock it all in. Todd sat beside him and placed a hand on his back. He wondered if the gesture was too intimate and familiar in the light of day, if any claims could be made after their curiosities were already satisfied.

Linc took a deep toke. "You good?"

"Yes."

"Are you sure?"

"Maybe we'll talk about it one day but, for now, I'm good."

Linc searched his eyes, stroked his cheek. Maybe it wasn't intended when he did it, but Linc's finger traced an outline of a long healed scar, as if he knew.

twelve.

"Ever been to the Hamptons?" Sidney asked William, tossing him the basketball, hard.

William caught it, but thought his stomach would cave from the impact. "The Hamptons? That's some white people shit." He bounced the ball a bit, took the shot. Missed.

They were in Sidney's backyard and it was the end of the school year. Sidney and William were seventeen. Even back then, Sidney was impossibly tall. William was tall, but Sidney was taller. And on this day, warm as it was with a setting sun filtering through towering dogwoods in the Baptistes' small backyard court, Sidney was godlike. Molded from gold. Shirtless and lean with broad shoulders and rippling abs. "My dad has white people money now," he told William, catching the rebound and dunking like he had an audience. He almost brought down the entire backboard. "He finally made senior partner at his firm." He tossed the ball back to William who was nearly thrown again.

"Dope. So when are y'all getting a real court?" William had zero game but he figured the appropriate dose of shit talk would distract from his lack of athleticism. Competition was the lifeblood of their friendship.

"Nobody says 'dope' anymore."

William took another shot. He didn't miss this time.

"You shoot like Karl Malone," Sidney went on. "When you're mad." A grin.

"Why would I be mad?" William asked, tossing the ball to Sidney as hard as he could.

Sidney caught it firmly between his hands. The momentum didn't shake him one bit. "If you wanna go, just say you wanna go."

William was aware of the Baptistes' yearly trips to New York, but a pass through the Hamptons was new information. "What do you even do in the Hamptons?"

"Dunno. Play polo? Drink champagne?"

"That shit sounds boring as shit!" William laughed.

Sidney laughed with him and dunked again. "Rich people are boring!"

It steadily became dark out. Although the sun set an hour later now, William's mother enforced a ridiculous curfew on the days he didn't work. He was supposed to be home half an hour ago. William hated being at home; being at the Baptistes' every night he and Sidney weren't on the schedule would always be the better option.

"I'll go," he said. "Are you really going?"

"In a few weeks. You think your mom would trip?"

"She's not the problem. Work is the problem. Unlike you, I can't afford to go in part-time or take days off."

"So it's a money thing," Sidney mused.

William shook his head. "It won't make a difference. Never mind. I can't go." He was looking away, but briefly caught Sidney's concerned eye.

Sidney bounced the ball and took a shot from an imaginary three point line. All net. "You're going," he said. "I'm gonna make sure you go . . ."

The memory as a dream dissolved into day and Sidney's statuesque teenage form gave way to Travis's head resting against William's chest. William gently rubbed his arm and Travis turned to him, wide awake, then rolled his eyes and pulled away. "What did I do?" William asked. "I just woke up."

Travis was on his feet, searching the bedroom for his things, which must have been scattered all throughout the condo. "You always do this," Travis groaned.

Leaving the party last night they walked to William's car in silence. When Travis was secure in his seat he folded his arms and stared off into nothing. William immediately knew what he needed to apologize for. "I'm sorry I wasn't more attentive. There were a lot of people there I had to catch up with." No response from Travis. "Do you want me to take you home?" He dreaded the thought. His own place was so much closer and, although the train was still running, William wasn't comfortable dropping him off at a station.

"I know how to fend for myself," Travis said. "I mean, maybe I wish I could've been by your side more. I don't know. I don't have anything in common with the people there. They were all friendly, though."

"Before I start this car, I wanna know if we're having an argument. Am I taking you home?"

"You sound impatient."

"Travis, I'm tired and I wanna go home. I said I was sorry. What do you want to do?"

No response. William shook his head and started the car. He blasted Keith Washington all the way down Massachusetts Avenue just to annoy Travis, who thought William's fidelity to 90s Adult R&B was corny. Once they made it to William's condo he immediately pulled Travis into a firm, deep kiss. What followed was as intense and rough as Travis remembered and longed for—bent over various pieces of furniture, flush and without mercy against walls, hanging off the bed. William fucked him until he was drenched with sweat and exhausted, then gathered him in his arms before they fell asleep.

Now they were back to . . . William wasn't exactly sure *what* they were back to. "I always do what?"

Travis slid on his underwear, his small but shapely ass making William's dick stir once more. "How can I be mad at you after that?" Travis demanded. "You know exactly what I want and it frustrates me. You wanna know what I was thinking last night in the car? 'Travis, you have no right to be mad at him over this.

Men like him aren't exactly lining up to date you. Bitch, *why are you mad?'* But I couldn't say that out loud. I couldn't tell you how insecure you make me feel."

William sat up in the bed, astonished they were in the same place they were four years ago and at the rising panic in Travis's voice.

"When I'm with you, even *right now,* I keep asking myself, why am I here? Why does he want me? I keep waiting for the punchline, for it to turn out you've been punking me this entire time. And I hate feeling like this because I don't wanna be Berger."

"Who is Berger?"

"Ugh, I forgot. You haven't seen a single episode of *Sex In The City,* have you? Berger was this deeply insecure motherfucker Carrie dated in season six, and in every episode he'd whine about not being good enough because she was so much more successful than him and he was so trash that he dumped her on a Post-It. A fucking Post-It! Berger is the worst boyfriend in television history but—God help me—I *might* understand where he's coming from. And then you fuck me like that and I forget all about it until the next day when it all comes back. Sometimes I wonder if I have anything to offer you."

"Come here," William told him. His voice was deep and authoritative but silk. The combination was irresistible to Travis, who immediately climbed onto the bed and straddled him. William held tight to his waist. "I like that you're not afraid to be open with me but you can't give me or any man that power. You can't tell another man he makes you feel insecure, Travis, especially when you have every right to be here. You don't have to be like me and you don't have to be like anyone at that party. You're here because you're sexy and funny and you keep me on my toes. There is no punchline. *I like you.*"

"I keep *you* on your toes?"

"Every time I see you. You help me relax. You help me get out of my own way. And you do *this* to me."

Travis felt William pulse against his ass and he laughed.

"How about we spend the day together? You can take the lead," William offered.

"You mean I'm in charge? I'm the boss of you?" Travis stroked his chin. "Hmm ... What can I make you do today? Oh! I know." He clutched William's chest and leaned in. "I'm gonna make you watch *Sex In The City.*"

"Anything except that."

"I'm in charge! We might be able to knock out the entire first season today. I'll cook."

"You cook now?" William grinned.

"One of the many ways I've grown since our last try."

"We're not talking about instant ramen and Hot Pockets, are we?"

"You too good for instant ramen and Hot Pockets?"

"That's a trick question, right?"

"I'm in charge!"

William laughed to disarm him and in a swift move rolled over so he was on top. "You're not in charge yet." He tugged at his briefs and soon Travis's knees were pushed against his chest, just before William's face disappeared.

thirteen.

"AT FIRST I THOUGHT it was triggered by something—a feeling, an event. Maybe when I was upset or vulnerable, but it also happens when I feel perfectly fine. I realized it's a reminder. Any time I see myself in the mirror with those scars, it's like I'm being told there's something I haven't resolved. It doesn't happen all the time. But when it does, I—"

Seated before his laptop at William's slate breakfast bar, Todd minimized the video and dragged its icon to the cloud folder he shared with Dr. Walker. It was Monday morning and the rain came down in sheets, lashing the windows. The forecast said it would rain all week and the temperature would drop about twelve degrees. The merciful seventy degree average from his first couple of weeks in DC could have been a fluke. He hoped the weather didn't dampen his mood on his first day coaching at Definitions.

When Todd mentioned to Dr. Walker he was leaving the country for six weeks, she suggested he keep a video journal. She didn't want him falling out of the habit of talking about how he felt if they weren't able to connect. He committed to three videos a week. It wasn't long before he realized she encouraged video so he'd be comfortable looking at himself.

He opened another, recorded during his fourth week in San Rafael when the questions peaked. "I don't mind certain kinds of attention, I guess. I just don't want to be the center of it. I don't like being scrutinized or having to explain myself, and that's usually what it comes down to. It's well-intentioned, I get it, but it makes me uncomfortable. And I didn't come all the way here to talk about me. I go out of my way *not* to make things about me. I don't want to take up space, but everywhere I go, I do."

In the video Todd laughed faintly at what he was about to say. "I know how I look. It wouldn't be honest to pretend I haven't leveraged it in ways. I just want people to get over it." He stopped the video and didn't bother transferring. It wasn't anything the doctor hadn't already heard from him. *Pretty People Problems*—the phrase he'd used with her. She'd asked why he said it so dismissively.

"Let's be honest. I could have it a lot worse, right?" he asked. "I know why people stare and there's worse things they could be doing to me."

"People *have* done worse to you," she countered. "You're privileged in a lot of ways. That doesn't mean you aren't allowed to experience pain, Todd. It doesn't mean you have it all figured out. What did we say about misplaced guilt?"

"It's unproductive."

"Every painful thing you've experienced, you wear it. So when people stare at you, you feel scrutinized, judged, like maybe you could have handled things differently."

"If I was a stronger person, there would have been a different outcome."

"Close, but be careful accusing yourself of not being strong enough."

That feeling of weakness inspired the next video he clicked. "More than what it did to my face, the worst part of what happened was, for a long time afterwards, I felt weak. I fought Deacon because I needed to protect myself. But I loved him. I couldn't hit him as hard as he hit me. That's why he got back up. That's why he did what he did. It made me feel like less of a man. I was ashamed. I still am."

He paused the video and sipped his tea. The Incident. The moment that crystallized why he felt so broken and what pushed him into therapy in the first place.

THERE WERE REASONS DEACON'S birthday parties were legendary, starting with his Echo Park condo. South-facing floor-to-ceiling windows that allowed sunlight to pour in during the day. A floating staircase with a top landing overlooking the open living area below. The men he invited were the second reason. All successful, attractive and fit, mostly from the film, television and music worlds. Deacon surrounded himself with beautiful, unattainable men and now they crowded his home.

Todd sat on the steps and observed the scene. He wasn't sure Deacon even knew all these people but he and his friends had curated and pruned the guest list for weeks. One of those friends, Cole, planted himself next to Todd and placed an arm around him.

"You seem like you're enjoying yourself!" Although they were right next to each other, Rihanna's latest was so loud Cole had to yell. He had the romantic, devastating looks of a soap opera lead—piercing blue eyes, square jaw, jet black curly hair. But those looks hadn't landed him a role in the remaining soaps left on air. So far he had some catalogue work, an Old Navy commercial and a bit part in a gay indie film under his belt.

"I just caught him in the bathroom," Todd said, as loud as he could without anyone else hearing him.

"Coke again?"

"It's every day now. Can you talk to him?"

"Everyone does coke. Here, have some of this." Cole handed Todd his cup and he took a sip. It was cold and red and strong. "Deacon's older than the rest of us. Who's he gonna listen to?"

Todd chewed on it for a moment, wondering if he should tell Cole everything.

They'd met at the 24 Hour Fitness on Santa Monica Boulevard, just as Todd wrapped up undergrad. A spot here and a compliment there led to coordinated training schedules and post-workout smoothies, which graduated to dinners and eventually breakfast the morning after. Deacon had roughly the same composition as Todd—over six feet and powerfully muscled. But he was twenty years older and twenty pounds heavier. Handsome, maybe once he'd even been "pretty," but now there was a hardness about him. His eyes looked like they'd witnessed a war, or like he'd led one.

It was easy for Todd to fall in love with him, which made it easier for him to agree to put his Masters on hold and join Deacon's small agency. He was an instant hit, booking jobs easily in spite of his palpable shyness. He was lost in love and wanted to make Deacon happy.

Being in charge of Todd's career brought out Deacon's controlling side, paired with a significant drug habit.

"I have a friend here," Cole continued, "he runs an agency out of New York. He's had his eye on you all night. His guys do a lot of training videos for bodybuilding sites, you know the how-to videos for each exercise? He gets them in *Flex, Muscle & Fitness, Men's Health*—but they're all a bunch of white guys who look like me. No diversity at all. You should talk to him."

Todd shook his head. "Leave Deacon for another agent *and* another coast?" He couldn't fathom it. Deacon had become increasingly volatile since he was going through a hellish divorce and his wife's number kept ballooning. He took it out on Todd, raging throughout the condo, breaking things. Every now and again he'd put a fist through a wall. He always calmed down, tender and apologetic, drawing Todd back in.

"Deacon's a good guy but he's older, you know? He's not getting you in front of the right eyeballs. You should be doing more fitness stuff. You're really jacked now."

Todd let it slip: "I have no choice these days."

"No choice?"

Todd shrugged. "I've been pushing myself extra hard for the past few months."

"I can tell! You shouldn't be doing underwear ads. You're way too vascular. Are you training for something?"

Only my life. Todd knew he had to get away from Deacon, but for reasons other than the ones Cole was so oddly passionate about. When cocaine wasn't flying up Deacon's nose he discovered a new, arbitrary reason to scream at Todd—Todd wasn't dieting or training properly, and as a result wasn't booking the jobs Deacon wanted (Todd was in the best shape of his life), Todd was flagrantly flirting with or checking out other men (Todd had become increasingly shy around other men since being with Deacon), Todd didn't clean up after himself (Todd left the condo spotless since he didn't want to hear Deacon's mouth), Todd wasn't affectionate or didn't want sex enough (being screamed at like a child for days on end didn't do much for the libido). What hurt most was when Deacon told Todd he wasn't smart enough to complete his Masters. *You don't even have the interpersonal skills to go into that field. You don't know how to talk to people. Why would anyone feel safe with you? Just stand in front of the camera and look good.*

Todd couldn't bring himself to identify it for what it was—an abusive relationship. Who would he talk to? Who would believe it? Would their friends take it seriously? Could he tell William?

He forced the notion away. Deacon was just frustrated with the divorce and he had a coke problem. Besides, it wasn't like Deacon had hit him or anything. That's what Todd had been telling himself for the past several weeks.

Cole inched closer. "Hey, are you alright?"

Todd didn't realize it but his face had collapsed into tears. His body hadn't succumbed to sobbing; he was still a big, strong oak but tears were streaming hot and fast. "I need to leave," he whispered weakly, finally telling himself, *Yes, you are being abused.*

Cole didn't hear him.

Todd pulled away and rushed upstairs. In the bedroom he searched for his keys and realized they had to be in the kitchen somewhere. Back downstairs, squeezing through guests, trying and failing at his height to be discreet. As he checked a drawer a hand landed on his upper arm. "Todd, right?"

He wiped his face and turned. A man—medium height, blond—immediately held out his hand. "Sorry, I've been trying to catch you all night. I'm Nate. Cole might have mentioned—"

Todd shook Nate's hand, hoping he couldn't spot the panic in his voice or behind his eyes. "New York, right?"

"I know this probably isn't the right time to steal clients since it's his birthday and all but—" Nate slipped Todd a business card. "Give me a call tomorrow?"

"Sounds good."

Nate gave him a questioning look and disappeared into the crowd.

Todd found his car keys and made sure his wallet and phone were on him. Heart pounding, he slipped back into the party, making his way through the crowd as quickly as possible. The condo felt unrecognizable; it was difficult to tell where everything was, including the right path to the door, with so many people packed into it. But soon he reached his exit, and his heart pounded with the prospect of being in the safety of his car and on the road to anywhere. He wasn't sure where he would go or what he would do or if he would ever come back and get the rest of his stuff but he would finally be away from him.

Deacon's hand latched onto Todd's from the crowd and Todd faced him. Sweat beaded Deacon's forehead. His eyes were a mix of confusion and controlled mania.

Let me go, Todd mouthed.

Deacon's grip tightened. The keys' teeth keys dug into Todd's palm. And the card. He hadn't pocketed Nate's card and it was balled up around the keys in his hand. Its crudely bent corners made Deacon's grip excruciating.

"Let me go," Todd said aloud this time. No one heard him.

Deacon used both hands to pull Todd to him, then wrapped him in a hug. His lips were at Todd's ear. "I'm sorry. Just stay with me tonight. Please. *Please* don't leave me, not tonight."

Todd was swept into socializing for the rest of the evening

as a couple, with Deacon by his side. Todd coached himself through each conversation; he knew Deacon wouldn't make a scene with everyone around but he was sure not to do or say anything Deacon could use against him later, and only if Todd bothered to stay. Todd was determined to get out of there once it was over.

After the crowd thinned and the pulsating dance music gave way to mid-tempo R&B, Cole was in his face again, asking if he was okay. Todd told him he was fine. Deacon seemed not to notice. Cole hugged him on his way out, whispering in his ear. "Don't forget to call Nate."

The moment Cole was gone Todd looked around him and realized he was alone with Deacon in the kitchen.

Deacon held his arms out. "You stayed. Thank you."

"I need to go," Todd said.

Deacon took a step forward and Todd took an equal step back, his eyes darting around. Deacon stood between him and the exit. Todd's heart sank as he realized they were a good twenty feet up from ground level so leaving through the adjoining deck wasn't an option. The only way out was through the front.

"What's gotten into you?" Deacon asked. "It's my birthday and you're leaving? You're not happy in LA? You wanna run off to New York?" He withdrew Nate's crinkled business card from his pocket. "Dropped something."

"Deacon, I don't wanna argue, I wanna leave. You had your party, we pretended to be cool for your friends, now please let me go."

"I'm not letting you go until you tell me why."

"Because I don't want you screaming at me and calling me stupid again. I've been rationalizing this for months, making excuses for you but I can't anymore. You have a cocaine problem, for one, which came out of *nowhere*. You know how I feel about drugs. I told you about my dad. It's the reason I won't take the enhancements you think I need to get the body you want me to have *overnight*. I don't believe in *any* kind of drug use. And your anger. I understand the divorce has you under pressure but you need to control your temper before you hurt someone. *Like me.* Now are you gonna let me through?"

Deacon stepped aside. Todd knew it was bullshit but what choice did he have? When Deacon grabbed him as he walked past, it was gently, at the waist, pulling Todd close again. "Wait."

Todd swallowed the knot in his throat. It came back immediately.

"Are you going to New York?"

"I'm not going to New York."

"Then why did you have his card?" Deacon was sweating again, his eyes wild, his voice low and measured.

"He gave it to me earlier tonight. I'm not thinking about New York."

"Then where are you going?"

"I don't know."

"Don't lie to me."

"I'm not lying."

It happened too fast for Todd to properly right himself. Deacon shoved him back hard, sending Todd flying into the kitchen table. He brought it all down, mostly empty liquor bottles, a few shattering upon hitting the floor. None of the glass hit him but he sat stunned, his back against the capsized table top.

Deacon sniffed and brought his hand across his nose, wiping at a nonexistent dusting. "Don't ever lie to me!" he roared.

Todd knew he would have to fight his way out. Deacon was beyond reason.

"Get up," Deacon spat, standing over him. "Get off the floor. Let's go upstairs."

Todd reached for the neck of a knotty Seagram's bottle, priming himself with a deep breath. "You're gonna let me walk out of here."

"Put the bottle down and take your sweet ass upstairs. You could've left a long time ago but now all of a sudden—*on my birthday*—you've grown a backbone?"

Todd's face flushed with anger and embarrassment. His grip

around the bottleneck tightened, although he still couldn't imagine hitting Deacon with it.

"Big, grown-ass man scared of his own shadow. What do I have to be worried about? I've never seen someone so weak in my life. Put the bottle down."

Todd knew it was useless but he asked anyway. "Why do you talk to me that way?"

"Because I know you won't do anything about it."

Todd nodded solemnly. He understood it. Deacon had good reason to believe Todd wouldn't stand up for himself. But he did stand. On his feet with squared shoulders and chin jutted upward, Todd told him once more, "You're gonna let me walk out of here." His heart pounded so hard his body shook. His hand was so slick with sweat the bottle was ready to slip from his hand. "Please step aside."

Deacon breathed through flared nostrils, inches from Todd's face, not budging. Todd's eyes moistened as he stared into Deacon's, searching, pleading. Aside from rage, nothing was there. When he tried to fake Deacon out by stepping to the left and sprinting to the right, Deacon caught him by his collar, yanking him backwards and bringing them both to the floor before Todd had the chance to estimate a backswing with the bottle to connect with Deacon's head. He'd lost grip of his weapon upon hitting the floor and tried to shield his face against the punches.

Deacon got him in the nose, a sickening *smack-crunch*. He kneed Deacon in the groin, grabbed for the bottle again and brought it down on Deacon's head with a hollow thump. He fell back, no longer straddling Todd, wildly attending to the pain between his legs and the expanding knot on his head. Todd pounced on him, knowing he had to put him down. Make sure he could never get back up.

Teeth gritted. Hands around Deacon's thick neck. Blood and tears streaming down his face. Deacon's palm smashing into Todd's already broken nose.

Todd held tight, grunting and crying as Deacon fought for

release and wheezed, trying to draw breath. His eyes bugged. Face reddened. He couldn't breathe.

The grip loosened.

Todd stood, watched Deacon cough, struggling for breath.

"Don't get up," he told him. Todd realized how congested he sounded. His nose would never be the same.

Leaning against the counter for support, he wiped his face with the front of his shirt, horrified upon pulling it back and seeing so much blood. He pulled the keys from his pocket and turned to Deacon, who was once again on his feet. With a final show of strength he grabbed Todd by the collar and the waist of his jeans and sent him flying.

Todd twisted on his ankle. He didn't know he was headed for the deck doors, could barely hear Deacon screaming as the glass exploded. Todd didn't immediately feel it, or realize what happened until he was on the other side. He was disoriented. Up was down. For a moment he believed he was dead or dying. Realizing he'd just been thrown through glass was an out of body experience.

He looked at his hands, his arms, at the shards of glass embedded in them, the mess of blood surrounding the cuts. Blood flowed into his eyes as the pain set in. His entire body felt like a truck had run over him. He tried to get up but collapsed into the glass scattered on the wooden deck. He passed out. Later he would convince himself it was for self-preservation; he needed to play possum so Deacon would leave him alone. But mostly he hoped he could skip forward to a better day.

Sirens brought him back briefly. Someone was asking him questions, making sure he was alive. He was lifted onto a gurney. Darkness again. He woke up as they pulled glass out of him. They told him not to panic. He asked where Deacon was. He trembled through the pain. His face was on fire. He told them to call William. They assured him they would; they had his phone. An authoritative voice explained his weight propelled him through the glass. It was also what saved him; it caused the glass to shatter into smaller pieces upon impact, so there weren't any stubborn jagged shards large enough to puncture an organ. "It's also a good thing you didn't go over the rail." Before Todd passed out again he heard another voice, a female one, marvel "Shame. Such a beautiful face."

THE MEMORY BURNED. HE felt everything from that night two years ago—the anger, the shame, the glass. *I didn't hit him hard enough. Maybe I should have killed him.*

Todd transferred the video to the shared folder and shut his laptop.

"Look who's home," William remarked, emerging from the back. He was already dressed for the day but not in a suit this time—a burgundy pullover, dark jeans and black boots. He squeezed Todd's shoulder and grabbed an orange from the ceramic bowl at the other end of the counter. Todd caught a whiff of John Varvatos Artisan cologne. "Have fun Saturday night?"

"It was cool," Todd said brusquely. He had a bone to pick with William.

"I bet it was, and if I had to guess where you've been all weekend—"

"Don't bother. Who do you think you are?"

"Excuse me?"

"You left a bottle of Xanax on my dresser." Todd chuckled at the nerve. "William, you know how I feel about drugs and Xanax, specifically, was never an option, because of the side effects. And why do you have a prescription for it anyway?"

"Xanax are like Altoids at this point. I barely use it. It's there if you need it."

"I don't need it and I don't *want* it. I have ways of controlling my anxiety." He held up his mug. "Herbal teas. Exercising—"

"And lots of drinking. Yesterday I noticed a *significant* amount of Macallan missing."

"I was just pre-gaming before I went out the other night—"

"I don't want you becoming an alcoholic. You know why."

"And you know why I can't risk becoming a drug addict. I can replace your liquor."

"I don't care about the bottle, I care about you and I want you to care for *yourself.* And I especially want you to be careful when it comes to Linc."

"This again?"

"Yes. *This again.* Do whatever you want, it's your life, but you need to know what you're up against. If you fall for him, you're gonna fall hard. And when he becomes distracted because you're no longer the most beautiful man he's ever met, it's gonna hurt. I know him and I know you."

"I don't care."

William frowned.

"It doesn't matter where it ends up," Todd told him. "Let me live." *Let me have fun. Let me feel him. Let me.* "If I fall for him it's not your problem. If he lets me down it's not your problem. We're grown."

"You're right. I'm sorry."

"I can't have another man control my life."

William nodded. Before leaving he squeezed Todd's shoulder once more. "Good luck on your first day."

fourteen.

William was rarely interested in Julian's rants, mainly since Julian brought so much shit on himself. But William knew the duty of a friend was first to listen. Not to immediately understand, empathize or condone but to allow Julian the space to vent. So much space.

"I don't appreciate being told I get into relationships just so I can check off a box. I was with Blair because, for some reason, I liked his old judgemental ass. Same with Sean! I don't believe in wasting anyone's time. I wasted *his* time? He's in the best shape of his life because of me! What is he even talking about?"

William had bags. Design magazines, fabric and tile samples, a small bamboo plant he planned to gift a client and a frozen frap. A dark parka shielded him against what was now a drizzle. "Is that rhetorical or do you want an answer?" he asked, hitting the 5 on the elevator panel. "Because I have one."

"He's bitter and dateless," Julian went on. "When people are insecure they project all their shit onto you."

"If we're talking about the same Dr. Blair Covington, I don't think he has anything to be insecure about. Like you said, he's in the best shape of his life, he has *amazing* skin, he's a doctor—"

"I didn't call you to talk about how perfect Blair is. And he's a *dentist.*"

"I know! I was in three weeks ago for x-rays and a cleaning."

"Why didn't you say anything?"

"You want me to tell you every time I go to the dentist?"

"Yes, if the dentist in question is my ex. As my friend, it's your responsibility to tell me when my exes are spiraling."

"In this particular case, there's nothing to report. Blair was great last time I saw him and, from what I'm hearing now, in fighting form when *you* saw him." The elevator opened onto the fifth floor and William entered the main lobby of Kendall Design Group. The company name shimmered in silver letters against a red wall behind a long, white and currently unoccupied reception desk. The job was shared between the assistants and was rarely manned unless they were expecting appointments.

Yet William smelled the distinct scent of Prada cologne.

He set the bags down and walked the frap to his office. "I need to call you back." He ended the call before Julian had the chance to protest.

James West had been William's assistant for two and a half years, plucked directly from a George Washington University meet-and-greet and paid an enviable salary to do whatever William asked. Tasks often fell outside the realm of client matters but were never demeaning. They were just frequent, to the point William decided to give the young man a break today and run around the city in the rain gathering gifts and samples himself, allowing James more time to become acquainted with unexpected guests like Cintra Mason-Baptiste.

They sat on the heather gray sofa at the K Street-facing window, holding steaming cups of designer coffee and chatting comfortably like old friends. James's long locs were tied in an elaborate bun on top of his head and Cintra's cream boatneck sweater casually exposed one silky brown shoulder. "Oh my god, William, we have to bring James to the house!" Cintra exclaimed, rushing over to kiss his cheek. "He's so cute and fun!"

"He usually comes with," William assured her, breaking away to hang his coat. "Aren't *you* a surprise?"

"I haven't seen your office in a while. I was hoping you'd be here but by the time I started cutting up with James I forgot all about you."

"If James can make you forget about me then I apparently hired the right guy." William winked at his assistant.

"I was just telling her how you got the crazy idea you weren't accepting any new clients," James offered. It was meant to be teasing and conversational but made William's eyes narrow.

"Which is crazy," Cintra added, "since we both know you're doing my dream home. James and I were thinking minimal but not modern. Classic and tranquil, almost Southern, with lots and lots of white—*Bancroft white.* Bancroft or Decatur white rooms with dark, gilded doors and filled with vintage pieces, like this nineteenth century Swedish secretary's desk I restored. You're good at that."

"I still need to see the property."

"We're going today. The three of us."

"In this rain?"

She gestured wildly to the window. "It's letting up—"

"And I just hung my coat. I need a few minutes. I have to make some calls, check emails, put my feet up and stare out the window while I enjoy my frap. James can keep you entertained; he's done a fantastic job already. Now may I ask the both of you if I can have my office?"

"Fine," she said, then placed a hand on his chest and lowered her voice. "We need to talk about your boy."

THE HOUSE WAS BUILT in 1899 and possessed the historic charm Cintra demanded, at least from the outside. Up until that spring it was rented by a boutique staffing agency that relocated to Alexandria, so the interiors were neutral and lacked character. A few walls needed to come down to restore rooms to their original dimensions and the kitchen, having suffered nearly fifteen years of constant traffic by office personnel, needed a complete remodel. But the property still boasted the high ceilings Cintra wanted and its tall windows looked out onto Lincoln Park. And of course there was the brick-paved sidewalk outside an iron gate.

After the house, they strolled through an architectural antiques warehouse on Eighteenth. Cintra agreed with William foregoing pricey furniture showrooms in favor of salvage. She was an artist and loved projects. When Sidney first introduced them, William wanted to hate her but she wouldn't allow it. They developed their own relationship and language independent of Sidney, bonding over art and design, floating jargon that sent Sidney out of the room.

Everything here was worn and aged, dying for a sanding and a coat of paint. But it was a beautiful clutter, old headboards and stair parts, shutters and doors all lined up against each other based on color family and age approximations. Cintra was enchanted by the textures and mused about where these items once lived and the stories behind them. She had an idea for every piece that caught her eye and they hadn't discussed a budget.

"By the time we finish everything else, you'll have changed your mind at least twice," he reminded her. "We're trying to get a feel for your *eventual* living room. There's still a wall I'd need to knock down."

"You're right," she said. "Speaking of knocking down walls—"

"Don't do this—"

Cintra laughed. "I don't think a baby's in the cards for me and your boy."

William looked at James, who trailed behind and documented items with his iPhone. He got the message and made himself scarce before William returned to Cintra. "Don't say that."

"Sidney's forty, William. I'm not too far behind. What do I look like birthing and raising babies?" She sighed, frustrated but wistful. "I'm not saying it can't be done but there was a moment in the last ten years when we could've kicked it into gear. We were already in our thirties by the time we got married. We did everything so late . . . You've known him almost your whole life, William. Did I make a mistake?"

The day of their wedding, Cintra called William into her

bridal suite and asked nearly the same thing. He had the opportunity then. "What do you mean a mistake? You just did things differently. There's still time. Who says you need to have a kid before a certain age?"

She chuckled. "Well, my doctor, for one."

"I doubt he said you *can't* have a baby."

"He didn't exactly, but carrying and having a child isn't exactly a day at the spa, even for younger women. The older you get, the more precarious it gets. Luckily, I'm in perfect health. I've been avoiding the real issue here—it's Sidney." They soon came across an armoire that had seen better days. She gasped and inspected the tag. "It's only nine sixty-three. We should probably get this today."

"Along with the one hundred seventy-five dollar brass toilet paper holder you insisted on? Are you angry with him? You wanna break him because he doesn't want kids?"

"Talk to Sidney."

"But I'm talking to *you* right now."

Cintra continued her exploration and William kept pace alongside her, occasionally making eye contact with the sales associate. They let William browse freely with no interference since he spent so much there, so each glance was one of gratitude.

"A lot happened in New York, to the point where I stopped being a priority. Starting a family gradually fell out of the question. And now we're in DC. I want my Capitol Hill Queen Anne, brick-paved sidewalk and overpriced antique bath fixtures. If he's good at anything, it's spending money."

It slipped out before William could catch it. "I'm sorry."

"For?" Cintra drifted to an old medicine chest and ran her fingers along its gilded edges.

"I want the two of you to be happy."

She chuckled and turned to him. The cynicism etched across her face seemed accusatory and he was briefly terrified she knew everything about him and Sidney. "Happiness is incidental in marriage. People get married because they want things. If this was only about love and happiness, we'd be having a different conversation right now."

"But you do love him."

"Of course I do, that's the easy part. All I'm saying is, life-building is business. It can't be boiled down to emotions when you're also investing *years* of time and money. At some point, you'll want payoff. DC is his last shot."

"Last shot for what?"

Cintra brushed at the chest's peeling paint, revealing the character beneath. "For him to act like somebody's husband."

fifteen.

"*A Love Supreme, The Low End Theory, The Velvet Rope, Songs In the Key of Life*—especially side four—and *Aquemini*. Now yours."

"Wait, what do you mean side four?" Todd asked.

"I mean the original release on vinyl. Two records—side one and two, then side three and four. Side four has 'As' and 'Another Star' back to back." Linc's jaw dropped, as if he'd just become aware of this incredible fact himself. "Don't get me wrong, the entire album is a masterwork. But those two songs *together*—" He sat back, his lips curling into a satisfied grin. "Bruh."

Todd considered it as he chewed a mouthful of snapper and rice. They were at a small table in the corner of Linc's favorite Jamaican spot. It was cramped, hot and the food took forever but it was the best in DC according to him. A playoff game was on the flat screen mounted above the counter, the sound drowned out by the Gyptian blasting from someone's docked device.

"Top five, huh? I'm not sure I can answer that," Todd finally said.

"Everyone has a top five."

"But you love music so much more than me. The stuff you're into has way more cultural impact."

"Try me."

Todd took a breath. "Okay. *Listen Without Prejudice Volume*

One, Missundaztood, Are You Gonna Go My Way, In Search Of, and *Late Registration.*"

"I wasn't expecting a rap album at all, but if there had to be one, it makes sense you'd choose early Kanye."

"I'm not sure how to take that."

Linc laughed. "I think it's a perfect list. I'm impressed with the inclusion of George Michael."

"I feel the same way as you about two perfect songs being next to each other—'Cowboys & Angels' and 'Waiting for That Day'."

"Agreed."

"And *Are You Gonna Go My Way* is peak Lenny to me. Like, he could never be more *himself* than he was on that album."

"I'm partial to *Mama Said* but I don't think you're wrong. Your tastes tell me a lot about you. A lot of that stuff came out in my twenties and I identified with it because I was trying to figure out who I was. So much of it is about identity, man, especially that Pink."

"I listen to a lot of it every day. Dr. Walker says I'm drifting, like there are parts of me I haven't figured out or reconciled. It's why I can't move throughout the world as confidently as I should." Todd sat back and chuckled at himself. "I'm almost thirty. A man should know who he is by then, right?"

"I think we have it figured out by thirty *only* if we're lucky."

"So when did you know?"

"I'm thirty-six now and there's parts of me I'm not crazy about. The thing is, once you figure it all out, the next challenge is fixing it. I haven't fixed it. Maybe when I'm forty or fifty I'll be pristine." Linc was suddenly wistful. "I can't wait to be older, man. Like those sharp, worldly, sexy motherfuckers in their fifties who know everything and everyone and they're bursting with wisdom and style and class. Those are the Black men who inspire me."

"You're pretty much there now, right?"

Linc grinned. "I'm still a little rough, man."

"That's not so bad." Todd's eyes connected with Linc's before drifting to the game.

"So who you got?"

"Got for what?"

Linc tipped his head towards the TV. "In the playoffs."

"Oh! For the West, Golden State, obviously. For the East, I don't know. But this looks like the end of the road for Miami." The guys at the bar reacted loudly to the game, alternating between disappointment and smug victory depending on their side.

"So you follow it a little bit?"

"I mean, we all follow it during playoffs, right? I tried to play when I was younger. Sucked at it. Mom got me into it because I was tall and she was sure I'd make friends."

"Did you make friends?"

"Sure, when I filled out and started scaring people," Todd laughed. "I was the biggest person in my class by the time I graduated."

"You were probably better than me. I can't play any sport for shit."

"You're in great shape, though."

"All calisthenics at home or at a park. Never been good at team sports. I hit a heavy bag every now and then if I find myself in a gym, but I can't do that shit you do. I can't afford to eat that much. What made you start?"

"I'd tried everything else and lifting was the only thing that looked good on me," Todd explained. The door swung open and a young woman entered, rushed and distracted as she made her way to the counter. Maybe she was just getting off work. Her braids fell over one shoulder and her skin was dewy and brown. Todd faintly made out that she was picking up an order she'd called in. "And it's cathartic for me somehow. Kind of like, how some people are calmed by knitting or drawing. I know it sounds crazy but it's like meditation—the counting, the breathing and concentration. I can feel myself getting better at it while I do it."

Linc responded but Todd didn't hear him. He was too

focused on one of the guys at the counter—around the same age as Todd, tall and skinny with a beard and a ballcap—attempting to chat up the woman who did her best to diplomatically decline his advances. Linc said something about the ginger beer running through him and left for the bathroom. The woman told the guy *No* for, in her mind, the final time before grabbing her order and making her way to the exit.

Don't follow her don't follow her don't follow her don't . . .

The guy waited until she was on the other side of the door before he went after her. Or maybe he wasn't going after her, Todd reasoned. Perhaps he was done with his meal, furious the Heat weren't making the Eastern Conference finals at this rate and decided to get in his car and go home.

Todd peered out the window as she walked down the street towards the train station. "Hey, ma!" The guy was close. Clearly he wanted to make his presence known so he wasn't as creepy about it as he could have been. Todd looked towards the bathroom. Linc hadn't emerged yet. He made his decision.

Out onto Twelfth Street. It was just before nine so not quite dark. The air was still heavy and humid from the rain earlier and it was quiet out, far past rush so not very busy. "Where you going?" the guy called out, catching up to her and falling into step.

She sped up.

"I'm just trying to get to know you, that's all."

"I already talked to you at the bar," she said tersely.

"Well let me walk you to the train. It's dangerous out here."

She scoffed. "I'm fine. Go watch your game."

"Come watch it with me."

"No thank you."

"Just let me have your number and I'll leave you alone."

She stopped, sighing heavily. As she pulled out her phone, Todd intercepted.

"Hey, I think you forgot to pay your tab."

The guy turned to him. "What?"

"They're looking for you. They want you to come back and

pay."

"They know me there. I got it. I'm kind of busy right now, if you don't mind."

"I really think you should go back inside."

The guy's face twisted up, annoyed. "Who are you? Can't you see I'm in the middle of something?"

"I see that. I also see she's not interested."

"So you throwing your cape on for a bitch you don't know?"

"Come on, man, you don't have to call her that. Come back in. I'll pay your tab. Just let her go. She's not interested. Can't you tell?"

The guy looked at her but her eyes connected with Todd's. She didn't appear angry or afraid, just anxious and exhausted. "You have a good night," Todd told her, before facing her harasser once more. He folded his arms across his chest, emphasizing how massive his pecs and forearms were. The guy wasn't more than one-seventy, certainly not a match if one considered size and strength alone. But Todd wasn't a fighter, and was so far removed from being a DC resident at this point he probably wouldn't know what to do if a fight commenced.

She didn't see much point in sticking around for their match and resumed her walk to the station. The guy didn't bother continuing his pursuit, instead shaking his head and heading back for the cafe. "You gon' get fucked up out here one day doing that shit, man."

He went inside as Linc was exiting. "What did I miss?"

"Nothing," Todd said. "Let's finish eating."

"Tell me what happened."

"He followed this woman after she said she wasn't interested and . . . maybe he just wanted her number. Or maybe he wanted more. Either way, I could tell she didn't wanna be bothered."

"You were about to fight him?"

Todd shrugged. "If I had to. Just to give her the chance to go home or wherever she was headed."

"You were about to fight him?"

"What am I supposed to do?"

Linc smiled, putting his arms around his waist. "You could've gotten hurt. You don't know that dude. But you're right. You might be a little crazy, though."

"I didn't think you were into PDAs."

Linc searched Todd's eyes. "I'm not but you have me feeling and doing things I never thought I would." He didn't care who passed when he kissed him. When he pulled back, Todd's face reddened, flush with a feeling he wasn't ready to identify.

"You know you just put a target on my back, right?" Todd grinned.

"Hey, I got you."

Todd stroked Linc's beard, pulled him close and kissed him back. "Then I got you too."

sixteen.

THE FIRST THING ANYONE noticed about Baron Lauderdale were his hands. Large, strong, manicured. Thick fingers nimble with an artistic grace. When he closed them around his chef's knife one imagined if such a large fist ever knocked someone's block off. But they were always gentle like him, built like a defensive lineman but teddy bear sweet. Hands large enough to palm a melon just as easily possessed Julian's ass once.

When they were together he maintained a modestly-trafficked food blog that took off once he added Youtube videos. He refused to appear in them fully—*It has to be all about the food*—but visitors would comment on how beautiful his hands were and how sexy and smooth his voice was. "It's ridiculous no one knows how you actually look," Julian eventually told him. "Just appear in *one* video. Let them see you from the waist up. I'll hold the camera. You cook."

The video itself was for Baron's short rib ragu but almost none of the comments were in response to the recipe. They remarked on his solid, heavy build and his adorable round face. They were calling him "Daddy." It yielded over 15,000 views in one week, five times more than any other video he had up at the time.

Now he was Internet-famous with a thriving catering business and well on his way to 100,000 Twitter followers. Last Julian checked, Baron had appeared on a cooking segment for the local morning news. To his relief it wasn't on the same station as Sean Lively. He couldn't have the two of them comparing notes.

"I thought you hated Virginia," Baron remarked now, flattening a ball of dough against his island counter with a rolling pin. "What was it you said? *Virginia isn't for lovers, it's for bigots and Kate Gosselin haircuts.*"

Julian watched him work from a stool across the counter. "And nice houses! I did say the houses were huge. You have a lot of space here."

"I do. We could've had it together."

"Jesus, Baron."

"That's why you're here, isn't it? You randomly hit me up and said you wanted to see me. I'm assuming we have unfinished business. Or you want some—"

"What kind of wine do you have?"

Baron wiped his hands on a towel and went to a cabinet. "I got you. Cab. Bordeaux. How about a blend?"

"California red?"

A wink. "Of course." Baron uncorked a bottle and poured two glasses with the mastery of a seasoned sommelier and slid one across the counter. "Should we toast?"

Julian immediately took his first gulp.

Baron shrugged. "I guess not."

"I'm here because you were always straight with me without making me feel bad for who I am."

Baron casually sipped. "I did. And you dumped me anyway."

"Be that as it may, a lot of people lately have been telling me how I ain't shit. In the *nastiest* way possible." Julian recounted the breakup with Sean and Sean's assault of his character, then the showdown with Blair that followed. Baron returned to his pastry, smoothing butter across the dough and sprinkling cinnamon, sugar and pecans. When the butter was completely covered he patted the ingredients in so they clung to the dough, then rolled it slowly, his hands careful to keep the roll tight and the dough from tearing. Julian made sure to focus on Baron's face while he talked, otherwise he'd be enchanted by those hands and lose track of his story.

Baron cracked a smile as he listened, amused at how Julian had mastered positioning himself as the victim in these situations, completely unaware he was the common thread in his own troubles. When the dough was rolled into a log, he cut it in eight parts and Julian stopped. "Are you making *cinnamon rolls?*"

"New recipe I'm working on." Baron wiped his hands again and took a sip. "Okay, so what I'm getting is you want me to tell you everyone is picking on you and they're bitter and jealous and need to leave you alone. Do you want me to beat them up too?"

"You trying to be funny?"

"You're funny enough for the both of us. You know, whenever you start off on one of your tangents all I can think about is how you had a nanny growing up."

"First of all my parents were very busy and second of all she wasn't a nanny."

"You told me a West Indian lady *who is not your mother* raised you. You're the only person I know who had a nanny. That shit blows my mind every time I think about it."

Julian rubbed his temple. "What does that have to do with anything?"

"Nothing really, it just falls in line with what we all know about you today. You see the world completely different from the rest of us. I'm not gonna beat up on you about it, but you need to understand why anyone who tries to love you gets so frustrated. Come here." Baron grabbed a small bowl and dipped a finger in. He pulled it back covered in white sauce. "This is the glaze I'm working on for the rolls. Taste it."

"You want me to put your finger in my mouth?"

"Yes."

It wasn't anything he hadn't done in the past. A perfectly normal gesture when two people were in love and one was a chef. Julian went to him, took his hand and sucked the glaze off his index finger. He did it in the most perfunctory way since he knew Baron was up to something. "It's fine," he told him.

"Just fine?"

"You're a fantastic chef."

"Thank you. A fantastic chef with a huge house, big enough for a dog to run around—"

"Oh please. Romulus hates Virginia more than I do!"

"Have you seen my yard?"

"Yes, and your smoker and your two-car garage. We won't work. We tried."

"Look, I don't have all these issues everyone else has with you. But I know why you left me. Or, why you *said* you left me, which sounds like bullshit but in a way it makes sense."

Because you always need to be the boss. It was a good enough reason, Julian thought as Baron pulled him close. They both had their alpha tendencies and clashed often as a result. The only time Julian ever submitted was in bed, and Baron was the only man he'd ever completely submit to without expecting a return.

"The rolls need an hour to rise," Baron whispered, sucking on Julian's ear. "Let's go upstairs."

"I didn't come here for this."

"You a goddamn lie. I know you ain't been letting that white boy hit. I know for a *fact.*"

"You can think whatever you want," Julian shot back, placing a hand against Baron's chest but not exactly pushing him away.

"You let Sean fuck you?" Baron pressed.

"None of your business."

"You can tell me."

Julian sighed. "No."

That was all Baron needed. He swept Julian up in a kiss. Julian's body went weak in a way it hadn't in years. Baron's kisses were sweet and intoxicating, his arms enormous and warm. He squeezed handfuls of Julian's ass and remarked on how much he missed it. Julian mumbled around Baron's tongue, something incoherent about squats. "I want you to sit on my face," Baron told him.

Upstairs was urgent. Hands fumbling to tear away clothes, Baron's mouth devouring every inch of Julian's body. Julian surrendered to him immediately, although he resisted a bit since Baron was new again. On his back, strong thighs wrapped around Baron's waist. Breath suspended once Baron was fully inside of him. Curses whispered as they rocked the bed. Julian grabbed the back of his neck and pulled him in for more kisses. He was reminded of how deeply he once loved him.

Later, with the cinnamon rolls forgotten and a reinvigorated storm pounding against the window, Julian felt rotten. The sex was what he needed, but he was overwhelmed by regret as Baron smiled at him and ran his fingers up Julian's back. "I'm so sorry," Julian whispered, nearly choking on the words. "You were good to me, really fucking good to me then."

"You don't have to apologize to me."

"Yes I do, and you're not the only one. I end up with these dudes and don't know what to do with them. And some of them turn out to be quality-ass people." He got up and began to dress. "I don't know why I can't get it right."

"You need to be honest with yourself about what you want. Or don't. Or who . . ."

"Who?"

"Listen, folks end up in relationships all the time with the wrong people. You want one kind of person and get with someone who looks the part, then he turns out not to be once you really get to know him. It happens. Sounds to me like you keep doing it over and over again, hoping you find one that fits." Baron climbed out of the bed and went to Julian, taking his chin in his hand. "You gotta figure out how to love someone for who they are, even the parts you don't like. Or be single for a while."

The rain wasn't as punishing by the time Julian was in his truck, driving up George Washington Parkway, but it was steady. Baron tried to get him to stay longer, to wait until the rain had passed completely. Julian was too afraid of getting comfortable and giving his ex the wrong idea. He had other exes to contend with. Apologies needed to be made, air needed to be cleared. He quieted the part of himself that shouted the real source of all this.

It was hard enough admitting he'd been wrong about so much. He had to face Blair and, at some point, Sean. He could just see the look on their faces.

But anything was easier than facing the whole truth.

seventeen.

SEATED BEFORE A PLATE of duck confit with maitake mushrooms, Sidney Baptiste swiped through William's tablet. Along with James, William and Cintra had compiled a portfolio—photos snapped at the salvage warehouse, Google images, examples from the KDG website—approximating the look and feel Cintra envisioned for the new house. Every now and then a weariness crossed his face as he considered the budget. "I want to remind you," Cintra told him, "salvage and restoration. I can do a lot of this stuff myself. William's just here to . . . you know . . . wrangle the contractors. I paint and build things. These only *look* like expensive ideas."

Sidney smiled at her. It was a little patronizing. "This is all very nice." He placed the tablet back on the table and returned to his duck.

"I'll talk to my guys and come up with an estimate but I need the two of you to figure out how much you're willing to spend," William told him. "Hopefully those numbers aren't too distant. And like Cintra was saying, a lot of it is restoration projects. I don't even need to be involved in that—"

"Remember what you did for that restaurant in Georgetown?" Sidney cut in. "The mural in travertine? I was thinking I wanted something like that for the bathroom."

"Travertine wouldn't exactly clash with the fixtures but it definitely falls outside of the style we were thinking of and, I gotta be honest, I can't do another mural. I don't have the time and you don't know your budget. I might be able to find a good mosaic travertine and brown glass tile for the showers but again—"

"What was the name of that spot?" Sidney asked, unable to detach himself from the idea.

"Mykonos," William told him, a patient resignation shading his voice. "How do you know that? We never talk about my work."

"Re-acquainted myself with it on your website the other day," Sidney offered. "And a really intricate iron railing for the staircase. Something . . ."

"Mediterranean," William finished.

"Is that the word I was looking for?"

"Every idea you've had since we sat down is in the general vicinity of Mediterranean."

"We did the Greek islands last year," Cintra explained to William. "He's been inspired by it ever since. At first I was on board but then I started thinking about what would highlight and honor my work. A white, minimal space does exactly that."

Sidney chuckled. "If I'm gonna be spending all this money, why not go all out?"

"You got something to prove?" Cintra asked.

"Maybe I do." Sidney called over the server and ordered an entire bottle of 1997 Cab and a plate of roasted foie gras for the table. "And it's romantic," he said with a grin. "Who wouldn't want to come home to that every day?"

"I'm sure we can combine everyone's ideas in a way that doesn't clash or break the bank," William offered.

"I'm the artist," Cintra pointed out.

"And I'm the money," Sidney countered.

"Which is probably why your tastes are so ostentatious. That's what happens when you work with a bunch of rappers."

"You trying to call me tacky?"

"The word I used was *ostentatious.*"

"There's nothing *ostentatious* about Mediterranean."

"Having money isn't the same as having ideas and knowing

how to conceptualize a space that looks good and makes sense. What you have in mind is far too grand for the scale of the house, Sidney. It's big but not *that* big."

"You're the one talking about dragging in a bunch of old used shit and painting it, like we have a lot of space for that."

William sank in his seat as they hissed at each other, withdrawing his phone and texting Travis. *Wyd?* He was ready for dinner to come to an end. Sure, the herb-roasted rabbit here was his best meal in months and he had a quivering, nearly drooling, anticipation for the foie gras, but was it worth suffering everything else at the table? He'd come to dinner with Cintra's words from the other day weighing on him. *DC is his last shot . . . to act like somebody's husband.* It was a calculated move on her part. William was Sidney's friend of nearly twenty-five years. She had to know, no matter what, he'd always land on Sidney's side of things. Suggesting Sidney fucked up in New York would prompt William to at least question him, instead of tossing him blind, knee-jerk support in the name of Britches Over Bitches. Sidney was being an arbitrary brat right now about the project which was enough for William to pull him off to the side. He was also achingly fine, now more than ever. Sidney Baptiste was the only man who could put William on notice. What Langley referred to as "a nigga in a suit" was the balance of polish, confidence and nonchalance William had envied for years. He just couldn't evoke the swagger Sidney possessed. Tailored within an inch of his life in his navy blue wool and mohair suit, he projected money a little louder than William and had a cocky air about him. The way he asserted himself was influenced by the rappers he'd grown up listening to, often not concerned with the sensitivity of the listener. It was what endeared him to his clients in New York and made William crave him now even more than the foie gras.

Travis responded quickly. *On a hot date right now. You?*

William knew he was being silly but responded in kind. *Same.*

Travis: *Ugh. Let's drop these zeroes and link up.*

"So how long do you two need?" William asked. "A week?

Two weeks? I'm happy to wait a month or even a year if need be."

"And he says it with such a tone," Cintra gasped.

William leaned in. "I made sure I let it spread rather quickly that I wasn't taking on any new work for the next several months, but I'm doing this only because you're my friends. I need the two of you to make a decision. There's a window of opportunity here, but a small one. I say it's best if we stick with Cintra's concept. She's the artist and she's resourceful enough to know where to cut costs. It also makes more sense with the square footage and the style of home you're moving into."

Sidney waved his hand dismissively. "Do whatever you want."

Cintra cut her eyes at him and excused herself from the table. "Is there a problem?" William asked once she was out of earshot.

"I'm sorry. I'm under a lot of pressure at the firm. You know how Langley is."

"I do, but is there a problem *at this table?*"

Sidney shrugged. "I mean, a little bit. Y'all got together and came up with all these ideas without me. Like I won't be living there, too."

"Sidney, we could barely get you to come to dinner tonight, according to how busy you are."

He took an indignant sip of his wine. "Then you could've waited."

"Was it your idea to come back to DC?" William asked.

"What difference does it make?"

"Seems like it would make a world of difference for your attitude."

"William, aside from Mom's party, this motherfucker has me in the office every weekend. Court is closed on the weekend! And after this I'm going *back* to the office. He's putting me to *work.*"

"Why don't you just quit?"

Sidney vigorously shook his head. "Oh no. I have to meet every challenge he throws my way."

"Why do you still believe that?"

"I don't want him to be right about me."

William resisted the urge to reach across and take his hand. "He's *never* been right about you. I've been telling you this since you were seventeen. You can't spend the rest of your life trying to please him. It has to be exhausting."

Sidney squinted his eyes and laughed. "I don't want to please him. I want to shut him the hell up." He rubbed his hands excitedly as the foie gras landed at the table. Cintra returned and they put the topic of home design on the backburner. They stuffed their faces with duck and took a tipsy trot down memory lane and eventually out into the rainy April night.

Cintra clung to her husband as he opened an umbrella, shielding her from the elements and pulling her close. "William, that was so much fun! You need to come by. Langley is doing a poker game in a couple of weeks."

"He's bringing that back?" William asked, putting up his own umbrella.

"I told him I could beat him," Sidney said. "That's all the motivation he needed. And it gets me out of the office for a bit. You should definitely be there." There was a sudden softness in Sidney's eyes as he looked at William, a fondness in his voice. Cintra didn't notice as she drowsily buried her face in Sidney's collar.

"Yes," William nodded. "I'll be there. Just let me know."

"And we'll have that budget back to you by the end of the week."

"Perfect."

They embraced under their umbrellas. As Sidney and Cintra made their way to the car, William checked his messages. He'd completely forgotten about Travis.

He could practically hear his petulant voice through the text: *Don't bother.*

IT WAS AFTER ELEVEN when Travis opened the door halfway

to his Wheaton apartment. He was in sweatpants and a baggy t-shirt and didn't look particularly sexy or welcoming, like he was holding back a sneer. "I thought I said don't bother."

"I lost track of time," William explained. "There was wine and foie gras and before I knew it nearly two hours had passed. And by the time I got on the road it was raining, so that took even longer—"

"Oh there was foie gras! Well shit, why didn't you just say that? I already knew I couldn't compete with some poor tortured animal!"

"Travis—"

"I was looking forward to seeing you earlier. I *shaved* for you."

"Can you let me in, please?"

"You'll be fine. You have an umbrella."

"I drove almost forty minutes in the rain to come see you."

"William, I have to get up in the morning so I can be at my desk by 7:59. Unlike you, I'm not the boss."

"I'm sorry I didn't text you back in time."

Travis didn't budge. "I accept your apology."

William raised his voice and it bounced throughout the hallway. "Are you *serious* right now?"

"Don't come up in here getting all loud and ghetto, William—"

"It was *two hours.* You knew I was out. And I wasn't on a date. I was with two friends of mine *who are married* and we were talking about designing the house they just bought—"

"Didn't you say you weren't accepting any new clients?"

"I made an exception for them."

"Why?"

"I don't know why! Because they're my friends?"

"So that's what you're gonna be up to while I'm trying to date you? You made this huge point about swearing off work so you could have fun and focus on yourself and now you're out having dinner with *clients.* The math doesn't add up."

William didn't know what he could do or say at this point. Travis seemed dead set on arguing. Deja vu. He buttoned his suit jacket and turned on his heel. "Okay. I tried. Talk to you later."

Travis grabbed his arm before he could make it down the hall. "Wait, you're not actually leaving, are you?"

William's jaw dropped. *"Are you playing with me?"*

Travis opened the door wider and pulled him into the apartment. "If you don't get your tall, chocolate ass in here right now. I ain't shave for nothing!"

Once inside, William backed him against the wall. "You think you're funny?"

"I'm not playing games, I promise. I really was pissed in the beginning. But then you were about to leave and you're so fine in this suit and you have that sexy walk and I just—"

"I told you to stop getting cute with me," William whispered, holding Travis's chin firmly in his hand. William pulled his face close enough to kiss him, his breath against his lips teased him with heat. "What did I say would happen if you called my bluff?"

"I don't recall," Travis said, fully aware of what was next.

William's grip tightened. "You *will* recall."

"You said you would punish me."

"That's right. How do you want me to punish you this time?"

They reveled in the charade, aware Travis was in complete control of the proceedings. He wanted William to keep the suit on so he could arch his back and dutifully call him "Mr. Kendall," like a student who had misbehaved. As they drifted off to sleep, Travis drowsily asked him, "How do you do it?"

William faced the ceiling but his eyes were closed. "Do what?"

"Be you. Everything is so practiced and perfect. Is this what I have to look forward to when I'm forty?"

William chuckled softly. "Age might have something to do with it, yes."

"You make everything look effortless. I know I tease you about it and sometimes it scares me but to watch the way you move and listen to you speak . . . You always know what to do and how to do it. You never have moments when you're like *Oh my god I fucked this up?"*

"I'm a reflection of my beliefs and my values. I think every man should be."

"Every man?" Travis asked.

"You've been given this incredible gift—*life*. What's the point of having it if you aren't working to be a better man today than you were yesterday?"

"I don't think I've ever seen it that way."

"One of the hardest decisions I made was to slow down and not focus on work as much. I told myself there were parts of me that needed attention. There are things I'm still bad at and things I regret. Things that keep me up at night." William's eyes fluttered open and he turned to face him, gently stroking his cheek. "The answer to your question is yes. I have those moments."

Travis considered this. Then, "Isn't part of being a better man being able to forgive yourself? To not beat yourself up for not getting it right all the time?"

William nodded. "You're right. But forgiving yourself isn't enough. Not when you've done what I've done."

eighteen.

Two weeks into his gig at Definitions and Todd had managed to keep it from Linc. He wasn't intentionally hiding it from him, he just wasn't sure how or when to mention it. Today, when Linc offered to have Todd join him as he took shots along Washington Harbour, Todd explained where he'd be. Linc groaned. "I hope I don't bump into that fool. You got a membership there?"

Todd laughed. "Something like that."

"I'll just text you to come outside."

On instinct, Todd wanted to defend Julian. He was good at his job, up to the task of running the place and professional to a fault. The contrast between Work Julian and Social Julian were night and day.

Just as Todd was on his way out, Julian called him into his office. It was mid-afternoon and Todd didn't have any clients booked for the rest of the day. Julian sat at his desk munching on the most rustic homemade granola Todd had ever seen. "So it's been great having you here. People love you, obviously. Everyone thinks you're really nice and focused and patient. Most of us tend to go for a more militant approach here but what you do is fine the way it is. I only have one concern."

"Okay, what is it?"

Julian went on, his tone firming. "If you and the client are both in the mirror and you're helping with form, you need to make sure your eyes connect with them. You know, through the mirror. You need to have a full scope of what they're doing wrong and how to correct it. You *never* look in the mirror. If someone has injuries or a mobility issue, you can't be half-assed about that stuff."

"Got it."

"If anything is making it difficult for you to work with people then you need to let me know now." He stuffed a handful of granola into his mouth. "If I looked like you, you wouldn't be able to pull me away from a mirror. No fucking way. *Ever.*"

Todd blushed. "I understand. I'll see you later."

"You in some kind of rush?"

"Actually my ride is waiting for me, so . . ."

Julian pretended to gag, knowing exactly who awaited Todd. "Have fun."

The sun had returned and it was a breezy seventy-five out. Todd tossed his duffle in the back of Linc's Wrangler, a champagne 2007 model, before hopping in the front seat. Linc removed his sunglasses before kissing Todd urgently. "I missed you."

"You saw me this morning when I left your place," Todd laughed.

"It was a long seven hours."

"Stop."

Linc kissed him again. "No," he insisted. "I'll never stop. You smell so good. You always smell like you just got out the shower."

"Linc, I *literally* just took a shower."

Linc looked at him, grinning in the goofiest way.

"So you know I work here, right? At the gym with Julian."

The smile melted. "I figured it out on the way over. What's that like?"

"It's something to do while I'm here. So I'm not sitting around William's condo thinking about how I'll approach my dad."

Linc put the jeep into gear and turned up Teedra Moses. "I'll try not to hold it against you."

"He's pretty good at running the place. We have different training philosophies but he's a solid manager."

Linc squeezed Todd's knee as he drove. "I don't care."

"You know what? I think one day the two of you are gonna become good friends."

"Ha! How do you figure?"

"Because eventually you'll run out of reasons to hate each other."

They came to a light and Linc turned to him. "One of the things I really enjoy about you is your optimism, however misplaced it might be. People like me and Julian Keys weren't meant to be in the same room. It just doesn't work. There will always be friction. William has tried many times." He pulled off once the light turned. "I wouldn't waste your time worrying about it. Some folks ain't meant to hit it off. It's not the end of the world."

"I guess you're right, but the reasons you don't like him seem small. He's definitely shallow but look at the industry he's in. I don't think he's a bad guy."

Linc patiently sighed. "As I told you before, he's never struck me as an authentic person. Who has the time to chip away at layers and layers of bullshit before they can get to an actual human being? Not me. Maybe you're more adept at it from being in LA all this time."

"You might have a point."

"I wish I had it in me to give people a chance the way you do. Maybe being around you will rub off on me." He smiled again.

They found a parking spot along K Street. As they walked past the plaza and restaurants towards the water, Linc explained he was taking shots for the Waterfront's revamped website and it was perhaps the easiest money he'd make all year. He snapped quickly, standing at the end of the river steps with the Kennedy Center in the distance. The park was moderately populated and allowed him to get shots fully capturing the details of the landscape. After a while he turned to Todd and said, "Get in a few of these."

"I thought you weren't taking pictures of people today."

"I wanna take some of you, if you're comfortable. These can be for us."

Propelling through the glass door at Deacon's condo two years ago had brought Todd's modeling career to a standstill. Aside from the video journals he recorded on his MacBook, he hadn't stepped in front of a camera since. They'd pulled out the glass and reconstructed his nose and no one would know anything had happened to him. The doctors remarked on how healthy he was, how his diet and habits made all the difference in him healing so flawlessly. But he still didn't have the desire to return in front of a camera any more than he wanted to face himself in the mirror or stand before a room of strangers.

Now here was Linc, smiling in the sun with warm brown eyes and his Nikon at the ready. He felt protected by Linc since their first night together, so the apprehension was gone. It was replaced by something scarier but seductive, the same tingle in his stomach and heat against his neck he felt when Linc kissed him after Todd thwarted a harasser. He was falling.

Todd pulled himself together, hoping he looked cool. "Okay, sure. What do you want me to do?"

"Nothing. Pretend I'm not here." He gestured to the fountain towards the start of the park. "Take a walk by the fountain while I talk to you. Don't pose. Okay, pose a little but you don't have to look straight at the camera."

Once Todd's face caught the sun Linc snapped away. Todd, in his blue and white ombre Polo and pale jeans, seemed larger than life and had a freshness about him that made the shots recall a cologne ad.

"How soon can you get a suit?" Linc asked.

Todd directly faced him—*snap!*—and smiled. He knew the question of suiting would come up one way or another, he just wasn't sure if it would be Linc or William asking. "As you can probably guess, suits can be a challenge for me. I have a few back in LA that no longer fit so I was probably gonna have to get a new one anyway."

"Let's see if you can get one quickly. Between me and William that won't be a problem."

"Why do you want me in a suit?"

Snap! "I have a gig in a couple of weeks. A wedding at a mountain vineyard. I want you to come with me."

"You want me to be your date to a wedding?"

"I want you to be my date to the liquor store, the post office, the fucking gas station—I want you to be my date everywhere." *Snap! Snap! Snap!* "I know what you're thinking—weddings are romantic and taking a date is supposed to plant a bug or something. I'm not asking you for anything but company, I promise. Hopefully the weather that day is as beautiful as it is now."

"Linc, I'm flattered, really. But . . . you realize how I get sometimes."

Linc lowered his camera as Todd came closer, taken by the concern creeping into his voice.

"Sometimes it's hard to be around groups of people, especially new people. And I'm getting to know you, and I wanna go, but I don't want you to be disappointed or embarrassed if I come across as awkward or antisocial. I'm working on it."

"I understand. Weddings are very social and folks will have questions about you."

"But I'll start looking for a suit. Hopefully one of you can hook me up with a tailor who works fast."

"You don't have to come."

"What if I said *no* today, then change my mind later and decide *yes,* I *do* wanna go with you but then I don't have a suit? You're gonna look at me like I'm crazy."

Linc nodded. "I probably would."

"So let's treat this like a *yes.* If I back out, at least I have a suit that fits."

Snap! "I can't believe I'm finally taking your picture. Do you wanna see them?"

"I don't need to see them now."

Linc shrugged and checked the preview. "Okay. No problem. I don't think you would be disappointed in these, though." He scrolled through the shots quickly, briefly glancing at him when he noticed, in a sequence of them, Todd looked incredibly sad.

"What?" Todd asked.

"It's nothing. You're just hot, that's all." He went over them again, wondering how he didn't catch it before. Sometimes he snapped so fast he didn't know what he was capturing, so this wasn't unusual. Instinctively, he reached for Todd's waist and squeezed him. Todd's eyes, once soft and romantic, were contemplative then pained, as if something inside was torturing him. "But if there's ever anything you wanna talk about and maybe you don't feel like going to William . . ."

"I'm fine, Linc. I'm having a good time."

"But are you happy?"

Todd wanted to say yes, only because it sounded right and would save time. He understood he was happy at this moment with Linc. That he was having a good time certainly wasn't a lie, but he knew he hadn't been satisfied with his life since it was time for him to be in control of it.

"I don't wanna put you on the spot," Linc went on. "I'm just letting you know I'm here."

Todd smiled. "I'm a lot better since knowing you," was all he could confirm.

Linc searched his face for a bit, then nodded and returned to the photos.

nineteen.

Watching Sidney climb out of the pool—his dense muscles sparkling in the sunlight, trunks clinging to his ass—wasn't the first time William felt the attraction. But he was ready to admit what it was and what *he* was. Being at that East Hampton rental in the Summer of '93, courtesy of Langley's firm partner Douglas Sweeney, shifted his optics. Everything was expansive and beautiful and laid-back. William could finally relax and come clean to his best friend.

He didn't know what he would say or how, but it had to happen before they returned home.

Sidney's fourteen-year-old sister Nicole lounged beside him in her poolside chair, her oversized Hollywood sunglasses taking up half her face. He couldn't tell if she was asleep until she spoke. "This is *sooooooo* boring. Is this what people do all day here?"

"I don't think they have waterslides in the Hamptons," William offered.

Nicole gagged. "I'm not a kid, I don't *do* waterslides." Nicole's latest thing was to say *do* in place of *like,* in a bid to show how mature and refined she'd become. "We can't even play music here. It's *so* quiet." She glanced across the yard where Monica chatted with the first Mrs. Sweeney. "And she's always watching us. Can we do something without Mom eyeballing?"

William watched as Sidney made his way to his own chair and caught the shape of his dick clinging to his thigh. William adjusted in his seat, trying to hide his own growing erection.

There's no way he was explaining *that* to Nicole. He forced himself to think of things that would turn him off—poverty, famine, dead relatives. It helped a bit.

"Why are you always complaining?" Sidney demanded as he plopped down on the other side of William. "Damn, we can't take you nowhere!"

"I'm entitled to my opinion!" Nicole shot back, lifting her sunglasses.

"You better be lucky Dad wanted to take your spoiled ass anywhere!"

Monica, from across the way, clapped her hands three times, immediately silencing them. But only momentarily.

"I am *not* spoiled and don't cuss at me! I'll bust you upside your big head!"

Sidney laughed. "Try it and see what happens!"

Nicole's flip-flop whipped across William's face and nearly smacked Sidney in the head but he ducked in time. The other went flying right after. William caught Monica sip her martini and stroll over, cool and calm with her patterned tunic shifting against gentle summer breeze. She couldn't wait for her children to be grown so they'd be more interesting to her. Monica had no interest in being a disciplinarian right now.

Sidney shot up and started after Nicole, who screamed and took off. She would have completely circled the pool if he hadn't caught up to her and grabbed her, lifting her from the ground. She screamed and fought him as Monica took her time across the yard.

"Get off me!" Nicole screamed, flailing.

"Say sorry for throwing your shoe!"

"Say sorry for your musty underarms!"

Splash! Into the pool she went. Monica was mortified. Mrs. Sweeney stifled a laugh. Nicole bobbed to the surface, spitting water and vowing revenge. William doubled over in laughter from his chair. Sidney caught his gaze from across the way and headed towards him. William didn't understand what was happening but the closer Sidney got the more clear it became.

"Go ahead, Sidney!" William warned, guarding himself as Sidney charged him. "Stop playing!"

Sidney tried to reach for his wrists, but William kept dodging him. When Sidney almost had him, William grabbed him instead. "I said stop!"

"He plays too much!" Nicole shouted as Monica held her back.

Sidney shook his head, laughing. "Nope!"

Then William did it, he pulled Sidney on top of him. It was only to disorient Sidney, who expected William to shove him back or release him and make a break for it. But William also wanted to feel him, even if it didn't last long, even at the risk of Sidney becoming angry.

Sidney wasn't offended but pulled back quickly. In the split second he was against him, William could swear there was a glimmer in Sidney's eyes that understood exactly what was happening.

He was ready to make another attempt to drag William into the pool but Monica told him to chill.

THE FOLLOWING EVENING THE yard was filled with friends and firm associates. Langley Baptiste, newly minted as third senior, decided against inviting anyone to the event other than his own family. And it was just as well, if Langley was to believe what he heard about Sidney's behavior the previous day.

Catering staff weaved through tiki torches and the crowd of cocktail beach dresses, polos, button-downs and khakis. A small jazz ensemble played sleepy renditions of David Bowie, Duran Duran and Lenny Kravitz. Nicole enjoyed herself a bit more after making friends with a girl her age. Sidney chatted up a waiter as William was stuck playing Langley's "son" for the evening.

Langley didn't parade William around claiming him as his own but was eager to have William at his side as he chatted with guests. When asked about Sidney, Langley would offhandedly gesture "Oh he's around here somewhere" and explain that William was not only Sidney's best friend, but also like family and—just now to partner Brad Rothschild—"practically a third son."

"I've been working with you for years," Rothschild chuckled. "Had no idea there was a second."

"I mean like a third *child,* counting Nicole," Langley clarified.

"So what do you plan on studying, William?" Rothschild asked.

William hadn't adjusted to being on display but answered with confidence. "I was accepted into the Interior Architecture and Design program at GW."

"Interior Architecture and Design?" Rothschild asked, smirking. "What's that? Picking out cabinets? Choosing *just the right* wainscoting?"

"Sure. But I also get to make office spaces bigger—or *smaller*—for people like you."

"Do you see that?" Langley beamed, putting his arm around William's shoulders. "Now, if you ask Sidney the same thing he'll feed you some shit about basketball." Langley sipped his gin. "At least William knows what he wants."

"Sidney seems pretty serious about basketball," William told him. While Langley made it to as many of Sidney's varsity games as he could, he thought it was a passing phase, something Sidney did to make himself popular with the girls at school. He was determined Sidney followed his footsteps into the legal profession.

William scanned the crowd for his friend but there was no sign of him. He was uncomfortable having to advocate for Sidney while his own father disparaged him to colleagues. "And he's good," William added. He needed Langley to understand he was on Sidney's side no matter what.

Langley chuckled. "You're the boy's best friend. What else would you say?"

William mustered the courage to excuse himself and went

off in search of Sidney. For the second time moving through the crowd that evening, he was mistaken for staff. It infuriated him but he managed to explain he was a guest of Langley Baptiste. Langley would later tell him it was why he spent so much time personally introducing him—so they would know who he was and not project their biases onto him. Recently, Langley had become more comfortable advising William on such matters, how there would always be someone ready to restrict him to a binary no matter how well-groomed, articulate or educated William was. William wondered how often he had these conversations with Sidney and if Sidney bothered to absorb any of it.

William came up short searching for Sidney in the rental's expansive backyard so he went inside. As luck would have it, he found him in the living room, stretched out on the sofa in his linen shorts and shirt. He looked half asleep. "Hey. You alright?"

Sidney turned to face him and chuckled. "I'm cool. There was no point in me being out there."

As William came closer, the faint scent of alcohol reached him. *Gin.* He hadn't tried it himself but he knew it when he smelled it. There was more than enough of it in his own home. "Were you drinking?"

Sidney shrugged.

"How'd you get liquor?"

"Made friends with a waiter. He smuggled it to me."

"Your dad is gonna murder you, man."

"I don't care. Matter of fact, *fuck him*. He hates me. You should go be his son since he loves you so damn much."

Sidney was grinning but William could tell he was hurt. "If you plan on passing out, you should at least be in your bed. What if someone comes in here and sees you like this?"

"Bro, I don't care anymore. I don't even wanna be here. I don't care about these bourgie-ass white people or that stupid-ass jazz music. Fuck the Hamptons." Sidney lifted his glass to his lips to polish off the contents.

"Your dad just doesn't understand your passion," William

offered. "That doesn't mean he doesn't love you."

"Do I look like I care?"

"Okay fine, Sidney. I'll see you later."

Sidney managed to bring himself to his feet. Holding onto the arm of the sofa he told him "Bye! Arrivederci! Have fun being me out there!" William started for the backdoor, but Sidney said something else that made him stop cold: "Are you really leaving? *You're not gonna try to pull me on top of you again?*"

William didn't know how to respond, so he stood there. It was the first time since yesterday Sidney mentioned it. Up until now he hadn't so much as passed him a knowing glance.

"Why are you messing with me?" Sidney went on, approaching William from behind. "What are you doing?" Sidney wrapped his arms around William's waist as he begged, "What are you doing?" Sidney's cheek rested on the back of William's neck and William's heart pounded so hard and loud it rocked him.

"I . . . I don't know," was all William could muster.

"Why didn't you say anything?"

William faced him and he searched for the strength to keep from collapsing. Sidney looked more vulnerable than ever. Not cocky, confident or the least bit in control. He was completely bare. His eyes pulled at William. But William didn't know what to give into first—how much he loved Sidney and wanted to hold him or how much he wanted to strip him naked and fuck him in the middle of the floor. And there was the nagging insecurity that Sidney only did this because he was drunk. No way would he feel like this tomorrow.

Sidney looked beyond him through the window and the party out back. "You wanna go out there and hang with my dad?"

"Of course not."

"You think they would look for us if we disappeared?"

"I think if they know I'm with you, they won't worry."

Sidney almost reached out for him again, but the door

opened and girlish giggles filled the house. They parted before Nicole and her new friend caught them.

"What are you up to?" Sidney barked at his sister.

"Samantha knows about a party at the beach and we're riding our bikes up."

Sidney laughed. "There's no way Mom and Dad are letting the two of you *fourteen-year-olds* go anywhere." He said "fourteen-year-old" like it was a slur.

Nicole placed her hands on her hips and triumphantly laughed back. "Yes they will because you and William are going with us."

Sidney managed to sober up enough for the short bike ride to the beach. The girls suspected nothing. The closer they pedaled the louder Janet Jackson's "You Want This" became. They parked their bikes and walked towards the shore. A blazing bonfire and about twenty kids gradually came into view. The average age of the group appeared to be sixteen or seventeen. If there were any adults nearby, William couldn't tell.

"Do you know anyone here?" Sidney asked Samantha.

"No. We're crashing," she answered without a beat. The girls ran ahead as William and Sidney trailed slowly behind.

The two of them were silent as they walked, both terrified of speaking up first. Sidney found a dune where he could keep an eye on the girls and sat in the sand, kicking off his sandals. William sat a few feet away. Sidney's collar caught a warm breeze.

"I'm sorry," Sidney said, staring off into the water. "I don't know what I was doing. The drinks, I mean. I guess I meant everything that happened afterwards." William still didn't know how to respond so he let Sidney go on. "But I don't understand it. I don't understand why it feels right. I mean, I know it's *wrong,* but . . . you're my best friend and . . . we're close. We trust each other. Maybe that's why I felt so comfortable."

William chuckled. "Comfortable? I've been scared this whole time."

"Of what?"

"You could've beat my ass yesterday at the pool."

Sidney shook his head. "I don't think I would ever hit you, man." He faced him. "I'm glad you came."

"I'm glad I did too."

Sidney gazed across the beach. Nicole and Samantha were socializing with a few other girls and looked like they were having fun and behaving. "So what are we gonna do?"

"What do you *wanna* do?"

Sidney leaned back, propping himself on his elbows and faced William. "I want you to come here."

William's heart was already beating out of control the moment they sat but now it pounded double-time. He took a few deep breaths to slow it, looked around to measure the risk of being caught and wiped sweaty palms against his shorts. He brought himself closer to Sidney and leaned over, grabbed the back of his neck and pulled him in for a kiss.

William resisted the urge to fall into him, to crush Sidney's body with his own and grind him into the sand. He didn't think he'd ever be able to come up. He restrained himself as best he could, even with Sidney attempting to pull him in deeper, even as good as he tasted with the lingering hint of gin.

"We gotta stop," William whispered in between kisses. "Someone might see us."

Sidney relaxed, folded his arms behind his head and stared at the sky. He smiled. "We're gonna be up all night."

MONTHS LATER FOUND SIDNEY back from Syracuse on holiday break. They were trying again in his room, like they did in the days leading up to him going away. Sidney was nervous and a little scared, but also excited to be with William. He didn't want to disappoint him.

"You gotta relax," William urged. He held Sidney's waist as Sidney grinded on top of him. William figured it would slide in a lot easier this way.

"I'm trying."

"No you're not. What are you afraid of?"

"Shouldn't you be wearing a condom?"

William shrugged. "I don't know. Should I?"

"What if one of us has something?"

"Something like what? A disease?"

Sidney nodded.

"I don't mess with them nasty ass girls you mess with so I wouldn't have anything."

Sidney sighed and climbed off of him. "It's just not working. Let me do *you* instead."

William laughed. "Yeah right."

"Then we don't have to do it then."

William pulled him close. "Your mom is gonna be home any minute. We need to keep trying while we have time." Monica and Nicole were out Christmas shopping. Langley, as usual, was elbow-deep in a case. William couldn't recall the last time he saw Langley after the Hamptons.

Sidney grabbed William's dick, which seemed permanently erect no matter what. "Let me just suck it."

"I'm tired of that."

Sidney huffed and William kissed him in response. Sidney tried to pull back a bit but William held on tightly. He was beginning to notice, while William was far less athletic, he could be aggressive when he wanted something. It wasn't the kind of force Sidney felt threatened by but it put him on notice. "I wanna keep trying," William said, his hand possessively grabbing Sidney's ass. "C'mon, before your mom gets back."

"Okay I have an idea. Lick it first. That might relax me."

William frowned. "You want me to lick your *ass*? I don't know about that."

"I suck your dick all the time—"

"That's not the same thing."

"Why are you so stubborn?"

"I'm not being stubborn, I'm just saying it sounds nasty."

"If you don't like it you don't have to do it again."

William considered it. Although he never said it aloud, he

loved Sidney. Maybe this would work. William was so hard it hurt but he wanted to be patient with Sidney. It occurred to William that Sidney wasn't relaxed because he was so pushy.

So he was tender until Sidney no longer desired tenderness and they took their awkward, at times painful, curious and fun route to the finish line.

They learned more about each other and the world that afternoon than in their combined lifetimes.

He always thought after his first time with Sidney they'd hold each other and kiss and talk. Figure out their post-college plans, sneak in a nap. Once Yvonne Kendall's laugh filled the house, they had to pivot. They scrambled to get dressed as William wondered why in the hell his mother was downstairs. No matter how often she demanded William let her know he was there, Yvonne never stopped by. She was too busy working. And when she wasn't working she was drinking.

They rushed down to help with the bags. "Look who I bumped into while I was out!" Monica told William. "I invited your mother to have dinner tonight."

William grinned. It was all he could do.

"Don't look so excited," Yvonne said, playfully slapping William on the arm. He couldn't smell any alcohol on her breath so that was a relief.

"What have you two been doing all day?" Monica asked.

"Mortal Kombat II," Sidney told her.

Monica tsked. "Gruesome. William, I can't believe we haven't invited your mother over. You've been spending all this time here and we never sat down to really get to know each other." She shoved two heavy restaurant bags into his hands. "You two can set the table."

William was shaking by the time they all sat down. William had never gone into great detail about his mother, other than how often she worked and worried about him. Sidney had a feeling, by observing William's body language, they were on the verge of learning why he'd been cagey on the topic of her, especially when his eyes bugged at Monica pouring her a glass of wine.

"Dig in," Monica urged, taking her seat. "You know we don't say grace when Langley's not home."

They spooned ravioli, salad and meatballs onto their plates. Yvonne politely asked Sidney about school and he explained, while monitoring William from the corner of his eye, that he was pursuing criminal justice since it made Langley happy and would track to law school. Sidney went into exhaustive, granular detail about his classes, teachers and his smelly roommate. Then he went on and on about basketball and how he felt less than confident in his abilities. After a while William understood what he was doing; he was keeping Yvonne engaged. Monica was at first pleased, then increasingly suspicious of Sidney's enthusiasm. Nicole, as usual, was annoyed.

"You should eat your food, Sidney," Monica suggested. "No one else has been able to get a word in. What about you, William?"

William shrugged. "I mean, it's school."

"You should be proud of yourself," Yvonne said. "I'm actually surprised Monica doesn't already know, since you're always over here."

"I haven't been over here since school started," William responded in a measured tone. "That's why she's asking."

Yvonne sipped her wine. "Excuse *me.*"

"I'm not doing that well," William went on, picking at his food. "It's not what I expected."

"It's college, William, of course it isn't," Yvonne interjected.

"I was telling Sidney the same thing," Monica offered, attempting to mitigate the tension. "They're not gonna treat you two like kids."

"The program is way more strict than I thought it would be. That's all I'm saying."

"Your grades are fine, William," Yvonne told him.

"They could be better."

"I'm trying to be encouraging. I can't encourage my own child now? When I was in school I *wish* my mother had given this much of a damn about me. Look at me."

"Are you about to yell at me in front of everyone?"

"If I have to!"

"Well you don't *have* to."

"*Why can't you let me be your mother!*" Yvonne screamed at the top of her lungs, slamming her hands down. It shook the entire table, rattling plates and silverware. They were silent. Monica's hand clutched her chest, her mouth agape. Sidney lowered his head, worried making any eye contact with William would embarrass him further. When Yvonne realized what she'd done she quickly apologized. It didn't matter. William bolted from the table and rushed upstairs to Sidney's room. Sidney followed.

"What's going on with your mom?" he demanded as William shrugged into his coat.

William didn't answer. He slung his backpack over his shoulder and made way for the door. Sidney blocked him. "Move," William growled.

"Nawh, tell me what's wrong with her." He grabbed William by the arms and stared him directly in the eye.

"I'll fight you."

"No you won't."

William relented, taking a breath and sitting on the bed. "She works a lot. Sometimes I think she hates me. When my dad went M.I.A. he left her with a lot of debt. I had to cut back hours at the store for school. So she drinks as much as she can when she gets the chance. I love her but it makes me sick."

"You think she has a problem?"

"I don't know. Maybe? I don't know why she's pretending to care about my grades all of a sudden. Last time I came to her trying to talk about school she asked why I didn't have a drink for her. I can't come into her room empty-handed."

"Sounds like she has a problem."

"I need to make sure my grades are perfect. I need to make sure I'm the best at what I do so I can take care of her, so she never has to worry about money again. So she never has to drink again."

"It's not your fault, William—"

"But I can *fix it.*"

"You don't have to. You're always giving me advice about my dad, right? Let me have a chance." Sidney smiled softly. "We're supposed to look out for each other, right?"

Sidney stayed true to his promise over the next several years. Girlfriends were incidental and temporary; they always returned to each other. Then Cintra happened. William didn't take her seriously in the beginning. She was beautiful, more beautiful than Sidney's other girls, and possessed a cool confidence that didn't shrink before Sidney's own. When William noticed how pragmatic she was, how committed she was to quality and artistic detail, it clicked.

Cintra was the closest Sidney had come to finding a woman who was like William. And it pissed William off.

twenty.

A SMALL BATTLE ERUPTED between Cintra and Sidney before the game. She was convinced she was playing tonight. Not so. Sweeney and Rothschild were Langley's guests and William was Sidney's. The sixth was Monica's brother Fred. The six of them, *the men,* would be playing. "But I'm great at poker," she explained, leaning against the bathroom door frame. "I'm better than you. We both know that. Even your father knows that."

Sidney was fresh from the shower with a towel at his waist, lathering on shave cream in the mirror. For Cintra, this was his most ideal form—bare-chested and fresh-smelling, engaged in conventional male grooming rituals. It was one of those small things that made the prospect of a husband so enticing, just watching him every day being a man in the most routine, mundane ways. "He likes it with six. And remember, *you're* the one who invited William," he told her.

"When I thought I was playing."

"But Langley never said you *were* playing."

"But I'm here."

"In his house."

She groaned and reached for the straight razor he'd grabbed. "Let me do that for you."

"I got it, Cintra."

"You're gonna nick yourself. Let me shave you."

He pulled the razor out of reach. "What's wrong with you right now? You wanna get cut or something? Just give me some space while I do this."

"You always need so much space."

"We're staying at my parents' house until ours is *perfect*. Of course I need space. Don't you?"

A flat chuckle. "You needed space in New York, too."

"I don't like what you're doing. I don't like how you sound."

"Sidney, I'm your *wife*—"

"But you sound like *him* right now. I don't like being doubted. I don't like hearing that I'm not good at what I do. I can shave my own face. I can play poker. I don't need you telling me how to be a man—"

"Oh, not this!" she spat. "The only one who's insecure about your manhood today is you. I come to you for closeness. I come to you because I need you and expect you to be a contributing part of this marriage. I'm not criticizing your damn manhood! Your father really did a number on you, didn't he? Is that what tonight is all about? So you can beat him at something?"

Sidney took a breath, faced the mirror, pulled the skin of his right cheek taut and glided the blade down. The strokes were clean and careful, but brisk. "I contribute to this marriage each time I walk into that office. I contribute to this marriage when I pretend you haven't spent an outrageous sum on something that *looks pretty in our home*. I support your career as an artist—no questions asked. Don't you ever tell me I'm not a contributing part of this marriage."

"Thank you, Daddy Warbucks, I appreciate the pile of money you let me sleep on every night! How did I function before I met you? In case you forgot, I have money, too, and had plenty before I married you. I was doing fine. You think you're doing me a favor by giving me the bare minimum?"

Sidney waited for his hand to stop trembling before he started on the neck, the most difficult part.

Cintra went on. "If you pretended, for once in the last few years, to love me with something other than your wallet, I'd be thrilled. You don't have to spend another dime on me, Sidney."

He stopped, holding onto the sides of the sink. "I'm doing my best."

"Sidney—"

"No, I'm talking. *I'm doing my best.* I'm doing more and giving more and *being* more than a lot of other men. You didn't marry a bum. I'm not a loser and I'm not a bad husband. All of this shit—being back home, being at Sweeney, doing this house—it's a lot for me right now—"

"Sidney, you're bleeding—"

"You want me to make more time for you? *Done,* but only after I can make some for myself."

Cintra pulled a square from the tissue box on the sinktop and brought it to the cut on his neck. She was pissed but didn't want to argue anymore. "We can finish this after the game," she told him as the doorbell sounded. "That must be your first guest."

WILLIAM DIDN'T BELIEVE LANGLEY *liked* Bradley Rothschild. Aside from whiter hair and slightly sagging skin his smirking, punchable face hadn't changed much since William first encountered him as a teen in the Hamptons. His face seemed perpetually on the brink of telling a series of racist or sexist frat boy jokes. Considering the psychological stakes of the game, the consistency worked in his favor. Rothschild could have had the shittiest hand but no one at the table would likely know until Showdown.

William, for his part, maintained a classic poker face and consistent betting patterns, staying out of the posturing at the table as best he could. Langley had a particular interest in Sidney this evening. He didn't just study him to evaluate his gaming demeanor, he wanted to rattle him. "What was that upstairs an hour ago?"

Sidney calmly sipped his scotch. "I don't know what you're referring to."

"Sounds like you and the wife were on the verge of nuclear war up there," Langley chuckled.

"Can we focus on the game right now?" Sidney matched the current bet, eager for the heat to be off him. William quickly followed.

"I only want peace in my home, son. Cintra's a good girl but she's always been a little too . . . mouthy. Ten years and you haven't put a button on that?"

"I'd appreciate it if you didn't disparage my wife in front of company."

Sweeney, a slighter man compared to his partners, waved it off. "Oh, come on! We're family. Langley is right. I don't mind entertaining all of that progressive women's lib nonsense but we can't let our wives bark at us. Not without consequences."

William's stomach turned. He didn't like where this was headed. A chuckle spilled from Rothschild's tightly smug face, causing his enormous gut to jiggle.

"Relax. I'm not talking about slapping her around," Sweeney clarified, pushing thin frames against the bridge of his nose to keep them from sliding. "But you can withhold things. Say *no* more often. You know they hate spending their own money."

"You can withhold *other things,*" Rothschild weighed in, adding chips to the pot. "And when she starts begging for it, remind her who's in charge."

"It's 2016, I don't need to *control* my wife," Sidney said, exasperated.

The older men at the table, including Uncle Fred who dealt this round, exploded in laughter. "Hilarious!" Sweeney declared. "Of course, because of the times, you can't do what you would've done maybe fifty years ago, but you can't relinquish *all* of your power. Just like that?" Sweeney shook his head, suddenly serious. "Maybe you're right. Maybe you don't need to control her. But every marriage involves an exchange of power."

Langley gestured with his glass in agreement before taking a sip of his ever present gin.

"You can't be this naive, son," Sweeney went on. "How often does she get her way?"

"What difference does it make?" Sidney demanded. "We both

get our way, when we can."

"Because of control."

"Because we respect and love each other."

"How nice. That sounds so beautiful, so precious. Don't tell me you've never gone to bed just a bit resentful because you could have told her *no* and didn't." Sweeney took a brief peek at his hand, face down on the table, and considered the flop before raising the bet. "If you wanna feel equal in marriage you gotta wield some control. That's the only way the damn thing works."

Sidney cut his eyes at his father before responding. "What you call control, I call compromise. Sometimes you gotta make sacrifices to keep the people you love happy."

"And there's nothing wrong with that. But it's good to remind her you won't be making sacrifices every time. I know too many men who live in that regret, drained of their will to live—*their fucking blood*—because they're living a lie. They had to become a completely different person because of *love.*" Sweeney dismissed the concept with his hand, as if the four letters spelled something far more distasteful and burdensome. "Damn right it's 2016. It's 2016 and you still think marriage is a goddamn Disney movie, when you know far more about the world than any of us did when *we* got married."

"Or you can at least tell her to lower her voice so everyone doesn't know your business," Langley said, bringing the conversation full circle. "Every marriage has problems, but you need to squash it internally. As quietly as possible. Don't want anyone thinking you've lost *control.*" He winked at Sidney, which infuriated his son.

Sweeney eventually took the pot on a relatively garbage hand—Jack High—simply by controlling the energy at the table. Sidney was pissed for folding so early. The other partners were equally annoyed, knowing they should have expected this after years of playing and working with the man. Doug Sweeney was an exquisite liar, capable of constructing entire worlds based on falsehoods. It swayed jurors.

All Sidney wanted was a single win. After the second and

third rounds, with Langley and William claiming the pot respectively, he left the table. William found him on the deck smoking a cigarette. "Jesus, I didn't know you smoked," he remarked.

"Sometimes I do. Cintra yells about it and I don't blame her."

"You do know I smoked after you got married," William offered. "I got fat and started smoking. I was a little cranky after that wedding."

Sidney didn't face him, instead he stared off into the dense woods behind the house. "I guess that's my fault, too, huh?"

William chuckled. "Yes, but I eventually came to accept it. Cintra's great."

"She's perfect."

"So what were you two fighting about?"

"The same shit we always fight about. She wants me to do more, to *be* more and I just . . . I thought I had it all figured out. I thought I got it right."

"Define *right.*"

Sidney flicked ash into the breeze. "You're asking a lawyer to define his concept of *right?*"

"I think you and I believe the same thing. I just need you to confirm it."

"In this case, *right* is a sense of order, of completion. Checking off all the boxes. Doing what a man is supposed to do."

"So tell me this," William said, stepping closer and leaning against the railing, "do you ever feel like you're performing?"

Sidney took a puff, faced him. "You think I'm faking my marriage? You think Doug is onto something?"

"Maybe it's some lingering resentment I have. Maybe it's how frustrated you are all the time. I love Cintra but I just want . . . I want you to tell the truth—*to someone.* Yourself, at least."

"I thought we settled this."

"Did we?"

"I don't know what you want me to say."

"I want you to tell me how you could turn it off," William

clarified. "How marriage means you get to claim you stopped feeling things. Those feelings never go away, Sidney."

Sidney stubbed it out, tossed the butt over the rail. "I need you to stop."

"What happened in New York? What brought you here? Why are the two of you fighting?"

"She said something?"

"She thinks I should talk to you, try to figure out what your malfunction is. But I already know the answer. You don't wanna be in that marriage. You married her to shut your father up."

Sidney's jaw clenched and his eyes briefly flashed in anger. "You've had too much to drink."

"Proving your father wrong can't be more important than something that felt so good to you, something that made *sense* for you."

"I've been getting shit from every angle all night and *I want you to stop,*" Sidney hissed.

"You hated him more than you loved me," William said defiantly, not caring who heard. "We said we were gonna take care of each other—"

"We were kids—"

"I know what it's like to perform. Everyone I meet thinks I'm perfect. There's stuff I wanna talk about but I can't because I don't connect with anyone the way I did with you. You took a lot from me when you got married. And you denied yourself, too. You're probably putting her through hell right now. Is that why you bought her a house? To get her off your back?"

Sidney slumped into a nearby chair and put his face in his hands. "You want something I can't give you."

William's eyes stung. He never cried. "I haven't been vulnerable since I've been with you. I would like to be sometimes. Ever since I knew you were back I've been trying to distract myself with someone else and that's not fair to him. It's always been you, Sidney."

Sidney looked up, exhausted. Frustrated. Trembling. "What do you want me to be honest about? How would that free me?

It will hurt my wife. It'll make her hate me. And my father will hate me even more. I don't believe you have any admiration for that intolerant asshole."

"So your hands are tied? You're gonna be your own prisoner for the rest of your life?"

"What you're asking me to do is impossible. Even just saying it—"

"Sidney, I love you. *I love you.*" William approached the chair and crouched before him. They were close enough to kiss. "I love you."

"I can't, William."

"All this pressure you feel to be the perfect husband, to be the perfect son—it's not healthy. You can't live for everyone else."

"But what you're asking me, it's only to benefit you, isn't it? Because you miss what we had. This isn't about living my truth, this is about *you.*"

William stood and went to the other side of the deck. "You're right. I do miss you. But it breaks my heart to watch you falling apart like this. Before anything else, you're my friend. If I never get to touch you again—and I *do* wanna touch you—I just want you to be happy. With or without me. I swear."

Sidney almost responded but Langley slid open the door and stuck his head out. "You two ready for round four? It's your deal, Sidney."

twenty-one.

His stage name was Black Suede. As far as Christian Pavlovic knew, the dancer had retired. Black Suede was once a mainstay in the club scene in Southwest, DC, until the construction of Nationals Park and a marriage ended his career. But he was here now, with dense muscles, a thick beard and a sexy gap, only wearing only a decorative sheath that covered thirteen inches, grinding to The Weeknd's "Often." Something alien or celestial powered him. Black Suede wasn't a go-go boy, he was a *performer* who hit all the important marks—body, face, and superior dance ability. While other dancers allowed their muscularity to render them stiff, Suede had the flexibility and grace of a more delicate man, while maintaining an intimidating, arresting degree of dominance.

Amid a shower of flying bills, the dancer's eyes connected with Christian's. It was finally his turn. He was, after all, one of the grooms. He beckoned Christian to lie on the floor, on his back. Suede had a trick up his sleeve. The other men at the party cleared a path and in a swift move Suede executed a flip-roll, landing in a split on Christian's waiting face. More bills rained on them as everyone cheered. Christian, drunk and heady, inhaled the dancer's sweet, musky scent. Suede leaned forward and proceeded to grind his ass against Christian's face, nearly performing a live sex show for everyone in the suite.

Eventually he helped Christian up, whispering "Congratulations" in his ear before returning to the rest of the crowd. Christian was breathless, cursing himself for falling under the dancer's spell and believing, if only for a split second, he would have him tonight.

Someone shoved Christian's ringing phone into his hand. The screen flashed insistently with the incoming call—*JULIAN KEYS*. Cristian groaned and answered. "What do you want?"

"We need to talk."

"Not right now. I'm kind of in the middle of my bachelor party."

"I know. I'm downstairs."

"You're at my hotel?"

"Come down. I'm in the lobby. I only need five minutes."

Christian ended the call and slid the phone in his back pocket. He made sure everyone was completely engaged by the performance before he slipped out. He found Julian at the lobby's bar in a black Under Armour tank top and gray sweatpants. He looked a little more broad than Christian remembered him. They'd been apart for over two years, long enough for Christian to fall in love with and become engaged to a man who didn't behave like a child.

Christian supposed it was his own fault to expect so much from Julian. Theirs was to be a strictly casual arrangement, Training Partners With Benefits. but it was so habitual and downright comfortable they thought it was the perfect foundation for something more serious. Julian was eager to get back into a relationship and Christian had developed a fondness for him. He wasn't quite in love with Julian, he knew that in the beginning, but the prospect of something consistent and familiar enticed him.

I should've known better, he thought as he took the stool beside him.

"You look like somebody wore you out," Julian remarked.

"You drove two hours to ruin my wedding?"

"No. I drove two hours to apologize."

Christian didn't believe him. The bartender hovered and Christian waved him away. He'd had enough already. He did notice the dirty martini awaiting Julian nearby. "You need an idea of what you did wrong in order to apologize, Julian."

Julian looked him over, a twinge of envy stirring as someone else had made it official. Christian, the son of Croatian immigrants, had the tight, beefy physique of a rugby player with a slight tan and buzzed raven hair. Tonight he was in a polo and cargo shorts that showed off impressive calves. "I do know. I've always known," Julian told him. "The arguments we had always seemed to be about one thing but it was way more than that."

Christian shook his head. "No. It was about *one thing*. You wouldn't let me fuck you."

Julian cringed. "That's not why we broke up."

Christian knew Julian was right in a way. He had some deficiencies in his personality, things that stretched Christian's patience to the limit, but he would've endured any of it if only Julian would submit to him. "Yeah, sure," Christian sniffed. "You know, I bumped into Sean recently. We had an enlightening chat about you."

"I can only imagine."

"He said he had the same issue."

Julian took a healthy sip of his martini, determined to avoid any derailments. "I don't want to talk about Sean. I just wanna say I realize I was immature and I wouldn't allow things to progress how they should have."

"Including how you never let me be the top."

"You knew I was a top when we got together."

Christian laughed so loud he drew the attention of the lone desk agent. "Bullshit!" he hissed. "You were never a strict top. Maybe you were with me and Sean. *I wonder why.*"

"You wanna lower your voice?"

"You came all the way down here to bullshit me because, I guess out of the blue, you're feeling some kind of guilt or something? Or, I was right the first time and you just wanna ruin my wedding. Couldn't this have waited?"

"No. I need to say this now."

"Then be honest about everything. I'll indulge your apology, so long as you're ready to admit you would *never* let a white guy be on top."

"Christian!"

"You talk a good game about loving whoever you wanna love but the rules for your boyfriends differ based on race. They get to have you however they want. That's all I'm saying." Christian gestured to the bartender. "As a matter of fact I'll have a shot of blanco. Make it two."

Julian finished his drink and tried to figure out what to say next.

Christian leaned in. "Here's the thing, Julian. I don't give a damn what you're going through, or the real reasons you came here. If you're gonna call me out of my bachelor party and expect me to entertain you *the weekend of my wedding* when I wasn't even *thinking* about you, then it will be on my terms." He downed the first shot. "Say it."

"But it's not even true."

"What about Blair? Baron? You mean to tell me you were a total top with *those* two? And don't assume I haven't compared notes with at least one of them."

Either Baron had run his mouth or Christian took a shot in the dark. "Okay fine! I'm sorry for not giving you any ass," Julian relented.

"It's also about the lie, Julian. You said you never did it and never would. Turns out there were men you would absolutely do it for." Christian brought the second shot to his lips and allowed it to linger. "I'm not married *yet.*"

"And?"

"I have a little bit of freedom for the next ten hours. Show me what you got."

Julian laughed. "You've lost your mind."

"You used to twist me into a pretzel." Christian took the shot and joined in the laughter. "What I wouldn't give, Julian . . . Your ass is amazing. It drove me crazy to be denied that." He threw his head back and groaned.

Julian signaled for another drink. "Thank you, but—"

Christian squeezed his thigh. "At least let me eat it."

"Your party must be lit. You're drunk as fuck right now."

"I am. But I need to get this out of my system. They got me a stripper and he's the most beautiful man I've ever laid eyes on. I'm about to explode."

Julian had only to guess the stripper was Black and muscular, as his fiance was. Christian had a type. "I meant what I said. I didn't come here to ruin your wedding."

"You wouldn't be ruining a thing, now that I think about it."

Julian briefly considered it. Christian was clearly inebriated and dying to sow a few remaining oats. As tempting as it was . . . "You're partially right," he admitted. "But it's not what you think. I denied you that one thing because I wanted to end the relationship. I would have given you anything you asked for if I wanted to stay."

Christian's eyes narrowed. "So you're telling me I still can't fuck you?"

"I'm in love with someone. I've been in love with him all this time but I've been in denial."

"Who?"

"Can't say just yet."

"Does he know how you feel?"

Julian shook his head, his eyes forlorn. "I can never tell him. He'll just tell me I'm not taking responsibility for my relationships failing. All this time I've been looking for *him* or a feeling that reminds me of him in you and everyone else I've been with. That's why I'm here apologizing. I wasted your time."

"So the entire time we were together, you were waiting for me to be someone else?"

"More or less."

"That's probably the most self-aware thing you've ever said. You must be tired of *yourself* at this point."

"I'm tired of being shouted down about how awful I am."

They were silent for a moment. Christian put his arm around Julian's shoulders. "I accept your apology. Maybe it's because

I'm drunk, but I'm willing to give you the benefit of the doubt here. Any growth is good, even if it's belated."

"I appreciate that."

"If you want, you can come up to the party."

"I'm not trying to get drunk and stuck here overnight in *Virginia* of all places."

"Fine, but I wouldn't be me if I didn't at least invite you to the wedding. If you can stomach it."

Julian smiled. "I might be able to do that. And I really am happy for you."

"Are you?"

A shrug. "It was the right thing to say."

twenty-two.

In a room down the hall from the bachelor party, Linc tenderly kissed Todd's ankle. He craved a puff or two but Todd didn't seem as cool with the smoking as he first let on. Todd often bristled at the mere mention of any drug—cocaine, Ibuprofen, the innocuous Chief. So this was the alternative. Linc started at the ankles, then behind the knees and got lost somewhere between Todd's thighs. He inhaled him.

Breeze stirred the curtains from the open balcony door. The hotel itself was fifteen minutes from the vineyard, on a sprawling hilltop facing the Blue Ridge Mountains. It was quiet out. Two bottles of champagne—gifts from Roderick and Christian—waited in a bucket of now-room temperature water. Linc considered opening it, just because it was the romantic thing to do. He was, after all, in love.

Todd laughed a little. "Your beard . . ."

"Does it tickle?"

"Yes."

Linc rose to a kneel and gazed down at Todd, eager to get inside of him once more. They'd arrived at the vineyard late afternoon so Linc could take test shots in the event hall and on the lawn. Christian invited them to the bachelor party but they declined. They couldn't wait to get to their room. Todd was ravenous, instantly falling to his knees, freeing Linc, devouring him. With quickened breath and closed eyes Linc swayed slightly, disoriented. It almost slipped out—I love you.

If you say it with your dick in his mouth you'll just be confirming everything people say about you.

"Stop for a second." Linc hurriedly shoved himself back in and sat on the edge of the bed. "I need to know where your head is."

"You just interrupted it—"

"I mean *you*. You know this ain't no fling for me, right? Not at this point."

"It's not for me either. I thought we both said as much."

"We've been dancing around it."

"I have to go back to LA eventually. I have to finish school. I wasn't expecting any of this."

"I don't think we ever expect it. It's supposed to be inconvenient."

Todd sat next to him and fell back, staring at the ceiling. "It feels good. When I'm with you, it's like I'm right where I'm supposed to be. I've been through hell, Linc. I need more time to tell you all about it but . . . I think I'm ready for you. Whatever it is, whatever we call it."

"We gotta go slow. I need to figure this shit out because I haven't always gotten it right." Linc laughed but Todd knew he was dead serious. "I just know I'm in love with you."

Todd ran his hand inside of Linc's shirt, caressing his back. "I probably fell for you the first night. Or the morning after. You make me nervous. You scare me. The way you look at me is like . . . I think you're challenging me. You know I always have to say the right thing, that I believe people, deep down, are good. And that I worry they'll disappoint me but maybe you won't, even though you've only heard the worst about yourself."

Linc turned to him. "I've heard the worst because I've done the worst."

"I don't care, Linc."

"Maybe you should."

Todd squeezed his thigh. "I just wanna enjoy today. Come here."

They fucked, they napped, they drank water, they fucked

again. Now Linc wanted more and was sure Todd did. Todd always wanted it. But Linc rose from the bed, switched on the desk lamp and grabbed the room service menu. "If we don't eat we'll pass out."

"I've done intermittent fasting," Todd joked. "I'll make it."

"The kitchen is about to close. We should get food."

"Order anything. I trust you."

Todd went to shower. He knew he was avoiding it—discussing the parts of Linc he'd been warned about, not only by Julian and William but Linc himself hours earlier. So maybe he was a little promiscuous. Maybe he'd cheated on a partner in the past. Had he called him stupid? Was he controlling and abusive? Had he pushed him through a glass door?

There were worse ways to be a boyfriend. Todd knew.

Linc was tender. He was engaged. He offered Todd his full attention, never interrupted or dismissed him. He was proud to know him. He admired him. Todd wasn't sure if any man he'd been with, much less Deacon, had treated him so well, had this much respect and reverence for him.

No, he decided as he emerged from the bathroom, *I don't care what you've done. You're as perfect as you need to be. And you're mine.*

Over stacked burgers, fries and champagne, Todd asked how Linc felt about the couple getting married—Roderick and Christian.

"Because one is white and the other is Black?" Linc laughed. "I know I've said some shit and I don't wanna offend you—"

"I'm not talking about me or my parents. I'm curious how you feel about *this* couple."

"I mean, love is love. Roderick seems cool. Look, I'm getting paid a grip to shoot this wedding."

"So you didn't react when you met them?"

Linc shook his head. "Absolutely not. My thing has always been that Black men know who we are in the world, not just what we think of ourselves but how people see us. You can't walk around oblivious to that shit. That shit will get you killed out here, no matter how put-together you are. Roderick doesn't act like one of those Black men." He leaned in. "And if he was, I'd take the job anyway."

"You see yourself married?" Todd ventured.

Linc almost choked. "Me? Nah. I'm not built for that . . ."

Todd let it hang.

He didn't revisit it the next day when they were surrounded by it, nestled in lush green foothills. The temperature was a perfect eighty and the air carried a sweetness—vines that bore clusters of plump grapes, freshly manicured grass and love made contractual. Todd watched guests arrive from a distance, far off on the lawn, taking in the beauty.

Linc helped style him for today—white trousers and a gray blazer, a dark blue shirt and a pale blue tie, burgundy brogues, a patterned pocket square. At first Todd was worried he'd appear ungainly but the result was sleek and refined. Linc's tailor was a magician. Before they left for the ceremony Linc squeezed his shoulders and told him, "You look amazing. You look like my man."

Now Linc was across the way, snapping photos of the wedding party in front of the vineyard's quaint barn. He worked efficiently; everything needed to adhere to a strict schedule. Todd loved watching Linc work. He instantly put his subjects at ease and treated them like stars.

He made everyone feel beautiful.

Todd squinted his eyes, not believing what they told him. Then he held back a belly laugh. No. It *couldn't* be. That wasn't Julian Keys marching up the path to the vineyard lawn in a smart beige suit and sunglasses, carrying what appeared to be a shiny, wrapped wedding gift. He stopped to chat with Christian for a moment, exchanging a brief hug before he made eye contact with Linc.

Linc threw his head back in a silent groan. Julian shook his head in disgust and made his way inside the event hall. Linc gazed across the lawn and frowned.

Todd was in hysterics.

twenty-three.

"So moving. I'm touched," Julian muttered at Todd's side during the vow exchange. Roderick and Christian's words bordered on saccharine, with gestures towards the union itself being revolutionary, society's denial of their humanity and right to love and how The Power of Love was all they needed to stand up to it. *I walk only in love and I want you to walk with me for the rest of my life.* Julian was relieved when it was over. "Get me to the wine."

Todd chuckled at the cynicism and glanced at Linc, who was so stealth he could have been invisible. Just because the vows were corny didn't mean they were wrong.

The guests stood and cheered before being ushered into the event hall for the reception. Todd and Julian, as late additions, sat at the last table behind blank name cards and empty wine glasses. Julian removed his tie after complaining about how tight it was. Todd was starving, his palms were sweaty.

"You got that look, man," Julian remarked, impatiently tapping the side of his glass as the servers took their sweet time filling them for the toast. "I can't believe he brought you to a wedding. Nope—I can, actually. That dude is working you."

"What do you mean?"

Julian lowered his voice since they weren't alone at the table. "You let him take your picture, didn't you?"

"What difference does it make?"

"I'll take that as a yes. You know all this is a show, right? I'm talking about this wedding."

"Why are you being so negative?"

"Because one of them tried to fuck me last night."

Todd glanced across at Christian and Roderick who made their rounds as everyone waited for each glass to be filled. They were in matching gray suits and cotton candy pink shirts and misty-eyed smiles. They couldn't be more perfect. "That was last night."

"And today is a new day?" Julian sniffed.

"Even if it's a facade, shouldn't we try to believe it for the next few hours?"

"Do you hear yourself? You need to believe in this shit because of *him*. Look, it's none of my business what you do with Linc, but I hate to see a good man play himself."

"Julian, I don't care what he's done. I've already seen the bottom. I know what the worst looks like."

"Okay, I'll back off," Julian promised as his glass was filled. "You're grown. You got it."

Julian didn't grunt during the initial toast or the speeches that followed. The two of them eventually got to know the other guests at the table over wedge salads and poached salmon, Julian leading with a crass charm and harmless schtick. He made a few jokes at Todd's expense about how pretty he was, but Todd had consumed enough wine by then that he endured it with a modest grin.

Linc didn't drop by. Todd reasoned it was a combination of being consumed by his gig and avoiding Julian. But it annoyed him nonetheless, more so when he came to realize Linc had been missing for quite some time.

"Jesus, they've played three Beyoncé songs and your knee hasn't even twitched," Julian remarked. "No shoulder-shimmy, no nothing. Something must be wrong. Your boy is scared to come say hi?"

"I wouldn't say he's scared," Todd managed. "What's going on with you today?" *Distract me from my paranoia with your entertaining nonsense.*

Julian sighed. "I'm being an ass, aren't I?"

"That's most days, but today you're a little more goal-oriented."

"Man . . . Well, first of all, would you consider me a friend?"

"Yes. Of course I do."

"So whatever I tell you stays between us."

Todd nodded.

"It's William, man."

"What's William?"

Julian reached for his glass but it was empty again. He shifted. "He was my client once, that's how we met. And he was a different person—physically, I mean. He smoked. He was kind of overweight. But you already know this."

"No, I don't."

"How often did you see him while you were living in LA?"

"He visited a few times when I first started school and then it tapered off. He didn't start visiting heavily again until after . . . It was mostly phone calls, Facetime."

"And you never came here to see him? Your family?"

"No. My mom was all I had before she died. Her family wasn't so into her having a Black son. And my father is another story."

Julian considered this, making a mental note to grill Todd for details later. "Well, yes, William had a tire." He gestured around his midsection. "And he wanted to get rid of it. I helped him." Julian never knew what William's issues were when they first met. He had no idea what led to the weight gain. He never bothered to ask. Not when they worked out together, or when they had dinner after a session. William would talk about everything—his love for interior design, his favorite singers, how much he admired independent Black businessmen who never sold off. Never once did William's love life come up, but it always lingered below the surface. "Then he fired me," Julian said with a fond grin. "You know as much as I do that coaching is about teaching your client how to do this without you. He didn't need me anymore. But I wasn't letting him go. I made him my friend."

Todd was speechless. A server returned with two bottles. Julian reminded him they both had red and their glasses were filled once more before he continued. "When you have a man like William in your life, you hold other men to a standard. Well, I don't know if you've ever done that so I should speak for myself here. But he's The Prototype. And I can't have him."

"You never told him how you felt?"

"I couldn't. You know how he is."

"Are you telling me you're intimidated by him? I don't know if I believe that, Julian."

"William makes his intentions and his interests very clear. He doesn't treat me like someone he takes seriously in that way, like a *man*. The line was drawn off rip—*We are platonic.* It makes you wonder what type of man he likes. You think, to be with someone like him, all you need is to be in his league. For me that meant owning a business, having an education, being in shape, having my shit together."

"A lot of us think that's enough for any man," Todd added, taking a sip.

Julian considered his talks with Blair and Baron and wished the server would just leave the damn bottle at the table. "We've all been lied to. In your twenties, all they tell you is how hard you have to work just to be good enough for whoever you happen to fall in love with. What do you do when that's not enough?"

For the first time, Todd heard something in Julian's voice resembling pain. He had a better idea of who Julian was and what powered his perception of adulthood. *Acceptance.* "I don't have an answer," was all Todd could muster.

"So are you in love with Linc?"

"I am."

"I know I asked you this before but what is it about him? And I don't mean it in a shady way. It's one thing to like him but what made you fall in love with him?"

"He represents a part of me I left behind when I moved. He's home. I've needed him all this time and I didn't know it. He's a good man, Julian."

"And he's been gone this entire time."

"I think he's taking pictures by the vines," Todd offered.

"Oh."

Todd rose with wine induced determination. "I'll find him and when we get back, the two of you can have a talk. Like adults."

"Yes, we can have an *adult* conversation about how he needs to stop bathing in frankincense," Julian cracked as Todd disappeared into the crowd.

Todd moved quickly, offering a friendly smile when he caught a glance and making sure eye contact never lasted a split second too long. He'd managed to keep a low profile the entire afternoon, never leaving his seat at the end of the main hall. Now the guests, mostly single gay men, were wine-drunk and inspired by the beauty of the vineyard and vows exchanged two hours earlier. They all urgently wanted that kind of love for themselves and Todd appeared unattached.

He didn't make it to the vines. Descending the steps outside the hall, Todd found them in the gallery, seated at a long, plush bench. Two empty wine glasses sat between them. They were enamored with one another, locked in intense conversation. Linc, whose back was to Todd, gestured with his hands to punctuate his points.

His companion glanced up as Todd drew closer and his face was shaded with either resignation or mild disappointment, as if he knew who Todd was and wasn't ready to accept him into their conversation. He appeared no more than twenty-four with defined cheekbones, full lips and a swimmer's build. Todd realized this man had to be a model of some sort and perhaps his reaction was governed by a competitive instinct. Todd had gone on enough calls to know that look.

Linc faced him and stood, coming to meet Todd as he advanced down the gallery. "Hey. Are you okay?"

"I'm great. I just . . . well, I didn't see you inside. Are *you* okay?"

"Yeah, they're partying. I took a couple of shots and now I'm pretty much done. My camera's in the truck." He gestured to the young man on the bench who rose to greet him. "Todd, this is Gabriel."

When Gabriel shook Todd's hand his posture was challenging, in spite of not matching Todd physically. "Good to meet you, Todd." His wide grin came with a sprightly English accent.

"London?" Todd ventured.

"Yes. East Ham," Gabriel told him. "Like Elba."

"I think Gabriel would be a great addition to the book," Linc added. "So he's been telling me all about the culture over there and his family and the ways we romanticize London as if things are any better for us over there."

"You should visit some time," Gabriel offered.

"I've been," Todd said, more defensive than he intended. "Not Newham specifically, but other parts. For work."

"You have a very familiar face, Todd. You're a model, I take it?"

"Former."

"Ahh, yes, well it has to come to an end eventually, doesn't it? I often wonder where I'll end up once I age out of it."

"Enjoy it while it lasts," Todd snapped, catching the shade. "Are you coming inside?" he asked Linc.

"Eventually. You seem to be enjoying yourself with Julian."

"I would like it if you joined us." Todd's hand reached for Linc's.

Linc's eyes were soft and yielding. "Okay, baby."

"Is that J-Lo I hear?" Gabriel wondered aloud. "I think I'll accompany you."

"Stupendous!" Todd exclaimed as they made their way back.

Linc stopped, allowing Gabriel to go ahead of them. "So there's a problem."

"You asked me to be your date to this wedding. Then you disappeared. And then I find you talking to this very attractive guy and . . . I'm not the jealous type but I don't think that's right. No, I *know* it's not right."

"Listen, I wanted you with me. But I thought you knew once we got to the actual event I'd be working—"

"That wasn't work."

"I explained to you that it was."

"Does *he* know that? Because he seemed way too comfortable. And territorial."

"I didn't flirt with him."

"Linc, I've seen you work a room. You don't have to try that hard. You didn't have to try that hard with *me*. I thought we were on a path."

"We are."

Todd found the courage to say exactly how he felt. "So you know I've heard things."

"I figured," Linc said.

"I keep avoiding that conversation. Any time someone says you have a reputation, I look the other way—"

"I wasn't doing anything wrong."

"Linc, it's wrong. I get what you do for a living and I love that you're so charming but I don't think it's necessary for you to be that charming with *everyone*. It sends the wrong message. I'm not saying you can't meet or talk to people but you don't have to make them feel like you're about to sleep with them just to take a picture." Todd took a breath, realizing how upset he sounded over something so small. "I'm sorry."

"I was planning on being by your side whenever I could, because I know you get nervous around people. But when I saw Julian I figured you'd be okay. Clearly I was wrong."

"You're missing the point. I don't need a babysitter. But, I'm sorry. I'm not ready to have our first argument. I don't like how it feels—"

"Don't apologize. I fucked up." Linc took his waist. "You're not saying anything I haven't heard before. It's that thing I need to work on. I'm with you. I got you. Todd . . ."

"Yes?"

"You want me to go in there and make peace with Julian, don't you? If it makes you happy, I'll do it. I'll do whatever you want me to do. For the rest of the day."

Todd broke into a smile. "Then you get in there and do it."

Joining the table was the first step. Acknowledging Julian without sneering was the second. Todd's closeness made it bearable, his hand resting possessively at the top of Linc's thigh or occasionally caressing the back of his head. Todd was more relaxed than normal and it had everything to do with unlimited petit verdot and Gabriel spreading his considerable charms elsewhere. It made Linc smile faintly; he wouldn't have guessed Todd would be the one putting him at ease this time.

For several minutes the three of them sat in silence, occasionally nodding their heads to the pop classics spun by an exuberant and accommodating dj. Julian quickly downed his sixth glass of wine and let loose. "You wanna know why I really couldn't stand your ass? You said *Liquid Swords* is the best Wu album when everyone knows it's *Cuban Linx.*"

Linc threw his head back and groaned. "Who the fuck is *everyone?*"

"Everyone with ears!"

"Genius has a better voice, smarter lyrics and his album is overall better-produced and way more efficient. It's not up for debate."

"If you were a pretentious music writer in the nineties or a backpacker, yes, of course you think it's the best. Y'all think everything that isn't massively popular is better by default. And if I hear one more person call *Liquid Swords* 'dark and cinematic' as if *every* Wu album ain't dark and cinematic!"

"*Cuban Linx* is about three or four tracks too long because Rae couldn't edit or sequence an album if his life depended on it."

"Do you hear yourself right now? Every track is Hibachi!"

"I didn't say the album wasn't good, it's just not as good as *Swords.* Slightly overrated by comparison. But still in the top five Wu solo joints."

Todd leaned in. "No idea what any of this is about but it's a great way to begin."

"What tracks would you leave off, then?" Julian demanded.

"'Glaciers of Ice', 'Ice Water', and 'Spot Rushers', easily."

"I can't believe you love this dude," Julian said to Todd.

"So give me your top five," Linc challenged.

"Overall? Or Just Wu?"

"Overall top five Hip Hop albums."

"Easy. *The Blueprint, Life After Death, Purple Haze, Flesh of My Flesh Blood of My Blood, It Was Written.*"

Linc loudly guffawed. "Not surprised! Are you sure you got enough New York shit on there?"

"New York is all that matters in this conversation. The sooner New York takes it back, the better."

"I kind of agree but only because the shit that's coming out now is a dumpster fire."

"Everyone sounds like they're having a seizure in autotune!"

Linc chuckled, then caught himself, steering it into a false coughing fit. The turnaround couldn't come that quickly. Too much shit had been talked, too many sneers and eyerolls exchanged. He held up a finger, signaling he needed a sip of water. Todd pinched the back of his neck, aware of the jig. His lips were at Linc's ear, a tender, sexy whisper, "Thank you."

"Okay I'm out!" Julian proclaimed. He stood and buttoned his suit jacket, swaying a little but determined to make himself scarce. "I don't need to see whatever's about to happen."

"You're not getting on the road, are you?" Todd asked him.

"That would be a bad idea, wouldn't it?"

"Have someone drive you back to the hotel." Todd tossed Julian his room key. "We're in 720. Take a nap."

"What are you doing?" Linc demanded.

"I'll be two, three, hours. Tops," Julian assured them. "And remember what I told you today stays between us." He gave Todd the eye-to-eye sign and was off.

Linc shifted. An unfortunate outcome of Todd's affection was that Linc had become painfully erect, straining the fabric of his trousers. Going back to their room was now out of the question. Todd, noticing his distress, pleaded, "I couldn't let him drive home like that. It's a two hour trip."

"I love this quality about you, how you hold open doors and stop what you're doing to help someone who's struggling with something heavy. Never stop being sweet and generous."

"I'll try not to."

"But today that shit is a gross inconvenience. A legitimate cock-block. Julian can get his own room."

Todd offered a mildly disapproving look. "Linc . . ."

"And what were y'all talking about?"

"Like he just said, it's between me and him."

"You know he wanted me to ask you."

"I don't know if Julian is that manipulative."

"Whatever." Linc took a swig of wine and placed Todd's hand in his lap. "So what are we doing about this?"

"There's nothing we can do. Not right now."

"Are you sure?"

Adrenaline surged through Todd as his eyes drifted to the windows and the barn beyond.

Could they?

The inside was clear with a few low stacked bales. No longer a working barn but a decorative refuge from the vineyard's tours. A barn for the sake of a barn. There was no door, only a hollow rectangle that allowed a powerful shaft of sunlight to pass through. Todd used a stack for support with Linc behind him, trousers at their ankles. For a split second Todd worried they didn't have protection until he heard the crackle of plastic. He stifled a yelp when he was full of Linc. His knees buckled and he righted himself. Linc didn't take long.

He moaned and trembled and fell against Todd, asking if he needed to finish. Todd told him, "No. That was for you." They pulled up their pants before they could be discovered and re-entered the hall as discreetly as they'd left. Todd briefly exchanged glances with Gabriel, who kept a safe distance. As if to toast, or more likely send a message, Gabriel smiled and raised his glass.

twenty-four.

Yvonne delivered the news matter-of-factly with no preamble, knifing through a fried boneless chicken breast sitting atop a waffle and sauteed kale. The stack was slathered in hot sauce and maple syrup, a mix only permissible at brunch. "He's been dead for about six months but I only found out the other day. You know I don't feel any kind of way about it but I thought you should know." She chewed and took a demure sip of her orange juice. Yvonne Kendall was a tiny woman, with a stylish silver pixie and large hoops dangling from her ears. Today she wore a chic Ann Taylor cream blazer and red cropped pants.

"Happy Mother's Day," William returned, tipping his mint julep in her direction.

"William . . ." She cut her eyes at him disapprovingly. "I'm not exactly thrilled about this."

"Are you sure?" he asked with wide eyes.

"I stopped wishing him dead twenty years ago. I deserve some credit."

"So how did it happen?" William was genuinely curious, as he would be of the details of anyone's death. He didn't know much about Henry Battle's character outside of Yvonne's reports on how trifling he was, so the immediate cause that came to mind was a weary bounty hunter who could clock out.

She waved her hand like she was dismissing a gnat. "Heart problems. The *good* news, as it turns out, is that he had a heart to begin with. It just seized up on him and gave up." His mother made a tight fist and opened it explosively to demonstrate how it all went down. "Just like that. At least, that's what I hear. You think they brined this chicken in sweet tea? Here, baby, taste this." Yvonne cut him a corner and deposited it onto his plate.

"How old was he?" William asked her.

She sat back and her eyes drifted upward. "I'll say seventy-two, seventy-three. It was probably time anyway. I'm surprised he made it that long."

William surveyed the other families in the restaurant treating their matriarchs to Sunday brunch. A father was present at a few tables. He wondered, out of those who were in their kids' lives, how many were even welcome. He also often wondered if the importance of a father being present was an overstatement, if they could all be counted on to solve more problems than they created.

Henry Battle. In his prime he was smooth, refined and as beautiful as his son. He had an imposing presence, one that compelled and commanded with few words. People just gave themselves to him.

"Apparently you have siblings scattered across the country," she went on. "Not a surprise considering *his reach.*"

William had always suspected this; it informed his urgency in asking about Henry as a boy. He longed for siblings throughout his childhood and, upon becoming so close to Sidney and Langley, stopped yearning for both a brother and a father figure. "How much did you dig up about him?" William asked his mother suspiciously. "There has to be more."

"Oh William," she sighed and concentrated on her plate.

"I'm sorry. It's your day. But you brought him up—"

"Because he's dead. Should I have sent a text?"

"Fine."

"So back to you. Tell me more about this new friend."

"No!" he laughed. "It's nothing serious. He's not new, really."

"Go on."

He sighed. *"It's nothing serious.* I'm just going out. I'm having fun."

"That's all I wanted for you, William."

"You want me to be married with a house full of adopted children."

"Eventually. And you'll get there. I can tell you're in a place where you can start building that for yourself." She clutched her chest. "This is exciting."

"I hate to disappoint you. I *never* want to disappoint you—"

"William, no—"

"I already know this will be temporary."

Yvonne dramatically rolled her eyes, wiped the corner of her mouth with a linen napkin and gestured for the waiter. "We're done here."

William laughed. "You're not gonna hear me out?"

"I know what you're about to say. Let's get the bill."

"He's fun and responsible but he's not the one."

"The *One?*" she asked with a frown. "What the hell is this? *The Highlander?*"

"*The Matrix.*"

"Or *that.* You're forty-years-old; that's too old to be talking about The *One.* Ain't no *One.*"

"Yes there is, Mom."

"Well, where is he?" She turned her head left and right, scanning the restaurant for potentials. "I don't see him. I've *never* seen him. What does he look like?"

"He's perfect."

"Then why isn't he *here?*"

William shrugged. "He doesn't know who he is."

Yvonne threw up her hands. "They never do!"

"I know what you want for me but it can't work without the right person. It *can't.*"

She studied him for a moment, her eyes a mix of concern and deep regret. "You've always been such a perfectionist. And I know why. It's because of *me* and what I put you through. I'm sorry."

"You've already apologized, millions of times—"

"Your father is not your fault. You've spent so much time making up for his failure that you haven't focused on *you*. You have to *enjoy it*, William, even if the person isn't quite right. Don't wait for somebody. I'm not gonna watch you do that. I'll die first. I'm telling you right now, I'll die before I watch you waste your life like that."

"I don't wanna talk about me anymore. This is your day," he reminded her.

"Don't worry about me, don't worry about Henry's dead, sorry ass. Think about yourself. Take care of yourself. You've earned it!"

"Like I said, I'm having fun. I'm not wasting my time pining for anyone." A lie. He was certainly pining. Maybe not in the beginning when he first encountered him at Monica's party. But now, especially after their chat at poker, it was a full-blown ache for Sidney. At times it showed up as a fond, romantic longing but it was mostly a nuisance and no amount of bouncing Travis on his lap would overcome it.

"You better not be. You're *old* now," she remarked.

"Here we go."

"Nope. We're not going anywhere. This is where we've been parked."

He indulged her for the next hour and a half. They had the same lighthearted disagreements and he gamely suffered the same nagging judgements. The familiarity of it was comforting if not entirely productive. Eventually, Yvonne reported on the rest of the family, mainly her sister's side and the cousins who were in a financial bind. Backed up student loans, rent, outstanding traffic tickets, other obligations that placed them in a tenuous position with the law. She explained her hesitance to relay these messages, but many of them found William intimidating and wouldn't come to him directly. He promised to reach out and make arrangements the way he always did.

He drove her back to her Le Droit Park home. Once she was safely inside, he couldn't make himself pull off. A sickness overcame him and he cut the engine.

Henry was dead.

It shouldn't have meant anything to him. His memories of his father were faint—tall, booming voice, an intense masculine cologne that filled the room, ambivalence. William didn't even remember how Henry felt. He remained just out of reach. A phantom.

Now there was no chance of having any kind of relationship with him. Not that William needed one. But maybe he still wanted the choice.

He wondered if Yvonne was truly over it. Sure, she had a few more days to process it all, but had she moved on as quickly as she'd encouraged him to? You don't mourn someone who ruins your life but, for the sake of decency and order, you mourn a parent, no matter how little of a parent they actually were. Right?

He felt more sick when he considered Todd's non-existent relationship with his own father.

William started the car just as his phone rang. The One.

"Yeah?"

"That's how you answer the phone now?" Sidney asked.

The words tumbled out. "My father died."

"Shit. I'm sorry, William. Do you need anything?"

"I don't think I do. What's up? Are you with Monica?"

"No, I'm at the house. The *new* house. I was seeing if you could come by but now I'm not—"

"I can be there."

"You don't have to."

"Twenty minutes. Sit tight." William ended the call.

TEN YEARS EARLIER. A bachelor's night out in Manhattan. Sidney had pretended, convincingly, to get shitfaced just to have his best man escort him to his hotel room. Once they shut the door, they clumsily kissed as they tore each other's clothes away, stumbled and fell onto the bed and into a comforting rhythm, pacing themselves once it set in that this time was their last. William's mouth at Sidney's throat, quickened breath behind tender lips, pleading for him to call off the wedding. "I'll give you anything you want. I'll be whatever you need me to be. Just don't do this."

Sidney stroked his face back then, his voice full of regret—"I can't"—making William kiss him deeper and pull at him with greater desperation, to grind against him more urgently. William told him repeatedly "I love you. I need you," and, for the first time, reversed roles with Sidney.

It almost worked. He'd denied him the pleasure for so long, always insisting Sidney had girlfriends for that. This time, William needed to do whatever he could to win his man back. Sidney never appeared happier, his body never quaked before in as much ecstasy as it did then. The love radiated from him. They slept in a tangle of brown, sweaty limbs.

And he woke up and married Cintra anyway.

Now he sat at the bottom of the stairs in the home he just bought, his face buried in his hands after floating the word *Divorce.*

Any other day, Cintra would be in the basement or out back restoring an antique piece while contractors worked on the rest of the house. But today she and Nicole had taken Monica to the spa for Mother's Day. It was also the contractors' day off so the house was deathly silent. The walls were Decator white, just as Cintra had specified, and the interior was larger since knocking down a wall. William's oxfords against polished hardwood floors had echoed throughout when he entered. It smelled of freshly dried paint and sanded wood. Nearly perfect and ready for its new owners to move in.

"You know this can wait, right?" Sidney asked with exhausted eyes. "I feel so selfish."

"I'm trying to figure out how I should mourn, if at all. You're not inconveniencing me, Sidney." William sat next to him. "Are you ready to tell me what's been going on?"

"I wanna give her the house. I mean, this is what she wanted.

She deserves it. I think you were right. I didn't buy the house to get her off my back but . . . this might be the first of many things I give her to make things easier."

"Have you talked to her about this? Divorcing?"

"No. But I can package it the right way, offer her things, make it less painful." A weak smile. "It's gonna hurt no matter what. I've seen a lot of divorces. It's like watching two people tear the ground apart with their bare hands and try to put it back together all by themselves. It's ugly. It's necessary."

"So what's changed since poker night?"

"Nothing," Sidney said. "She still resents me. The distance. The fact that we didn't get pregnant earlier. So whenever she's not working on something for this house we're arguing over every little thing. This house is all I got right. But I'm tired." He rested back on his elbows, stared at the ceiling. "People feared me in New York, the way they fear Langley. Almost never set foot in a courtroom. Things were handled quickly behind closed doors—money, contracts, disputes. Then I would go home and fuck my wife until she passed out. Then there were parties, so many parties. Temptation everywhere you looked. The best liquor. The best drugs. I could do whatever I wanted. There were no limits."

"And you gave in?" William asked.

"Nothing happened. I came close. What got out wasn't the full story. There was never a woman."

"I see."

"Everything you ever heard about the industry is true. These dudes swear up and down they're not gay but . . . Fortunately for me, what my wife believes—what my father believes—is what everyone else believes. Loft party, invited by a client. Got there and it was all men. I knew I should've turned right back around but . . . There were a lot of fine men there, like the most unattainable, attractive men in New York. I'd never seen anything like it. I was drawn in. And I had the time of my life. In the back of my mind I knew there was a reason I was invited. Who better to protect everyone's secret than me? My reputation was built on keeping secrets. They needed me there."

William nodded.

"That was my introduction," Sidney continued. "When I wasn't working I was hanging out more. The parties got more intimate, more exclusive. The last one turned into something else. And I was high off… shit, I don't even remember, but I was fucked up. There was a hotel room. And someone was pushing me back on a bed trying to pull down my pants." His voice cracked. "And there was another dude next to him, coaching him. Those dudes were gonna try to fuck me, one after another. And I was high enough to let them. But I snapped out of it and left. Lucky for me there were women in the room earlier that night, so by the time the story got out, all anyone knew was that there were groupies in a hotel room and I stumbled out drunk or high, zipping my pants. No one knew it was just dudes there at that point. Cintra almost killed me when she found out. She swung a bat at my head but I ducked."

"Sounds like her."

"Langley demanded I come home to be closer to family and so I could focus. She agreed with him. I didn't have to pass another bar, so I didn't have an excuse not to do it. But if I can't be my own man it doesn't matter if I'm in New York or DC. Everyone thinks New York did something to me, that it changed me. Truth is, I was miserable the entire time. And I'm miserable now." He finally focused on William. "I wish I'd trusted you. I wish Langley didn't have such a hold on me."

"Your father is a hard man to say no to," was all William could muster.

"If he can't sell you an idea he'll force it on you," Sidney agreed. "For the longest time I believed nothing could make me feel like less of a man than disappointing him. That's how fathers make you feel, that your manhood is anchored entirely to their principles, not your own." Sidney realized what he was saying and regretted it. "I'm sorry. I didn't mean to—"

"No, I understand what you mean. I didn't need Henry for that."

"You've always had a better relationship with Langley than me."

"I've also defended you to him. Sometimes I thought I wanted what you two had but not like that. Just *having* a father isn't enough. I've been thinking about this all day, since Mom told me Henry died. Like, would it have been any better if he stuck around? I'm not so sure. But you need to understand, my relationship with Langley was shaped by *Langley*. I never went to him."

"He was using you."

William nodded.

"And I need to get this out. I'm sorry for what I did to you. I convinced myself you were something to be ashamed of so I could make the decisions I made. I couldn't deal with the fact that you're the love of my life. I still can't deal with it. It changes so many things."

William shut his eyes to fight a sudden stinging. There weren't any promises in Sidney's delivery, nothing William could safely imply, but hearing it was unexpected. "You have the worst timing, Sidney."

Sidney's eyes were sad and fearful but he managed to smile. "I have no idea what my life will look like after this. I don't know where I'll end up, if I stay here or go back to New York. I know for sure I'm not staying at Sweeney. But I'll need you, William. As a friend, at least. Can I have that?"

twenty-five.

Gabriel. Todd had forgotten him after the wedding but here he was again, in chic black and white and seemingly the centerpiece of Linc's collection. He sat in the quarter lotus, completely nude with his eyes closed and facing Heavenward.

Todd and a few others gathered at the photo, which took up the entire wall, remarking not on the composition but the subject. His full lips, his flawless, youthful skin, his abs etched in onyx. *Is he here? I heard some of the models were here. I wonder how tall he is.* Etcetera. In order for this to happen, Gabriel had to undress at Linc's studio.

None of the shots Linc had taken of him were here, not the ones from the harbour or the candids at the vineyard. Linc explained that in the best photos, the ones that suggested a story, Todd appeared sad. *Melancholy* was the word Linc used. If Todd wasn't willing to discuss that sadness, then he couldn't be a part of the collection, could he? The focus of the exhibit and the book was the story behind the photo, what made these men who they were, what had brought them to this point in their lives and how much farther they believed they had to go. The humanity of his subjects was most important, and for that Linc needed text.

Todd was not giving him text.

That was how the tension began. There was no pronounced resentment, just an undercurrent of dissatisfaction and a slight distance, but a complete change from only a couple of weeks ago. Todd would ask a question and Linc's responses were clipped. He didn't seem as excited to have Todd in the room. Maybe they'd settled into a rhythm; maybe things were simply less new. Maybe Linc was just immersed in his work. The book was coming out soon and the exhibit was sooner. He had to concentrate on his art.

That's what Todd told himself.

Presently, he wondered how many men in the collection Linc slept with. It was a notion he'd tried to ignore since Julian first introduced it, but he wasn't literally surrounded by the possibility back then. So many gorgeous men had stepped in front of Linc's camera.

Todd had the urge to leave. His eyes drifted to the gallery entrance and a newly-arrived William who wasn't alone.

BREE DOWNED HER LYCHEE martini and adjusted the straps of her tiny black dress. She wasn't used to getting pretty, not like this. She regretted drinking so fast; she was already teetering in her heels. Now Mel's arm draped around her shoulders, nearly causing her to topple. The scent of weed and Polo Red, hair in neat cornrows. He towered in a long sleeveless tee that exposed tattooed arms and wore a cluster of black and silver bracelets on one wrist. "Did you see my picture?" he asked, gleeful.

"It's lovely, Mel," Bree said. "The Modern Day Hendrix angle is working. I can't believe you're actually here. I recall the two of you agreeing to not be in the same room."

"I'm still in the book, so I consider this a professional courtesy."

"But do you know . . . never mind." Bree now realized there was truth serum in lychee, and it was delicious.

"Do I know what?"

"I was gonna ask if you knew who else was here but that doesn't matter. I need to put this down." Bree scanned the room for any surface before shoving the cocktail into Mel's hand. "Are you able to confirm you were actually invited?"

"I wasn't *not* invited," he said, "and it's not like there's security at the door. It's an open event."

"I think you've forgotten what an invitation is. It doesn't matter if *anyone* can just walk in, you're not just anyone. You're the artist's ex-lover—"

"And one of the subjects. I came to look at myself, not Linc. Why are you litigating where I show up? You're supposed to be happy to see me."

"Yes, I forgot, being happy to see you is my job."

"At least pretend."

"It doesn't matter if I'm happy to see you. I just don't want any drama. And he's in an easy mood tonight."

"Of course he is. He's *easy.*"

"Why can't you be a little less . . . you know . . . You're a lot right now. Your bracelets are loud. You're very tall. We know a lot of people here and they'll have questions." Bree placed a hand on his shoulder, considered how she'd say it and let the words tumble. "He introduced me to a new person tonight."

"What kind of person?"

"*That* kind."

He laughed too loud for her comfort. "Nah, you wellin'."

"I wish I was. And I don't know who else Linc might have told. But he seems very into him."

"You mind telling me who?"

"I mean, you don't need to know that right now."

Mel pointed to the picture of Gabriel. "Is it him?"

"Of course not."

"Yeah. Linc's dating history is on the lighter side." Mel surveyed the room. He briefly landed on a photo of William Kendall and chuckled. Bree didn't ask for context; Mel always laughed to himself about one thing or the other. After a series of gestures towards each display followed by a "No" from Bree, he gave up. "So he's not in any of the photos?"

"It would appear he's not."

"Then let's find him."

"Mel—"

"It'll be fun. I won't say a word, just wanna see him."

"This matters more to you than I thought it would."

He scratched his chin. "Let me guess. Tall. Lightskin. Kind of skinny—"

"Definitely not skinny."

"Ah!"

"Dammit."

"So muscular? Thick?" He scanned the crowd. It could have been anyone. "That motherfucker."

"Ugh. You *do* care."

"You're supposed to mourn the relationship, Bree. If you can't respect it while you're in it, then at least do it afterwards. Do you see me out here with a *new person?* Why are you looking at me like that?"

Bree shook her head. "You shouldn't have come, Mel."

"I need to smoke."

"You smell like a Death Row Records tour bus in the nineties, a smoke is the last thing you need right now. You two have been broken up for a while, remember? Since Christmas, by my count, based on the *tiny* bit of information I got from the two of you."

"But it wasn't that long ago he was trying to come back."

"The fight at my house did it. I could tell just by looking at him. He was done."

"I was done too but I've been *single.*"

"And that was your choice. But this is Linc we're talking about."

"Point him out to me."

"So you can do what?" Bree asked. "Throw a drink in his face? This is a classy event. We're sipping cocktails and listening to Nina Simone. You can't come in here smelling like weed and starting fights. This ain't *Basketball Wives.*"

Mel did another scan. His eyes landed on William, this time in the flesh, who'd just arrived with a date. More relaxed than usual, not in a suit this time but a cream polo and tan trousers, presumably not to steal Linc's thunder. Mel was momentarily distracted before his survey guided him to the lone figure standing before a large screen cycling through images from Linc's collection. He was massive compared to the other men there, slabs of muscle packed on his shoulders and chest, the density and detail of his back visible through a pale blue graphic tee. Mel squinted. From his angle he could tell he wasn't only fit but had the features of a romantic lead, or an Armani model. "Found him."

TODD WAS ALONE WHEN William arrived at the exhibit and he thought of the Portrait Gallery event when Todd was too shy to mix with the crowd until he was properly fueled by his drink. He thought of Todd's solitude in his rental just outside of LA where he lived for two years after his fight with Deacon. He thought of how Todd never mentioned his friends at school or the other models he might have befriended. Aside from William, no one was permanent for Todd, so he often chose solitude when it didn't choose him.

Todd caught his gaze and smiled. It was a sweet, hopeful smile. Then he drifted, alone, to the next display. He didn't have the same gravitational pull as men with larger personalities, men like William and Linc, so people admired him from a distance, nervous about how to approach him. He managed to take up space and still be the smallest person in the room.

News of Henry's death had stirred William. It forced him to consider his regrets, as death often does, and Todd was at the top of the list. *I'm so sorry, Todd.*

"Deja vu, right?" Travis said. "I feel like we've done this many, many times before."

"Oh?" William asked.

"We met at a party like this. We met *again* at a party like this. You bourgie types love your art exhibits."

"Don't you mean *us* bourgie types? No one has to exactly drag you to these events."

"I'm usually just here for the liquor."

They were greeted by Linc, in his favorite glen plaid vest and trousers, white shirtsleeves rolled to the elbows and free of the camera that usually dangled from his neck. He hugged William tight and long, grateful for his presence after having not seen him for weeks. William mentioned the house he was remodeling and it seemed they'd be talking shop for the next several minutes. Travis attempted to break away but William grabbed his hand and pulled him back in. "Travis, have you met Linc?"

Linc snapped his fingers. "Portrait Gallery, right?"

"I saw you there but we didn't speak." They shook. "Once I bumped into William it was a wrap. But I've met you before. Way back. When I dated him the *first* time."

"Forgive me if I didn't—"

"It's okay. I probably wasn't around long enough for you to remember me."

William tensed. "Looks like I'm still paying for that."

"We have banter now," Travis added.

Linc nodded. "Impressive."

"So you took these?" Travis asked. "You're a good photographer. Wait. Is that *you?*" He turned to William, then to the screen playing the slideshow at the end of the hall. "Oh shit, that's *you*, William." In the photo, William faced a glossy, transparent canvas, his blurred shoulder in the foreground. The canvas was covered in an intricate blueprint and bore his reflection. He held a marker and had a distant look in his eyes, captivated by something other than his plans. Before transitioning to the next image, a caption appeared at the bottom: *The Architect.* "What does that mean?" Travis asked them.

"There's a story behind each image," Linc explained. "It's in the book. William builds things. He creates things. So that's the title I gave him."

"You make him sound calculating."

"It's what he does. At work."

"So what's the story?"

"It's in the book," Linc repeated. "Everyone gets a paragraph or two."

"And your story is about your job?" Travis asked William. "Come on. There has to be more to it."

William put a reassuring arm around Travis's waist. "That's all there is to it."

Travis, still dissatisfied, let it go.

"If you two want drinks, the bar is right there." Linc pointed. "And don't be afraid to make a request at the dj booth, as long as it's on-format. Enjoy yourselves. It was great meeting you again, Travis."

Linc made his way to the next set of arrivals and Travis turned to William. "I'm not sure if I like him."

TODD WAS GONE. IT took Linc a while to notice. He was too busy introducing the collection to his guests while covertly keeping an eye on Mel. At no point did he realize Todd slipped out. Moving to the back of the room he withdrew his phone and checked his messages.

Had to go. Wasn't feeling good.

Linc didn't believe him. *I'll be by William's afterwards.*

He didn't wait for Todd to respond. He approached the circular sofa in the corner where Mel dozed, mostly upright with his head hung back, snoring softly. Linc sat beside him and nudged him with his thigh. "Wake up."

Mel stirred, immediately rolling eyes upon opening them. "What's up?"

"Enjoying your nap?"

"I was trying to."

"I don't have a problem with you being here but, one, you can speak and, two, it's kind of rude to pass out in a corner. Other than that, how have you been?"

Mel reached around on the floor for his drink, which was two-thirds done. "I'm still here."

"And your music?"

"You're real funny to me."

"Excuse me?"

"You heard me. But since you brought it up, I haven't written anything new. But this, what I learned tonight about you, is good material. I was convinced *this* time, you would get it. Does he know he's your rebound?"

"He's not a rebound. What difference does it make to you anyway?"

"The fact you even have to ask tells me how much time I wasted with your ass."

"I'm not trying to fight with you, man." Linc leaned in, resting an elbow on his lap. "I know you miss it but I can't give you that tonight."

"Sitting a little close. You sure your dude won't mind?"

"Don't worry about him. I'm trying to figure out what you mean. What difference does it make to *you* who I'm with now?"

"It doesn't."

Linc laughed. "Okay, Mel."

"The problem is you haven't given yourself time to learn anything. You jumped right into this, didn't you? Did you tell him why we broke up? Does he even know who you are?"

"We're not ready to have that conversation yet and I need you to lower your voice."

Mel glanced around the room, checking to see who might have heard them over the music. The only pair of eyes on them were briefly William's, as if he knew his name would come next in this conversation. As it often did. "How do you know you won't have the same problems with him that you had with me?" Mel asked.

"First of all, he's a much nicer person than you."

"If managing to eke out a remaining fuck about you makes me mean and nasty, I'll be that. How long did it take for you to move on after the last time I saw you? Did you take a day to think about why we didn't work? It wasn't because of my attitude, Gerel."

"We keep having different versions of the same conversation, and in each one of them you're perfect."

"I *am* perfect, according to you every day you tried to get me to come back to you. I was forced to grow while I was with you, you didn't give me a choice. And I had to do it fast. So it bothers me that you're out here booed up this soon after pleading with me. There's no way *you've* grown. And it's so sad." Mel gazed off into the crowd, making eye contact with William once more and quickly looking away.

Linc rose. It would be easier to deal with Mel's words later. "If I were you, I'd leave. You don't seem like you wanna be here anyway."

He faded into the crowd as Mel reached into his jeans for his cigarettes. Two left. This was meant to be his last pack. He made his way out onto the Barracks Row portion of Eighth Street and the balmy evening.

Mel was two puffs in when the main gallery doors opened and William stood alongside him.

twenty-six.

The December before. Rain whipped the windows of William's condo as he put the final touches on his tree. Thousands of tiny lights bounced off crystal garland, icicles and delicate, blown glass spheres. Real pine cones dusted with fake snow evoked a decorated tree left in a winter storm with all its brilliant lights intact. William's interiors could be nothing other than icy, clean and intentional. But something in him melted as Todd, on the phone from Los Angeles, first brought up the possibility of returning home.

"You ever feel like if someone stares at you long enough they can see everything wrong with you? Every awful thing that's ever happened to you? How bad your insides look? That's how I feel anytime I leave this house." Although Todd had filed an order of protection against Deacon, he'd taken the extra step of renting a house in Arcadia. He trained in the garage, not ready to return to a commercial gym. He did his best to fight his way back to normal. Things were quiet for him, stable, but he told William how incomplete it all felt. "I can't shake the feeling this never would have happened to me if I got right with Anthony. It's nagging at me."

"Is that what Dr. Walker told you?"

"She didn't come up with it on her own, William."

"Her job is to cycle through theories and guide you to the right one. Parents are an easy go-to. Especially fathers. I don't know the last time I saw Henry, but I found myself replacing him."

"With other men, right?"

"With a father figure. Not romantic relationships. But we're all different. Besides, if you really wanted to come home, Anthony or not, Christmas would've been a good time to do it." He stepped back and looked over the tree, his design eye taking account of the full picture and reconciling it with up-close details. "And you're in that house, alone, no tree, no mulled wine, no Temptations playing in the background. I get it. People stare at you because they think you're superhuman. You might *be* superhuman, you've survived a lot."

"I could have died that night. I *should* have died that night. No matter what I do, it's like it happened yesterday."

"I'm so sorry, Todd."

"You're not the one who did it to me. I was stupid enough to fall in love with him and let him convince me to get in front of a camera when I should've stayed in school. It was fun sometimes and I was able to put money away but that's not who I am. But I'd finally gotten to a place where I was confident and could look people in the eye. After that I'd lost control of everything. You've always been in control of your life, William. You'll never know what this feels like. I don't wanna be afraid of the world and how people who are supposed to love me could disappear or die or lie to me or throw me through a pane of glass *but I am fucking terrified.*"

"You need to trust yourself. You've come a long way and you don't have much farther to go. I promise."

"You think I should come back to DC?" Todd asked.

"I'm gonna tell you what I've always told you. A visit is never out of the question, but LA is more your home now. I just want you to think about coming all the way here and looking for something Anthony might not be able to give you. He made his choices. You weren't one of them. He doesn't deserve your time."

Todd dropped it. They ended the call. Guilt guided William to his wine rack, but that wouldn't do. He grabbed a bottle of

Blanton's, poured it into a glass and swallowed hard. What did Todd suffer alone in that house? How many people connected to Deacon had he cut off? How many other friendships had he ended because of his own shame and fear?

During other calls Todd insisted he was fine, which made it easier for William to ignore the whisper of pain in his delivery. Now Todd was more vocal, able to put it all within context, armed with the language of trauma-focused therapy.

So began the slow burn of William's panic. He poured another shot and texted Linc. *I need something strong.* His phone rang immediately and William told him, "Not something to smoke. I can't have that smell in here."

"Why are you suddenly asking me for—"

"Just help me out." It was late but William was determined, skating over the edge in Linc's voice. Maybe Linc was going through something too that night but he wasn't ready to ask what. "I don't care what it is."

"What's going on with you, man? You wanna talk? I can talk."

"I don't. I can't. Do what I'm asking you. Please, Linc."

Silence, then, "Okay, man. I got you."

Forty minutes later it wasn't Linc who stood before William's open door but Mel with a brown paper bag. "Wassup?"

William, in a tank top and lounge pants, didn't understand but let him in anyway

"Gerel is busy," Mel began. "Have you started drinking?"

"Yeah."

Mel shook his head. "I wish you'd waited."

William leaned against the breakfast bar and raised his glass. "It's not working."

"Do I even wanna know?" Mel asked.

"It's not like I would tell you anyway." It was odd having Mel here. William knew what he and Linc often went through, had even advised Mel about it on a few occasions, but this was his first time in William's home without Linc. "He sent you?"

"Yes." Mel hung his rained-soaked gear in the closet then proceeded to the bar with his bag. He withdrew a medium-sized jar, the liquid inside a deep murky brown. "You're drinking whiskey, right?"

"What the hell is that, Mel?"

"This is weed. You're a square, so I wasn't bringing you anything stronger than this, and you told Linc you didn't want to smoke so *voila.*"

"You have *weed-infused whiskey?*"

"Why'd you say it like that?"

"I just didn't know they made that."

"Yes, and it's highly concentrated so I need to pour it for you. What chasers you got?"

"Wait, just slow down for a second. I need to absorb this."

Mel opened the refrigerator and retrieved a half-done two-liter of ginger ale. "Absorb what?"

"You don't find this odd?"

"You opened the door."

"I mean, you're not a stranger but . . ."

Mel measured out what he believed was a suitable pour for a square like William into a small glass and topped it with the ginger ale. "To be honest, William, if I was you, I wouldn't question it. You needed Linc to help you out but he can't be here. So you got me instead, and I don't know enough about you to judge if you decide you wanna tell me why you're suddenly living on the edge." He handed him the glass. "Take a sip."

William sniffed it first. The smell of marijuana was so overpowering he could already taste it. The first sip brought a flush to his cheeks and he set the glass down. "I see what you mean."

"You ever smoke before?"

"A long time ago. I got so high I kept making phone calls all night because I was afraid I'd end up talking to myself."

"That's why I'm here. You thought I was just gonna drop this off and walk away? Then I gotta hear Gerel's mouth. I think I need some too."

"I knew there was more to this." William took his glass

and made his way into the living room. Maybe things felt awkward because it was so quiet. He cycled through his playlists, considered that Mel liked his R&B with bite and settled on *Here My Dear.*

"Did Linc tell you this was one of my favorites?" Mel asked from the counter. "I love vengeful, petty relationship drama on an album. Nice tree, by the way."

"Thanks. So this is in your top five? I'm impressed. You're kind of young."

"I'm also an artist. Has Gerel ever asked for your top five?" Mel sat next to him on his long, white sofa, distant enough to not make him uncomfortable.

"Of course. That's his shorthand to figure out how cool you are. Toni Braxton, Sade, Chante Moore, Maxwell are all in there."

"You like your R&B buttoned up," Mel laughed. "For me it's *Mama's Gun, Sign O The Times, Here My Dear, My Life,* and *1st Born Second.*"

"If we were doing top tens, *Mama's Gun* would be on mine."

They both sipped, anchored on common ground.

"You get lost in it," Mel mused. "From top to bottom, I can't think of a better sequenced, better composed R&B album, especially for it to have dropped when it did. They just weren't making albums like that, they still aren't, not even Erykah herself. It's the kind of album I would make."

"Would?" William asked. "You're not making music?"

"I go back and forth trying to figure out what I wanna do. It's an uphill battle. I'm *out.* "

"So is Frank Ocean," William offered.

"Frank Ocean is safe for people. He sits at a piano and croons about his broken heart. Plus, I don't have friends named Beyoncé and Pharrell. I might stick to writing. The only reason I sing now is because I don't trust anyone to perform my shit correctly. Can you skip to 'Anger'?"

William hit a button on the remote, skipping forward to track four. Mel was silent as he listened, staring into nothing, sipping his drink. He didn't sing along but his eyes stirred with every peak of Marvin's performance.

"What did Linc do?" William asked him.

"When you texted him we were fighting."

"He did sound tense."

"He decided to call my bluff tonight."

"And the bluff?"

"I told him that if I slept with one of his friends we still wouldn't be even."

"Maybe it's not my place to say but you shouldn't be in a relationship with a man who pimps you out as a debate tactic."

"I know," Mel said. "But I want him to feel how he makes me feel."

"This isn't the way. There's *no* way. You shouldn't be focused on revenge. Channel it into your art."

"Fuck art. I need him to feel some kind of hurt. He's too cool about everything. You can't be nonchalant at all times. I hate that shit. He takes nothing seriously. I want him to be *in trouble.*"

"You want to punish him, I get it."

"I was too inexperienced when I got with him. He knows more than me, he's done more than me. I could never expect him to change but he could make me into whatever he wanted me to be."

"He should have known better."

"You're not the first to say it." Mel stared into his glass, turning it in both hands so the contents swirled. "When he's good, when he's *present,* I'm pretty sure I love him. But then I have to ask myself if I've experienced love enough to identify it. I'm not even sure I'm qualified to be writing about it. It's fucked up how quickly you rejected me, though."

"I never explicitly rejected you but there's no way you thought I would—"

"But what if?"

"You're not my type." William pushed his glass aside, deciding even the small dose Mel had given him was too much. He was terrified he'd do something stupid like actually fuck Mel or, worse, open up about his guilt over Todd.

"Humor me. What is your type?"

"Clean-cut. Professional. Maybe even conventional."

"So you want someone like you?"

"Anything wrong with that?"

"I guess what they say about us is true. We all wanna fuck our reflections."

William relaxed into the cushions. "We want a person who reflects our values. Straight folks want the same thing, they just aren't accused of being narcissistic for it."

"Then you're not at risk of taking it any further than a kiss, since I'm not your type."

"A kiss?"

"A strictly therapeutic kiss for someone who's been kissing the same man for way too long. A kiss we've already been cleared to share."

William's head swam. He laughed, goofy and tingling. "Shit . . ."

"I wish you could see yourself now," Mel said. "I've never seen you this relaxed. It's hot."

"I'm sure it is."

"We'll keep it between the three of us."

"Mel . . ." In his haze, William hadn't realized how close Mel now was. It was Mel's heat that alerted him, less than an inch away. Words escaped William's lips, as lax as his eyes and the curl forming at the corner of his mouth. "Just a kiss . . ."

"Just a kiss," Mel assured him. William was planted. Mel climbed onto his lap, faced him, grabbed the sofa's back.

"This is a full body kiss," William said.

"You could escape if you wanted to." Their lips met first, instinct or habit brought William's hands to Mel's waist, then up his back, pulling him in deeper as Marvin narrated.

William turned away. "Just a kiss."

"You're hard right now."

William released him. "Yes, and you need to leave."

"It was nice."

"It was, but I can't save you from him"

BESIDES THE HAIR, MEL didn't look much different now from six months ago. His exterior longed to harden, he needed to best his emotions, but his vulnerability bubbled to the surface as he recounted his fight with Linc minutes earlier. "I basically told this dude I still care about him and he asked me to leave."

"In those words?"

"No. But close." Mel flicked the cigarette butt and it caught a breeze before landing in the middle of the street. "You probably think you wasted your time trying to help me that night, because we're having the same arguments, just not with the benefit of regular sex."

"You want him back."

"I don't think I do."

"I wasn't asking. You never intended for this to be permanent. You wanted him to suffer for six months and return to you having learned his lesson. You don't just want him to be a better man, you want him to do better at being *your* man." Mel was ready to protest and William held up his hand. "I know what you're about to say and it's a lie. I know that feeling. You're only invested in his growth if it benefits you. You're gonna be spinning your wheels for the rest of your life if you don't get over him."

"Sometimes I think you don't like Gerel."

William uttered a flat chuckle, a *tuh*. What a silly thing to say. "Of course I like Linc, otherwise I wouldn't be here."

"Maybe I'm reading you wrong."

"I think you are." William had spent too much time defending Linc to Travis that evening to be accused of such a thing. "I just don't like all of his choices. I don't like how people react to those choices. Linc talked about how brilliant you are, how much he loves your mind, but when you talk about loving him—I'm sorry, Mel—you don't sound that smart. A lot of us can stand to be more vulnerable, but not you, not in this case. You think he's never used that?" He stopped short of calling Linc manipulative. He took a breath. "I need to go."

Mel's eyes narrowed. "No, I think I'm right. You two . . ." He shook his head.

"What do you mean *you two?*"

"You're alike. And you can't stand each other."

"Oh please."

"You think I'm stupid?" Mel demanded.

"That's not what I said—"

"Did you see the caption he put under your photo? *The Architect?* Do you know what the rest of it says? I peeped it a few months back. It could've been a draft." Mel reached into his pocket for his remaining cigarette. "But he was real slick about it. That's supposed to be your friend."

There it was again. Between Mel and Todd, William knew he had to squash this idea that he and Linc were fake friends. "He and I have always been good."

Mel pointed to the gallery entrance with his unlit cigarette. "Go in there and ask him what it says, William."

"No, how about *you* go in there and yell at him and embarrass him in front of his guests? That's your thing, remember? You cooked up this nonsense that Linc and I hate each other because you don't want to admit you want him back. I was trying to help you make a better decision so you don't feel so stupid this time. But I don't care what you do. It's your life." William disappeared inside, not before Mel mumbled a callous invective that would have gotten his throat punched if William were a more savage man.

twenty-seven.

Linc was probably too comfortable apologizing without knowing his exact reasons for it. His delivery wasn't perfunctory but was too perfectly rendered—the regretful eyes, the timing, the palms facing outward. *I've done this many, many times and I know how to get it right,* he seemed to be saying.

Todd sat at the edge of the bed in William's guest room in his briefs. His eyes were distant and tired. "What are you apologizing for?"

"For whatever I did. Whatever made you leave."

"That's kind of dismissive and I don't need an apology from you."

"Then what *do* you need?"

"I need to train in the morning. Let's go to bed."

"Not until you tell me what's wrong."

Todd took a breath then leaned forward, elbows resting on powerful thighs. He knew how he would sound and hated himself for it. "When you took Gabriel's picture, did anything else happen?"

"He tried to suck my dick. I told him to chill. He left. Is that what you were worried about?" Linc was incredulous to the point of suppressing a chuckle.

"You have no reason to lie to me, so I believe you."

"But he's not why you left. Can't be."

Todd had briefly chatted with William and Travis before

leaving. Travis was overly enthusiastic about meeting Todd. He'd seen him before in ads and William had mentioned he was his houseguest. The few times Travis was at the condo, Todd was with Linc. Todd smiled through it the way he always did, eager to disappear. William was sympathetic. Maybe he knew what Todd felt then. "There was something about being in a room with all of those pictures and hearing the things I've heard. I panicked."

"Then why don't you just ask me what's up instead of worrying about what you heard from William or Julian or whoever? If you need the truth, when I was in my last relationship I fucked around *twice*. That's it. I don't fuck everyone I meet and I don't fuck everyone I shoot, if that's what you're worried about. And I already apologized for looking like I was flirting at the wedding."

Todd sighed.

"What, Todd?"

"I don't wanna walk into a room and feel like everyone is gossiping about my boyfriend."

"People will talk regardless. I don't know what else I can do."

Todd waited for Linc to strip down to nothing before he hit the lights. Linc's tone had been strained, bordering on condescension, his mea culpa powered by fatigue rather than love but Todd still craved him. Linc lay on his back, the covers gathered mid-thigh, so he was beautifully exposed and ready to be straddled. The tension over the past several days couldn't disrupt their passion, in spite of Todd's growing concern they hid behind it, used sex to ignore any issues.

"I didn't mean to ruin your night," he told him.

Linc chuckled bitterly. "You didn't. A couple people tried, though."

"Are we okay?"

"You and me? We're more than okay."

"Are you sure? Because now I can't sleep." A smile.

Linc climbed on top of him and immediately covered Todd's face in soft kisses. "I snapped at you. I'm sorry. I'm used to being shouted at. Worn down. My defenses went up kinda hard."

"Your ex?"

"He doesn't let up."

"So it was him tonight? He was there?"

"Yes. But I don't wanna talk about him now. I wanna love you." A deep kiss. Todd's hands pinned above his head. Although he was the strongest of the two, he was easily malleable in Linc's hands.

Todd squeezed him in his thighs. "It's hard to stay mad at you."

"You've been mad? Like *upset* with me?"

"Maybe a little worried about us. I get in my head, think things are worse than they are. I'm probably thinking about my last relationship, too."

"So what happened?"

"I'm not ready to talk about it."

Linc's thumb traced Todd's cheek. He almost asked again before Todd took his thumb into his mouth.

"Don't do that," Linc whispered.

Todd relaxed his thighs, gave Linc the space to slide down, kiss his body, pull off his briefs before Linc reached for the pile of condoms he'd haphazardly tossed on the nightstand during his last visit. Linc was more tender tonight than their first time, but Todd still cried out once he was full of him. Linc's mouth covered his, muffling any sounds as he slowly drove into him, and it all came with the silent assurance they were perfect. Todd had nothing to worry about. He was safe and Linc wasn't going anywhere. By the time Todd drifted off to sleep, drained and exhausted and flush with the heat of love, he had abandoned his doubts all over again, comforted, complacent and as silent as could be until the next disappointment surfaced.

twenty-eight.

The studio was a pit of humidity. Rafe glistened as he gently instructed the class to "Maintain Ustrasana by holding onto your ankles." Most could perform the posture, but it required them to face the ceiling and take their eyes off him. Rafe Ashton had a body sculpted from dedicated training by Julian during their time as a couple and his long, dark hair was tied into a man-bun.

Julian, in a kneeling position along with the rest of the class, reached backward for his ankles and thought it would be easier since he was so short and mastered it before, but he'd gained so much dense muscle over the years that his ankles were just out of reach. Drenched in sweat and miserable, Julian was convinced Rafe increased the temperature in there just to fuck with him.

He stole a glance at Rafe, who offered a soft smile with a wink that belied the fact they were all suffering in pure Hades. Even the ambient music spilling from the sound system was hellish.

"If you're having difficulty," Rafe said, "hold onto your waist."

Julian's eyes darted around. Everyone was confidently grabbing their ankles at this point. The instruction was for him.

Rafe wasn't cruel but could be playful. When Julian came to him that evening insisting they talk, Rafe agreed to it but only if Julian joined his hot yoga session. Even if Rafe's intent wasn't to expose a weakness, Julian was now acutely aware of how bad his flexibility was and cursed himself for not properly stretching after his lifts.

Julian grunted as he used momentum to reach his ankles and almost toppled to the side. "Your waist," Rafe reminded him.

A few years ago the two tried desperately to balance one another out. Julian was often hyper and aggressive while Rafe maintained a practiced calm. Julian helped Rafe build muscle mass and Rafe taught Julian breathing techniques and meditations. Their approach to fitness spilled over into other aspects of their relationship, including the bedroom. Rafe taught Julian to be more sensual, to look into his lover's eyes, to stimulate each other without reaching an orgasm. Julian tried unsuccessfully to rope Rafe into disagreements, if only to have him express a different kind of passion, to react in a way more familiar and human to Julian. As he next attempted the rabbit pose, Julian reconsidered his excuse for dumping Rafe—"You're too zen." Although Rafe accepted it, he was obviously too smart to believe it.

Thirty minutes later found them on a bench three blocks from Rafe's yoga studio, facing the DuPont Circle fountain. Rafe's hair—inherited from Sri Lankan and Japanese grandparents—was now loose and falling over one shoulder, at times fanning against a light breeze. Tall water bottles and gym bags sat between them.

Of all his ex-lovers, Julian regretted his treatment of Rafe the most. Combativeness wasn't a language Rafe quite understood, so no matter how difficult Julian behaved, he wasn't phased. None of this made Rafe passive, he just preferred to approach every circumstance peacefully. He naturally didn't understand Julian's distress tonight, why he seemed so anxious and why he was so apologetic. "We were great together," Rafe reminded him, ever the optimist. "We worked out and traveled and had the best sex."

"I'm glad you remember it that way."

"I wouldn't choose to remember it another way. Are you okay? You were tense earlier. I thought the class would help."

"You always think things can be fixed by twisting someone's body into impossible positions."

"And when you realize those positions aren't impossible, everything else falls into place, doesn't it?"

"Those positions are definitely impossible for me now."

Rafe's eyes were gentle. "They don't have to be. Tell me what's bothering you."

"I'm kind of fucked up right now. Realized I was going in circles. Been forced to look at myself. You ever have that?"

"Yes. It was a long time ago."

"And you've been zen ever since. I think I finally got it," Julian went on. "I'm in my mid-thirties. Shit wasn't adding up and now I know why and I owe you an apology."

"I knew this would happen eventually and I'm proud of you. You have clarity now. And you're so beautiful for it."

"You're making this too easy."

"What did I tell you at the end? *I'll be here when you figure it out.* Maybe you couldn't hear me over your ego."

In the past, the term would have sent Julian into a defensive rage, but he knew Rafe was steering him towards his oft-invoked Eastern philosophical concept of *non-self.* "I couldn't hear *anyone* over my ego, especially when I was being told some shit for my own good. That was hard to say, by the way. Even to you."

"So how will you use this?"

Julian gazed off past the fountain and the gradually darkening sky. "I don't know. Be alone, I guess. I need to be by myself."

"There's nothing wrong with being alone."

"The minute I had my shit together I thought I didn't have to do anything else. I thought I was perfect."

"God's gift to the world?" Rafe quipped.

"Exactly that. And once I had someone, like you, I wanted you to be someone else."

Rafe's calm veneer flickered a bit, like he was trying to locate a signal. "I'm not sure what you mean."

"You have discipline. It's what attracted me to you, and everyone else. But it all goes back to one person, someone I could never be with."

"Do I know who?"

"He doesn't even know."

"You think it's worth telling him?"

"There's no point in it. If there was a window of opportunity it closed years ago. We're friends."

Rafe's eyes twinkled with realization. "Is it William?"

Julian sighed.

"I like William. But he's disciplined in a different way. I think he holds himself to a standard and it might be causing a burden for him. I could be wrong."

"How do you figure?"

"I don't wanna judge him."

"It's not judging. You're just making an observation." Julian grinned.

"William's concerned with perfection, just as you are. He's good at it, but I don't think he can sustain that forever. How does he live in the moment? How does he find peace? He's aspirational. I think he represents what everyone—especially Americans—think they want, but you have to make a lot of sacrifices to live like that. I'm not sure it's worth it. But, again, I could be wrong. People can find calm in work and structure. Do you think you want what he has and that's why you fell for him?"

Julian didn't have an answer or the chance to offer it. A man approached from around the fountain—over six feet tall with an academic air. His hair was long and full, a few locs pulled back into a small knot to secure the rest into a loose pony that cascaded to his waist. Rafe stood and they embraced. "Julian, this is my partner Amir."

Amir's handshake was strong and assured. "It's great to finally meet you." His voice wasn't only deep, it was commanding, precise. A baritone that made Julian tremble from the inside out.

"What have you heard about me?"

Amir laughed. "All good things. You look familiar."

"He owns Definitions," Rafe offered. "Do you have ads, Julian?"

Julian tried to appear as casual as possible, even though his legs were ready to give out beneath him. "I'm on the side of a few buses."

"Amir teaches Egyptian studies and English as a second language."

Julian sized up Amir once more. "They pay you well."

"I'm good with my money," Amir offered. A teacher straight from the cover of a romance novel who spoke with the cadence of a king. Julian could hear lifetimes and galaxies in that voice. The thought of Amir talking dirty made the blood rush throughout his body.

"We were meeting here before dinner," Rafe explained. "You're more than welcome to join us."

Julian grabbed his bag. "No. The two of you go ahead. I actually have plans of my own."

He had no plans.

"It was great seeing you and hearing about your progress. We should get together sometime. The three of us." Rafe pulled him in for a bear hug. Julian wondered if Rafe felt his heart pound during their embrace, if he caught the brief glance in Amir's direction. Or the smile Amir offered in return.

twenty-nine.

"ALMOST AT THE FINISH line," Cintra mused as she tore plastic from the custom vanity she and William designed. It was for the powder room, low and wide enough to hold a vessel sink and the requisite toiletries. The top was polished cohiba granite with precise outlets for plumbing. She swatted nearly microscopic flecks of dust and stood back to admire it. "We do good work." She held out a fist but William wasn't much of a pounder so he gave her shoulder an affectionate squeeze.

He then circled the piece, inspecting each detail to make sure it matched their vision. "Now we have to get it in there."

"I know you're in your jeans today, William, but we have guys for that."

"Am I not a guy?" A grin. He waved over a worker from down the hall. "Do you know how many sinks I've installed with my own hands?"

Cintra backed away. "You got it, then."

The vanity and sink went in smooth, just below wall-mounted fixtures and a bell-shaped mirror. Cintra immediately brought in a glass vase of fresh white lilies and a basket of hand towels before whipping out her phone to document the progress. "I can't believe you aren't more excited about this. You know this is the most important room in the whole house, right? Your guests talk about you when the bathrooms aren't on point."

"We still have a short way to go. I reserve excitement for the end. Anything can happen between now and then."

She laughed. "One time in your life, I wanna see you make a fuss. About *something.*"

"Maybe you will one day. Excuse me." He reached into his pocket for his buzzing phone and stepped a few feet away. James was in the middle of a crisis back at the office and William was needed as soon as possible. William didn't bother asking what; his trust for James ran deep. "I need to head back to the office. James needs me."

"I was headed in that direction anyway," Cintra told him. "Maybe I can ride?"

William was a rigorous planner and considered every possible outcome for each decision. But there were the occasional outliers when it came to work. Expensive or rare pieces could be damaged in transit, a supplier could run out of materials, a contractor might come down with the sniffles. William thought he was always prepared, that there was a Plan B and C. That no matter what happened he'd never succumb to surprise.

He hated surprises. He didn't appreciate when fate snatched the choice from him. The only thing worse was when the choice was snatched by someone close who knew he preferred to be in control.

When Cintra offered to ride with him up to KDG's suite, he thought nothing of it. He figured she was being nosy and wanted to share a brief air-kiss with James before she went about her own business. He never guessed a surprise awaited him and she was in on it. Or that it would be so loud the minute they hit the main lobby.

William froze. He wasn't startled or shocked. His heart didn't pound uncontrollably. He was confused because he didn't know the context and was annoyed something was planned for him behind his back. He grinned nonetheless.

James was in front leading the cheers and applause. Scattered among the crowd of staff and business acquaintances were Travis and Julian with Langley way in the back. "You won!" James told him.

"What did I win?"

"The 2016 National Design Excellence Award."

"I didn't even submit us for that. I didn't think I would—"

"*I* submitted you for the McKeene project right before the deadline. You won!"

"*I won?*"

"You won, William!"

He exhaled. James hugged him and Cintra followed. Soon everyone was all over him. Someone popped a champagne bottle and turned on the music. Slices of cake were passed out. They didn't give him a moment to breathe. In the middle of it all, he learned Cintra had called him to the house so James could prepare the office for the surprise. William playfully threatened to fire him.

"And why did you invite Travis?" he hissed in James's ear.

"Because I thought he was important to you."

William glanced at Travis who had found his way to Cintra, comfortable and pleased to see a familiar face. "I don't want you to get the wrong idea but—"

"Is he just a piece?" James ventured.

"He's a friend, but do me a favor and try not to dip too far in the personal contacts unless you absolutely have to, okay?"

James nodded in the affirmative and walked off. And here was Julian, squeezing William in a bear hug and nearly lifting him from the floor with his powerful arms. "Congratulations, my dude! You finally got that award!"

Once he was released, William got a better look at him. He hadn't seen Julian in weeks. "I appreciate it."

"So where is it?"

"You mean the actual award? The National Society of Architecture and Design has an annual banquet at the Omni in a couple of weeks. I was already going but now I'll be there to accept it."

"So who are you taking?"

"I usually take James but I'll probably bring my mother along this time. Why, you wanna join us?"

Julian laughed. Nearly blushed. "Nawh, I was just asking. I'll probably be at work anyway." He was anxious and awkward, as if William were someone he was only just getting to know. "So what have you been up to?"

"I've been taking it easy," William said carefully. "Found out my father passed away."

"Shit, man. Are you okay?"

"We weren't close. I don't remember what he looks like, frankly."

"I'm still sorry to hear it."

William glanced at Travis once again as Julian went on. Their eyes connected. Julian squeezed his upper arm. Travis flinched.

"I just came through because your boy called. I need to get back. We should catch up, though, have some drinks. A bite. I see Todd more than you these days." Another laugh.

"Yeah, sure. Let me know when you're free."

"We're both busy but we can make it work." Julian hugged him again and grabbed two slices of cake on his way out. William wondered if he was high.

"That was Julian, right?" Travis asked later. "I think I remember him from before." *Before* was how Travis referred to their courtship four years earlier, a time so distant for William he was constantly surprised how much Travis recalled. "Even back then . . ." Travis shook his head.

"Back then what?"

"He was crushing."

William offered a perplexed look before saying goodbye to a few guests. The party wasn't meant to last beyond half a sheet cake and two bottles of champagne and rapidly thinned. Someone offered to treat him to happy hour afterwards but he declined.

With William to himself once more, Travis continued. "You said he used to be your trainer and you became friends. Why?"

"Julian wanted to start his own business so he surrounded himself with other business owners. He was not *crushing* on me."

Travis chuckled and sipped his champagne. "Okay."

"You're being messy."

"He doesn't look at you the way I look at *my* friends. He looks at you like he's in love." Travis shrugged. "Or maybe he just admires you because of your *business acumen.*"

William gently took the glass from Travis's hand. "That's enough for you. It was great seeing you today," he told him, gentle yet firm. "We'll get together later and finish this."

"Fine. Hopefully by then you'll realize I'm right." Travis winked and went for the door as Cintra and Langley approached to say their goodbyes. Just as Travis was leaving he stopped to greet Todd, who was on his way in. William's mouth went dry and he immediately downed the remainder of Travis's champagne. He searched for something nearby—the back of a chair, any surface—to stabilize himself. He took deeper breaths. Tried not to appear so shaken.

Todd reached him first. "I'm so sorry. I would've come with Julian but I had a client. Congratulations!"

William succumbed to his twentieth or thirtieth hug that afternoon. Wondered if Todd felt how shaken he was. "I appreciate it."

"Looks like everyone's leaving."

"Yeah. We all gotta get back to work."

"Is this your first award?"

"First major one, yes."

"I'm proud of you."

"That's very sweet, Todd, thank you."

Cintra politely intercepted, exchanged introductions with Todd then squeezed William. "Okay, babe, I'm out. It was fun fooling you. Are you good?"

"Still in shock." William glanced at Langley, whose grin was wide and full of teeth. Not at all friendly or even cordial if you knew who Langley was. It was a grin that ate William alive, made his flesh crawl and burn. The same grin Langley wore at Sidney's wedding reception ten years ago, when he sat across from William and all of this began.

"You mind if we have a chat in your office?" Langley asked, his hand tight on William's shoulder. "Won't take a minute."

"I'll see you two later," William told them before following Langley down the hall. He didn't look back but hoped Todd and Cintra would just leave. Everyone needed to leave. The party was over.

They entered his office quietly, William locking the door behind him. He was dizzy. His stomach had steadily dropped since Todd's arrival. Langley strolled to the small bar, grabbed a bottle of gin and poured a shot.

"It was only meant to be for a few weeks," William said. His voice, normally strong and measured, trembled with uncertainty. He immediately regretted his choice of words.

"How long has he been here, exactly?" Langley asked.

"Not long."

Langley walked his glass to the window. Stared out into K Street. It was hot and bright out. "Why is he here?"

"Things weren't going so well for him in LA. He needed a change of scenery."

"Sit."

William did so without question, not sure what to expect. He'd never known Langley Baptiste to be a violent man. Intimidating and imposing, yes, but never someone who exacted physical harm. He couldn't recall a time Langley raised his voice. He never had to; he made the point with his physicality.

"We agreed he is never to come to DC, *for any reason.*" Langley seethed. His shoulders squared. "You had one job. He has no reason to believe there's anything for him here."

"He's an adult. He's gonna come and go as he pleases."

Langley chuckled. It was flat and spiteful. "Remember when you would come by the house for a cigar? We'd sit on the deck and catch up. About work, the family. *Especially* family.

We'd talk about how men like you and me always have to *carry* our relatives. Your aunt and cousins. *Their* kids." A casual swallow of gin. "I know everything about everyone in your family, the ones you help, the ones you'd rather didn't exist. I·know everyone's financial issues, their troubles with the law. How important they all are to your mother. I have friends at every precinct—all seven districts—friends who won't be as patient or lenient with them once I say the word."

"Langley—"

"Your family's had it relatively easy, William, and not just because of you. You think I'd have gone into our agreement without some form of insurance? Everything you have today is because of me, you understand?" He downed the rest of his drink and went to William, crouched low and gripped the back of William's neck. It was so rough and so tight Langley could have made a closed fist. Even as he struggled, William realized it could have been worse. If Langley knew the truth—that Todd had come back to see Anthony—Langley might have sent him through the window and out onto K Street. His lips were at William's ear, intimate and threatening. His voice was low but to William it roared. "You get Todd out of DC or I'll destroy everything I helped you build, you goddamn faggot. Do you understand me?"

thirty.

PRIME'S SUNLIT LOUNGE WAS empty but for William and a lone female bartender. He sat in the corner at a small table, before a rectangular plate of calamari with bok choy, an Old Fashioned and three shots of Wray & Nephew. It was the next afternoon and he'd convinced the manager on duty to give him the top level an hour before regular service. William appreciated the space and calm of the lounge when it wasn't busy and considered it neutral ground for his meeting with Linc.

Todd had fallen hard for Linc, just as William predicted. Linc had become his anchor in DC and the only person at this point who could ever compel him to leave.

William unconsciously rubbed his neck, sore from his encounter with Langley only twenty-four hours earlier.

When he spotted Linc at the top landing he considered Mel's accusations. It wasn't jealousy Mel had implied, but something more damning, that William loathed the parts of Linc that reflected himself and vice versa. So maybe Mel was a lot smarter than William initially thought. Petulant and petty but perceptive in the way artists could be, a grain of insight buried beneath emotional carnage. Here was Linc now in his retro jersey polo, snug gray trousers and driver's cap, camera strap looped securely through his fingers. He considered himself a cultural custodian of sorts, someone who preserved a notion of classic—not regressive—manhood and conveyed it through his personal brand. He knew how to work a room and used charisma honed over several years to get exactly what he wanted from people. And that was only where their similarities began.

After a tight hug, William gestured to the shots and Linc knew this was serious.

"Congratulations again on your award," Linc offered as they sat. "I wanted to be there yesterday, but work. You know how it is."

"I appreciate it either way. Now I have to pull together some kind of speech where I appear humble. I've been waiting a while for this. I'm not sure I can do it."

"Then don't," Linc said. "Who do you need to be humble for?"

"Everyone. You know me, I can schmooze but I don't politic too much, that's probably why it's taken so long to get this. But at some point you have to play along. Talent only takes you so far."

"I get tired of being on my best behavior all the time, just so I don't offend someone's weak-ass sensibilities."

"You sound like Julian."

"That was violent! Get up there and say what you feel, even if it's *I deserve this.* So what's on your mind, man?"

"Have a shot."

"Now?"

"I want to make sure that by the end of this you don't resent me."

"Why would I resent you?"

William nodded to the set of glasses on the table, inviting Linc again to take one. His friend did so and smiled, enjoying its familiar burn. He followed with a ring of calamari and watched William intently. William wasn't exactly nervous—not that he ever would be—but he tread carefully. What he had to say was likely the last thing Linc wanted to hear.

"It's about Todd," William began. "And Melvin. And you."

Linc sighed. "You gotta get the fuck out of here, William."

A chuckle. "You wanna take another shot?"

"Do you see me laughing right now? You need to mind your

business. Todd is grown."

"You love him? I mean, do you *really* love him or are you temporarily infatuated?"

"You gotta be kidding me right now."

"Linc, listen to me. Todd wants to get back to normal. He can't do that with you in the picture. I could see if the two of you were being casual, but he is *in love with you—*"

"Fuck you mean *back to normal?*"

"You know he's in therapy, right?"

"Yes, I know. *And?* Normal is relative."

"Normal was *his* word. Did he tell you why he's in therapy?"

Linc shrugged. "Not exactly but I know some of the shit he's been through. I know who his father is and what happened to his mother."

"So you also know how his last boyfriend beat the shit out of him and pushed him face-first through a glass door?"

Linc fell silent, staring at the remaining shots and deciding how he would pace himself. He'd only briefly considered that Todd's scars were evidence of violence in a previous relationship. Todd's size and strength were enough to convince him to abandon the notion altogether.

"You're probably thinking Todd's not a small man." William went on. "But Deacon was just as big and he had a coke problem and anger issues. He took everything out on Todd because Todd is so passive. Todd's doctor has him convinced he wouldn't have ended up in a relationship like that if he didn't have issues with Anthony. That's why he came here to resolve things with him."

"And that's why he stopped taking pictures?" Linc asked.

"Yes."

"How bad was it?"

"There was a broken nose. Some deep cuts on his face. You almost can't tell."

"I can tell."

"He looks away when you try to make eye contact, doesn't he?"

"In the beginning he did. I just thought he was shy."

"I'm gonna ask you again. Do you love him?"

"I do. But I need to have a conversation with him. See where his head is."

"He needs the space to deal with it right now but he's not gonna tell you that. He's ashamed. But he also seems to love you a lot. I don't think he wants to push you away, but he needs to address this."

"Sounds like you want me to dump him."

"Linc—"

"What did you tell him about me?" Linc asked, his fingers hovered over the next shot glass. "You've been on this for a minute. He already doubts me because of you."

"I said you're easily distracted. He told me the same thing—to mind my business. But I can't. He needs to put this stuff with Deacon and his father behind him, as much as he possibly can."

"*I'm* not abusive. You can say a lot of shit about me but not that."

"I wasn't suggesting you are."

"You're suggesting *something.*"

"Mel is a mess. I talked to him at your exhibit. He wants you back. Poor thing. What do you do to these boys?"

Linc took the shot. "Fuck you, William."

"What do you think Mel is gonna do next time he's in a room with you and Todd?"

"I can handle Mel."

"The last time you tried to *handle* Mel you sent him to sleep with me instead of cutting him loose. Everyone around you *told you* to cut Mel loose. I know what's best for Todd right now and I need you to cut *him* loose. Please."

"Who is Todd to you? You've known him for ten years but he was on another coast the whole time. I don't have any friends like that. I *see* my friends, especially the ones who need me the way you claim Todd needs you."

"I visited Todd plenty of times."

"Never talked about him. Never pointed to an ad and said, *This is my friend.* He was a secret until recently."

"So I'm supposed to hand you a dossier for every friend I have?"

"You don't have to hand me shit, but if he's been so important to you all this time, why haven't you acted like it? Why do you care so much today? And how long before he was pushed through a glass door did you know his boyfriend was abusive? Shit ain't adding up, man. Maybe your problem is with me."

William noticed the lounge wasn't as quiet as when he first took his seat and now downtempo house music played on a low volume. It was probably just loud enough to buffer their talk, which was likely to increase in volume. "I don't think it makes a difference, Linc. The point is, Todd has bigger things to focus on. You have the information now so hopefully you do the right thing."

Linc shook his head in disgust. "I wish you knew how crazy you sound right now. Let that man be."

"Todd's not happy!" William didn't expect he'd be the one to raise his voice. He relaxed back into his chair, clutching his Old Fashioned, and brought it back down. "You can see his scars? You're looking at him that closely and can't tell he's in pain?"

Linc was silent again as he thought of the pictures he took at the harbor and the vineyard. He considered when Todd told him he'd been through Hell and everything Todd revealed their first night together. The pain had always been there. "I'll talk to him," he said. He downed the third shot of rum and nodded. "You want me to do this, I'll do it my way."

"That's all I ask."

TWO NIGHTS LATER. LINC apologized for the smell in his studio, the glassiness of his eyes, the dryness of his mouth as he kissed Todd. He'd spent the last hour sorting through his remaining photos, candidates for another slot or two, maybe even the cover. All reserved for Todd. *The Face.* Linc needed those eyes in and *on* his book. He also needed to let him go.

It was right there in the photos, the ones he wanted to *use.* Todd's sadness. *I don't think I should see you anymore but, if you don't mind, can I use this shot?* Linc lit up to make himself feel better about it.

Todd was energized as he shed his clothes in Linc's bedroom and talked about his sessions that day. "This is the week everyone is starting to see and *feel* progress and they're so grateful. So am I. Julian thought I was crazy." He gently shoved Linc back on the bed.

"You think you're just gonna get in this bed after invoking Julian?"

Todd laughed. "He's the last thing on my mind, really. I just like when—I can't believe I'm about to say this—I like when I'm right. These people need the energy and resources of a facility like Definitions, just not the parts that intimidate them. With me, they don't have to worry about any of that."

"I'm happy for you." Linc held out his arms and Todd climbed on top of him. "I love seeing you like this." He pulled him in for a deep kiss. "So what are you thinking about doing? This job obviously means a lot to you, but that wasn't your initial plan."

"I don't know. I'm enjoying it. I'm enjoying *you.* Everything's up in the air right now."

"Your place in LA—"

"The owner's cool checking in, as long as I'm paying on time. Why?"

"Are you any closer to figuring out your plans?"

"I guess I haven't thought about it as much as I should."

"I want you to think about everything that's important to you right now."

"Well you, of course." Todd smiled.

"Todd . . ." Linc was silenced by another kiss, Todd's lips trailing down his neck, lingering at his chest then moving down to his stomach. Lower.

It was so good he decided the conversation could wait.

"So maybe I should just stay here?" Todd suggested the following night. They were on a bench facing the Tidal Basin, flanked by cherry blossom trees. It was dusk so the sky was purple with bursts of amber reflected in the water, the Jefferson Memorial aglow just across. Linc casually snapped with his camera as they talked. Having any conversation with Todd at home or near a bed or with any semblance of privacy proved impossible since they couldn't keep their hands off each other. All Todd had to do was lay beside him, draw Linc in with those eyes and smile. It was a wrap.

Now Todd stared out into the water, large Smoothie King cup in hand and his gym bag at his feet. "It only makes sense, right? Is there anything keeping me in California?"

"You tell me," Linc said. "What was keeping you there in the first place?"

"School, then love. But after that . . . I'm not sure. Fear, maybe."

Linc placed the camera between them and held Todd's chin. "I want you to tell me what happened to you out there."

Todd didn't immediately respond. He pulled away a bit, waited for a few passersby to advance down the path and took a breath before he continued. "My ex wasn't very good at talking things out. I ended up on the other side of a sliding glass door. The hard way."

"He pushed you?"

"Technically he swung me, really hard. I spent a lot of time hating myself for it. I was ashamed. Embarrassed. It's why I started seeing Dr. Walker. Sometimes when I look at myself I can still see what he did."

"What do you mean?"

Todd's voice was low, tenuous. "How I looked afterwards. The first time I saw myself in the mirror—the cuts, the bruises. They never exactly went away. I've been trying to figure out how to talk to you about it without sounding crazy."

"You think you sound crazy to me now?"

Todd shrugged.

"I keep asking if you're happy, if you know what your plans are, because I'll look at you sometimes and all I can see is this pain. I knew you were carrying something with you. And if you haven't dealt with it, then are you sure you need to be here? With me, I mean."

"We agreed it's not supposed to be convenient."

"I know, but . . . I didn't think it was this bad. You're talking about trauma, being reminded of it every time you see yourself. And on top of that you're worried about me flirting with other dudes. You're going through some serious shit right now—"

"I already know what I need to do. I just need to see Anthony."

"You think maybe you should worry about that first?"

"First?"

"Before you commit to me."

"No, Linc, I don't think that."

It was the most certain Todd ever sounded, so much Linc considered delaying the conversation once more. But he remembered Mel's accusation he hadn't grown and William's suggestion he never gave his lovers proper room to grow themselves. "I think it might be necessary, Todd."

"I don't understand what you're saying."

"I just don't want to be in your way."

"You wouldn't be in my way. You'd be by my side."

"Baby . . ."

Todd turned back to the water. "This isn't what I think it is, is it? You said the other night that we're okay. From day one, you said *I got you*. Has that changed?"

"Remember when you were talking about your therapy and said you have things you need to figure out? That you can't move as confidently through the world as you should? Don't you think you need the opportunity to do that?"

"Of course I do but this came out of nowhere. This doesn't sound like you."

"I don't wanna see you in pain, Todd—"

"I'm in pain *now*. You're breaking up with me."

"I'm not . . ." Linc sighed. He had to choose his next words carefully. "I need to give you your space, so you can confront your father, so you can put all this stuff with Deacon behind you—"

Todd faced him once more. "How do you know his name?"

"Huh?"

"Deacon. I never told you my ex-boyfriend's name."

Linc sat back and recounted their conversation. He could've sworn . . . *Shit.*

"Fucking William," Todd seethed. "This is him, isn't it? If he already told you what happened to me, why'd you bother asking?"

"I had to hear it from you."

"I can't believe him."

"Is he wrong, though? If he is, I'll take it all back. You think you're ready to be with me—hell, *anyone*—right now?" Linc reached for him but Todd recoiled. "Todd. Am I really what you need right now?"

"Do you realize what you're asking me? I already told you how you make me feel. You know I haven't been this happy in a long time. Why would you do this to me?" Todd was panicked and so loud he drew the attention of the couple the next bench over. "What did William say to you?"

Linc looked away. This was a disaster. His heart was breaking. "I'm sorry."

"Don't say that to me again. It doesn't mean anything anymore." Todd grabbed his bag and stood. Slung it over his shoulder. "You know this is ridiculous, right? Did you bother asking William why it was so important that *he* get to tell you something that was so humiliating for me? I wasn't ready for you to know but now you do and I can see it's a burden."

"There's nothing about you that could ever burden me, Todd."

"I don't expect you to be perfect. I don't need *you* at one hundred percent just to love you. I have parts of me that might be broken but I *am* working to fix them. And if I get clarity tomorrow it doesn't mean they stop being a part of who I am.

I'll have these scars forever. I need you to be able to look at them and not feel sorry for me, or like I need to finish working on myself so you don't feel like it's such a challenge to be with me. I shouldn't have to be perfect for you."

"Todd, I've never met anyone like you. You're a genuinely good person and it's the most beautiful thing about you. Not a lot of people can say that."

"But I'm not just that, Linc. You keep idealizing me like this and then you can't handle the parts of me that seem scary for you. That's why we love, so we can help each other get through the scary parts, so we can fill in the blanks for each other. And now you want me to be alone again. You want me to do it by myself because, what, it builds character? It'll make me more of a man? I was gonna tell you about Deacon, *after* I saw my dad, because I thought it would be easier for me. All I needed you to do was be there for me when I finally sat down with him." Todd realized people were watching him. His ears burned. "I need to go."

"Where?"

"I don't know. I already have a headache so I can't see William right now. But I need to get out of here."

Linc stood. "You need a ride? I'll take you anywhere you need to go."

"I don't need you to do anything."

"I love you."

Todd nodded. "I know you do. And I love *you*. You're the best thing that's ever happened to me but I can't look at you right now."

thirty-one.

THERE WERE FIVE BALLS left on the table with Todd in the lead. It was in this same bar ten years ago that William taught him how to hone his stop shot. *Pool can look sexy,* he'd advised back then, *but you need to master the most effective shot.* Todd balanced the cue on a freshly-chalked bridge and leaned in as house music thudded on the floor below. A grin spread across his face.

Todd had mastered the shot the night before he boarded the plane to California. He considered it the perfect cap to his time in DC. Nothing else needed to be pursued or achieved. He could finally put it all behind him and never look back. It was magic on William's part, Todd decided, how he stepped in so soon after Todd lost his mother, restored his faith in the world and convinced Todd he could confidently build a better life on another coast.

Now William was on some other shit. After his argument with Linc at the Tidal Basin, Todd found himself on Julian's doorstep with William attempting to reason through the phone:

"You've been through a lot. You didn't come here to end up with someone—"

"Did it occur to you that I might be happy with him, in spite of everything else? How could you possibly think you were helping?"

"You once thought you were happy with Deacon and he

almost killed you."

"Fuck you, William."

Julian didn't want to know what the issue was, but found it interesting that Linc's spot wasn't an option. Clearly Todd had beef with him too. Julian was happy to host him for as long as he wanted.

Presently, Julian observed from the bar as Todd sank the fifteen. One more stripe to go before the eight.

Todd's opponent smirked, pretending not to be impressed. "That's cute for you." He had a shaved head and eyebrows that dipped mischievously low in the center. He wore a snug Janet Jackson concert tee and vintage jeans. Occasionally he'd utter something in Spanish, most of which Todd easily deciphered.

Todd made his way around the table, mentally setting up the next shot. This was their second game. Todd won the first and they agreed to best three out of five. Everyone watching was mesmerized by Todd. Each time he brought his arm back for a shot it emphasized how broad he was. Tonight he wore a pale blue tank top because Julian had encouraged him earlier to bare more muscle. Julian didn't understand Todd's modesty. Todd, hesitant in the beginning, warmed to the idea after a pre-game drink.

"It won't just be cute after your second straight loss," Todd now told his opponent, uncharacteristically cocky.

His opponent's companion, who stood by to catch any drunken fouls, offered an instigating chuckle.

Todd chalked the tip of the cue. "I got time tonight."

His opponent rolled his eyes with a half-grin. "Shoot your shot."

Todd leaned in, brought the cue back and *crack!* The last stripe went down. The cue ball spun in place, punctuating the move for him. Todd strolled around the table again as it settled down. All that was left for him was the eight and it was against the rail. "Eight ball, corner pocket." Todd hit the cue ball with a Left English and it spun gently into the eight. The eight rolled slowly and came to a dead stop instead of disappearing into the pocket. The room groaned.

His opponent shook his head and tsk-tsked. "Aww, *pobrecito.*" He stooped down, brought himself eye-level with the un-sunk eight ball. "Want me to blow on it?"

Todd laughed. "You have two balls left. There's still plenty of opportunity for you to lose."

"You just back away from the table so you don't *accidently* bump the ball in."

"I don't have to cheat to play," Todd said. "And I'm not sure I caught your name. I don't wanna keep calling you Nephew all night."

His opponent laughed and sank one of his remaining balls. "The name is Omar." He made his way around to the other side to target the last solid, the six. "And I also got time tonight."

"Nice to meet you, Omar."

Omar wasn't able to sink the six but it ended up right next to the eight on the edge of the corner pocket, setting up a nearly impossible shot for Todd. "If you sink that, drinks are on me for the rest of the night," Omar promised.

Todd knew if he aimed for the eight straight on, the solid would pocket first and he'd lose. He decided to shoot for the rail so the cue ball would bounce back and smack the eight just enough to nudge it into the pocket first. "I'm gonna bank it," Todd told him.

"Fuck does that mean?"

"Means I like my liquor top shelf." Todd reached across with his cue a final time to make sure he had the correct angle before leaning into his shot. "Eight ball, corner pocket. You can start with a Sidecar." *Smack!* The cue ball hit the rail, bounced back and clicked the six. They both went in, eight ball first.

The room cheered. Omar came around and shook Todd's hand. "Who are you?"

"I'm Todd and I've been shooting pool for ten years. You ready for a third game or do I get my drink?"

"I'm not trying to get embarrassed anymore tonight," Omar laughed. He gestured to his friend nearby. "Todd, Mel. Mel,

Todd."

Todd regarded Mel for a moment. He was tall and lanky, with a warm sun kissed complexion and cornrows that hung just past his neck. Colorful tattoos decorated his forearms. Mel offered a quick nod.

JULIAN WAVED THEM OFF as they head downstairs. Julian enjoyed when Todd was uninhibited and whatever trouble he would get into with his new friends was fine by him. This could be Todd's night.

Julian faced the bartender for another whiskey and realized he had no business being here otherwise. He wasn't as excited about coming out as he thought he'd be, wasn't the slightest bit flattered or energized by the looks he received. He wanted to call William and tell him how he felt, even without knowing his exact endgame.

Was it worth telling William?

His drink arrived and an arm brushed against his. Julian ignored it. The voice followed, a smooth baritone that weakened him all over again.

"Julian? I thought that was you."

Amir. Julian was momentarily disoriented, unable to draw breath. Amir's locs were knotted on the back of his head. His eyes were the color of resin or ale. His lips were full and Julian wanted to suck on them.

"Wassup man. Almost didn't recognize you." It was all Julian could muster.

"Really?"

A weak grin. "I've had a few." Julian realized how broad-shouldered Amir was, how he was perfectly lean and muscular like a student athlete through his polo. He wondered what he ate. "So what brings you out? You don't strike me as someone who would be at a spot like this. No offense."

"It's cool. It's a friend's birthday. They're all downstairs dancing to that *oontz-oontz* music. I'm getting too old for this. How about you?"

"My boy needed a drink."

"And where is he?"

"Off having fun."

Amir gestured for the bartender, ordered himself a brandy. "So is your boy your *boy?*"

"You mean like my *dude?* Nah. A good friend."

Amir nodded.

"How's Rafe?" Julian asked.

"He's good. He's home, probably asleep."

"He doesn't mind you being out so late?"

"C'mon. You know how he is."

"What do you mean?"

Amir offered an incredulous look. "So you're gonna act coy? I see." The bartender placed his drink before him and he opened a tab. "Remember, he told me all about you."

"You weren't clear about what he said."

"I know you two used to play. Rafe doesn't go out, but he was perfectly fine with you going out, especially if you brought someone home."

"So y'all have that arrangement too?"

"Maybe."

"Now who's acting coy?"

Amir laughed. It was a powerful, masculine laugh that shook the room. "I'm not saying that's what I'm looking for tonight . . . maybe under the right circumstances. The right person. You never know." He took a sip. "So what about you? Aside from your *boy* needing that drink, what else has got you out?"

"Not a damn thing. Just here for moral support. Halfway thinking about carrying my ass home."

"You can chill and chat with me while our friends are having fun, can't you?"

"You're my ex's current. You don't think that's bad form?"

"I think we both know the rules don't apply in our case."

SEEING TODD UP CLOSE aggravated Mel even more. Linc found all kinds of men attractive for any number of reasons but Todd wasn't playing fair. Not with those eyes or that physique, both of which seemed crafted by God when He had the most to prove. Earlier that evening when Mel and Omar spotted Todd setting the rack upstairs, Mel stopped short, took Omar by the shoulder and whispered "That's him." Omar wondered if they should mention they were friends of Linc. Mel decided it was better to get to know Todd for himself, see what made Linc fall so hard for him other than his absurdly good looks.

They were now at the downstairs bar near the main dancefloor where, according to Omar, the drinks were stronger. "If I'm paying for them, I want to get my money's worth."

It soon became apparent that Todd didn't only look like a model, he'd been one at some point. Omar floated that he was a stylist as if Todd would find any kinship there, but it turned out Todd was a fitness model and anything Omar could say about fashion would mostly elude him. They found a comfortable volume in spite of the throbbing music and debated the differences between LA, New York and DC. Through it all, Mel realized Todd wasn't only attractive, he was exceedingly kind and not just for the sake of endearing himself to them. Mel didn't detect a petty bone in Todd's body and his aggravation skyrocketed.

Todd finished his drink and Omar paid for another round. "So you're originally from here?" he asked Todd. "What brought you back?"

"I wanted to see if anything had changed."

"And did it?"

"People don't shoot pool as well as they used to."

"You're funny. What else? What about the guys?"

Todd shrugged. "I dunno. I guess . . . I didn't give it a lot of thought."

"Why not? You know those LA dudes are fake. And the ones here . . . Are any of them even from here?" Omar laughed.

"When I got back here I was kind of focused on one person."

"That was your first mistake," Omar observed.

"You don't have to tell me."

Omar let it hang, glancing at Mel to see if he caught it.

"Maybe you'll make a new friend tonight," Mel offered, barely suppressing a grin. He began backing up to the dance floor in step to CeCe Peniston, jerking his thumb behind him and mouthing "Look what we got!"

"He's such an old head when it comes to music," Omar said. When he didn't get a response, he realized Todd was also making his way into the crush of dancing bodies. Omar gave in and for the next ninety minutes they alternated between the floor and the bar, fielding the occasional advance, sweaty and progressively more inebriated and relying on a bottomless reserve of energy. When Mel pulled the two of them close to his sides and held up his phone to snap a picture, Todd thought nothing of it. The moment was too pure for him, and without being armed with the knowledge Mel was the ex-lover Linc seemed so regretful about, it would never occur that it was Linc who Mel sent the picture to.

thirty-two.

Todd being away from the condo wasn't new for William, he would be gone days at a time when he was with Linc. But, if the conversation went the way William believed it did, Linc was no longer a factor, which meant Todd was with Julian now. He'd tried to pry the info out of Julian, who was being as weird as ever. "Todd may or may not be staying at the crib."

"Fine, Julian, as long as he's okay. Is he okay?"

"I can neither confirm or deny—"

"I'm not playing, Julian."

"He's good. I *won't* tell him you asked."

What he really wanted to know was if Todd was any closer to giving up on DC, but he couldn't exactly ask Julian that. Worrying about Todd and Langley's demands—not to mention constant, inconvenient fantasizing about Sidney—wrecked William's sleep. He was naturally exhausted when Travis brushed up against him after two in the morning. It was a move that would activate any man—his face buried in William's neck, hand reaching for his dick. William, groggy and fatigued, asked him, "What are you doing?"

"I can't sleep."

"I don't know if I have the energy for you tonight."

Travis was always wired, spoiled by William's aggression. He expected it to be rough and nasty every time. The occasional hand around his neck, the relentless swatting of his ass. He needed to be worked over hard before bed, otherwise he'd spend the entire night tossing, turning and trying to negotiate "just a little bit."

"I don't think you understand how privileged I feel to be having regular sex with someone I'm not ashamed of," Travis countered. "Do you know what it's like sleeping next to you?" He straddled William the way he always did and squeezed his chest. "I'm trying to get as much as I can while it lasts."

Any other time William would've dismissed it as paranoid, insecure babble but Travis was right this time. The clock was certainly ticking.

William managed a smile. "I'm an old man who needs his rest."

"I promise not to wear you out this time."

"Oh? So I don't have to toss you around the room until the sun comes up?"

"As much as I would love that . . ."

William was hard enough. He decided Travis could do all the work. William reached for the nightstand drawer to blindly search for a condom, but his phone buzzed almost on cue, flashing with Sidney's name. He watched it go off for a moment before sending Sidney to voicemail.

"You could've answered that," Travis offered, although he didn't bother adjusting his tone to match the statement.

William didn't have a chance to respond. The phone buzzed again. Travis climbed off and watched William take it into the living room.

"Do you realize what time it is?" William demanded, leaning against his breakfast bar without a stitch of clothing and feeling indecent in his own home.

"I can't sleep," Sidney told him.

"No one can and somehow that's *my* problem."

"My bad. Did I wake you?"

"No, but I wish you cared if you did."

A laugh. "You're funny when you're grouchy."

"You called me twice just to irritate me?"

A deep sigh. Some hesitation. "I miss my friend."

It was so simple and tender. William felt a distinct warmth—the flush of love. "Where are you?" he asked Sidney.

"In the basement. Having a drink. Guess what I found on demand? *To Sir, with Love.*"

William couldn't conceal his delight. "Of course you did! What part are you on?"

"'If you apologize because you are afraid, then you're a child, not a man.'"

"My favorite line."

"*Ours.* I wanted to live by that since I first heard it. But I ended up trying to live unapologetically. It's not really the same thing. Failed at that too. I think if I'd made a different choice ten years ago—"

"Remember what I said about timing?"

"Yes. But it's too late for me to apologize for what I've done, for any reason other than fear of how it can turn out. I've made such a mess."

"You're not making it any better by calling me at two in the morning. I'm not the right person. You know why."

Dead silence on Sidney's end. He must have paused the movie.

"What do you need?" William asked. "Setting all the mess aside, what do you need right at this moment?"

"Freedom. Not from my marriage, exactly, but from him."

"Langley."

"You always say *At least you had a father,* but you really don't know what it's like to have a motherfucker get under your skin the way he does."

"I might have an idea."

"I hate how he talks to me. You've heard that tone. I disgust him. Because I wanted to play ball as a kid? I'm a great attorney now, he should be satisfied with that. He should be thrilled! Is it the way I talk? How I dress?"

"Maybe it's not you, Sidney."

"What else could it be?"

"Maybe he's made mistakes himself and feels guilty and takes it out on you."

"You know I would kill for some dirt on him," Sidney chuckled. "With his perfect ass. Langley Baptiste makes no mistakes. If we could all be as flawless as him."

"No man is flawless. Not even your father."

"You know something I don't?"

William decided he'd offered too much. "It's a theory. Point is, stop beating yourself up. Talk to your wife."

"And then?"

"And *then?* Sidney, that's on you. Hold onto whatever freedom you can find after that."

"You're holding back."

"I am."

"Why don't you tell me what *you* need?"

William glanced up. Travis stood at the end of the hallway, a dark silhouette against faint moonlight bleeding from the master bedroom. "I should probably get back to bed," he told Sidney. "Think about what I said. Enjoy the movie."

"I heard you won an award. Congratulations."

"Thank you, Sidney."

They ended the call and William followed Travis back to the bedroom. Travis's body language had shifted. He knew what was coming. When William didn't fall back onto the bed and pull Travis on top of him, didn't possessively grab his waist or squeeze his ass, he knew. But William still pulled him close once they sat on the edge so it was okay, not as humiliating as four years ago. His hand rested gently on the back of Travis's head. He didn't explain the phone call, didn't invoke "work" as his reason this time or say "It's not you, it's me." He simply told Travis this would be their last night together. William didn't have to explain there was someone else. Travis didn't want him to say it, he needed to hold onto his dignity as best he could. As much as he wanted to believe this was casual fun, he'd fallen for William again. This moment needed to be painless and they both did their best to keep it that way.

But it would hurt like hell tomorrow.

thirty-three.

"Too zen?" Amir asked. "How do you leave someone for being too zen?"

"I was young and stupid."

"It wasn't that long ago."

Julian sighed. "So just stupid. He's a good dude. Good to look at. Great in bed. I just didn't have any connection with him."

"His calm is the best thing about him. It's great not coming home to confrontation or an attitude or passive-aggressive, petty bullshit. It's not how he wakes up. We could all be more like Rafe."

"Don't get me wrong, it's what drew me to him in the beginning. But in the end I didn't understand it. It didn't feel human to me. And the bottom line is, I had other things on my mind."

"Oh?"

"We can leave it there."

Although his sips over the past hour or so were measured, Amir had grown more relaxed chatting with Julian. He would lean in, brush his shoulder against his. It carried a hint of intimacy, if not outright violation. "We don't have to keep talking about him, you know. Every time I try to change the subject, you bring it back to Rafe."

"Do I?"

"Yeah, this entire time."

"I didn't realize I was doing that."

That laugh again. "You want me to call him? You need him to come hang out with us so you don't feel like something's gonna happen?"

"Pssh! Something like what?" Julian scoffed.

"I have no shame in admitting you're attractive. I might be curious about you. I'm sure you're curious too."

"Wow. And you're not even drunk."

"I've never needed liquor to say what's on my mind."

Julian lifted his glass to his lips and frowned upon realizing it was empty. "Well, what makes you so sure?"

"It's kind of obvious," Amir said, casting a sideways glance at Julian's crotch and his prominent erection. "I'm surprised you're not in pain by now."

"I think you're seeing what you want to see," Julian fired back, resisting the urge to readjust on his stool. How dare this man, damn-near a complete stranger, attempt to humiliate him like he was a hormonal adolescent in need of the nearest textbook to hide what only came naturally and, often, completely without warning? "Maybe you shouldn't be looking."

"Maybe neither of us should be looking."

"And on *that* note," Julian announced, signaling for the bill. "We were having such a nice conversation, Amir."

Amir nodded, amused, and slowly sipped his drink like he'd been doing all night. "Cool. You remember where Rafe stays, right? Not too far from here, actually. Right by Potomac Avenue."

"I don't care where he lives."

"I'm just saying, in case you wanna drop by."

"For what?"

"Because he wants you to."

"I beg your pardon?"

"You didn't catch the hint the other day, when he said the three of us should get together? C'mon, now."

Julian shook his head as he scribbled his signature on the receipt and pushed his stool under the bar. "I didn't catch anything. I'm out."

Amir grabbed his arm before he could make himself scarce. "He said you've been tense and need to relax. We can help you. Give him a call later."

IT WASN'T UNTIL TODD was in the passenger seat of Mel's parked Impala that he learned who Mel was. It came to him in a haze, literally. Mel was sprawled across the back and he and Omar passed a blunt through the seats. Todd declined so Omar offered the half-done liter of Coke in the console if he found himself thirsty. He wasn't sure how the detail revealed itself. Maybe one of them had asked Todd to clarify his remarks from earlier, why he seemed so bitter about focusing on one person when he returned to DC. When Mel mentioned he knew Linc, Todd didn't register any outward surprise. He was too gone, his consciousness hanging on by a thread. Mel went on, asking if Todd trusted Linc, becoming more and more agitated and detailed about his relationship with him. He had an axe to grind. "Don't be stupid like I was. Don't get dickmatized either. We can all do better."

"Wow," Omar said, almost choking on his pull. "That's still my friend."

"You knew me first, though. Linc is like your friend-in-law or something."

Omar poked Todd in the shoulder. "You good?"

"Yup." Todd stared at the ceiling, wondering why his eyelids hadn't dropped, confused by how he was lethargic and wired in equal measure. It was an alien feeling, kind of good, but it scared him.

"So y'all still talking?" Mel asked.

"I don't know," Todd said carefully. "We had a fight. I think he broke up with me."

"So *he* broke up with *you?* Look, he did you a favor. But you know how he does. Shows up on your doorstep looking all stupid and lonely and shit. *Baby, I'm sorry.* I swear all that nigga knows how to do is apologize and fuck, and only one of them he can get halfway right."

Todd stirred as his phone went off, nearly bumping his head. He answered after taking a deep breath to slow his pounding heart. "Where are you?" Julian demanded over the music. "I just looked for you downstairs."

"Oh. I stepped out. We're coming back in."

"What are you doing?"

"Hanging out."

"You left?"

"Julian, I'm coming back in. Don't move, okay?"

When Todd first swung his legs outside of the car and rose to his feet, his heart raced again and leaned against the roof to steady himself. Something wasn't right. Mel and Omar asked again if he was okay and he nodded. The bar was only around the corner, not a long walk. As they made their way back, Todd faintly heard one ask the other what exactly was in that Coke bottle.

They re-entered without incident. Todd spotted Julian by the bar and managed to introduce everyone. "This is Linc's ex," he whispered to Julian, like he was sharing a privileged, dirty secret.

Julian reached for Todd's shoulders. "What have you been doing?"

"He's had a bit much," Mel offered. "I think it's time for him to go home."

Julian smelled the weed on them. Everyone's eyes were glassy with a hint of mirth. But he knew Todd wouldn't dare. "A bit much *what?*" Todd teetered a bit and Julian grabbed his arms to steady him. "You aight?"

Todd convulsed. His hand flew to his mouth and he shook his head. Julian followed as he rushed to the bathroom.

Todd just made out the outline of a sink before he heaved into it. His body rocked violently. Everything came up, He stood hunched over it until he was sure there wouldn't be another rise in his throat. Julian was close by but made certain not to grab or crowd him, worried any gesture would worsen his condition. He simply said to him, "Let's get you home."

"What did I do?" Todd asked.

"I don't know what you did. Did you smoke something?"

"He was talking about Linc and how I shouldn't trust him."

It occurred to Julian that Mel was the same ex he'd heard about. "Okay, well, I think I warned you about that. Let's go."

Todd faced himself in the mirror. "If I could just stop bleeding," he said, voice breaking, still trying to recover his breath. "If I could stop bleeding I'd be okay."

"What are you talking about?"

"Nothing." Todd straightened, wiped his chin with a paper towel. "You can't see it."

"You didn't just drink tonight."

"No, that's all I did. I just had too much."

"You think they slipped you something?"

"I held onto my cup all night. I need to get in the bed."

"Do you want me to call William?"

"God no. For what?"

"He's known you longer. He's worried about you."

Todd pushed past him, back out to the bar where the crowd had peaked and the house was replaced with trap. Todd didn't expect Mel and Omar to still be there, he just wanted a bottle of water before he climbed into Julian's truck and passed out. But there they were, being shouted down by Linc, who Todd could just hear over the music. "We said no matter what happened to us, we'd never get this petty, this dirty! You knew exactly what you were doing when you sent that picture!"

Todd felt a familiar instinct. He wanted to go to Linc and squeeze him. His body craved him. It was followed by a flash of anger before he remembered how thirsty he was.

"And you came running," Mel shot back. "Why? And how did you know where we were?"

"I told you to stop geotagging your phone pics. Anybody can find your ass."

"Oh god, Linc! Didn't you dump him? Why are you so

pressed?"

Linc almost responded, but noticed Todd and Julian nearby. Todd could barely keep his eyes open now and, although he stood with his hands shoved into his pockets, he appeared to be leaning on Julian, who was solid enough to support him. "Linc, I'm fine. You don't have to stay."

"What's wrong with him?" Linc demanded of Julian.

"That's what I'm trying to figure out."

Linc faced Mel and Omar once more. "He's been drinking with y'all all night?"

"We stepped outside to the car for a little bit—"

"He doesn't smoke," Linc told them. "He doesn't *do* anything. Now if I find out y'all gave him something—"

"Completely by accident," Mel said.

"You ready to go?" Julian asked Todd, jingling his keys.

"I need water."

"I'm taking him with me," Linc said.

"Pssh! I got this!" Julian insisted. "He'll be fine. C'mon, Todd."

"I need water."

"We'll stop at the gas station."

"I'm taking him with me," Linc repeated. "All y'all niggas been drinking. He's not getting in the car with you!"

Todd gave the bartender a pleading look before he was passed a water, free of charge. He downed it in seconds and made his way to the exit. He just wanted to be out of there. Didn't care how he was getting home or whose home he'd end up at. They followed. Todd leaned against the building once they were outside and slid to the ground. "Give me five minutes." A heaviness settled in the back of his head. He didn't have the urge to vomit again, there was nothing left. He just didn't want to feel like his head would detach from his body and tumble down the sidewalk.

Linc wasn't done with Mel. "What did you give him?"

"We were just having a good time. You've really outdone yourself, Linc, he's beautiful." Mel gestured to Todd, whose face was buried between his knees. "You went from one pretty, biracial dude to the next, huh? At least you're consistent."

Omar, who could tell from experience how ugly this could get, reminded Mel it was time to go. It didn't register.

"And it's funny," Mel went on, "You used to tell me, *You're the most beautiful man I've ever laid eyes on.* But this one right here? *Shit.* Do you tell him the same thing?"

"As a matter of fact, I do, but the difference with him is, he's not a mean, hateful bitch." Linc instantly regretted his words, then considered how fed up he was by now and went back to meaning exactly what he said.

Mel was nonplussed. "He will be by the time you're done with him. Trust me."

Julian sat with Todd and placed a hand on his back. "How are you feeling right now, man?"

Todd merely shook his head in response.

"You got some real issues," Linc told Mel. "You probably already had them before me so it's not my problem. At least not anymore. You can leave now."

"Cool, but don't forget to tell him why we broke up."

"That has nothing to do with—"

"Oh it has *everything* to do with him. Y'all met through William, right? They're friends. Maybe he should know what kind of strange, fucked up friendship you two have. Competitive. Lowkey can't stand each other but comfortable enough for you to send me to fuck William so you could ease your guilt. Maybe *everybody* should know that."

"Wha' happen?" Julian asked.

Linc ignored him. "You're making a fool out of yourself right now. Go home."

Mel shrugged. "What I got to lose?"

"You are so foul," Julian said.

"Mind your business." Linc didn't bother to so much as face him, so he didn't realize Julian had risen to his feet. "This don't have shit to do with you."

"And I would've done it too," Mel continued. "But, you

know, William ain't shit either. Y'all are basically the same but he's bespoke and you're thrift shop."

"Now *that's* funny!" Julian declared, before asking Todd if he felt well enough to get up.

"I'm not," Todd moaned. "Give me five more minutes."

"I already told your ass he's coming with me," Linc spat.

Julian was amused. *"My ass?"*

Linc faced him, holding a tight fist on the other hand as if to prevent an involuntary swing. "Todd will be alright. What I need you to do is mind your business and carry *your ass* home. You good?"

"I'm real good, but since Todd's not fucking with you right now he's riding with me. Worry about your man over there. Nasty ass." Julian advanced on Linc. "And why you squaring up like you about to swing? I wish you would!"

No one could get to them fast enough. Linc threw the first punch and missed, the heat of his rage making it impossible to correctly anticipate Julian's speed. Julian barreled into him, sending Linc back against Mel who fell into Omar. They all hit the ground like dominoes.

Todd managed to raise his head and make out some of it. Mel and Omar quickly gathered themselves and attempted to pull them apart, the fight sending them all whirling into a trio of trash cans. A few bystanders who had witnessed the exchange of words were now trying to help break it up, but Linc and Julian were too fast and too strong.

Linc was scrappy and vicious, just as Todd suspected. A dirty fighter. He smacked Julian in the head with a trash can lid, which only stunned him for a split second. Julian was more brutish. A grabber. A wrestler. He yanked Linc by the shirt collar and slammed him against the side of the building. He screamed in his face, the insults, epithets and threats flying faster than anyone could hear. "You trying to see how fake I really am, nigga?"

"I already know how fake you are, bitch!" Linc spat.

Omar's arms were around Julian's neck, pulling at him,

pleading for him to release Linc. But the fabric of Linc's shirt was swallowed by Julian's fist, nearly choking him.

Todd found his strength and wits and stood, ready to diffuse it. But he froze, not from the heaviness in his head, which wasn't as present now, or the return of his nausea. It was the red and blue lights he spotted from the corner of his eye and the warning chirp of the sirens that followed.

thirty-four.

THE SUNLIGHT WAS PUNISHING when he opened his eyes. It didn't register immediately that he was at Linc's but this had been his first time sleeping downstairs.

The previous night came back to Todd as scattered puzzle pieces. The fight, the cops, Linc and Julian forced to apologize to each other like kids on a playground. In Linc's Wrangler, drunkenly telling Todd how much he loved him. Falling onto Linc's sofa. And now, the pile of blankets and pillows nearby on the floor.

Linc hadn't slept upstairs either.

Todd rubbed the back of his neck. He couldn't fully stretch out during his rest and now he paid for it.

Linc appeared with a mug in hand. Todd sat up, took the mug and slid over. The tea was spiced with vanilla and turmeric. He sipped silently as Linc explained everything. He was still furious with Mel—there was only so much he could ever blame himself for—but Mel was definitely too young when they got together. Todd realized he wasn't just hearing backstory, Linc was admitting for the first time he may have damaged Mel, used the fact that he was Mel's first love to excuse his recklessness.

"I was all he could see. I could get away with anything. I had my excuses—*I didn't promise you monogamy*. I should've let him grow. That's how I convinced myself that you taking a break from me was the right thing to do. I don't want to be all you can see. I can't do that to someone else."

"So what happened with William?" Todd asked him. He didn't want to be angry but what he heard the night before—if he'd heard it correctly—sounded unconscionable.

It took Linc a moment to answer and in that moment Todd noticed Linc's right eye was starting to swell. Julian had gotten a lick in. "I was mad. I just wanted to stop arguing so I said *If you want William then go.*"

"You think you have a temper?"

"No more than the average person."

"What's average? You got into a physical fight last night. You're thirty-six years old. I thought you two made up."

"I'm not like Deacon."

"Who threw the first punch?"

"I did. You might've been half-conscious but I was getting it from all sides. And I'm sorry, baby, but Julian has way too much mouth." Even Julian's apology last night was littered with insults. *I'm sorry I called you a militant, fake-ass Harlem Renaissance dandy. I'm sorry for calling you a walking Tumblr page, a ginger beer-drinking, self-righteous thinkpiece-ass nigga. I'm also sorry you're all of those things.* "He kept provoking me. He was in my face."

"Linc, those officers last night had a sense of humor. What if you'd ended up with two cops who didn't just force you to apologize to each other? You could've ended up dead or in jail."

"Baby—"

"I know. You're sorry. I'm sorry too. I was a mess. This is probably all my fault anyway. I should've stayed in last night."

"You had no idea what you were getting into."

"The last time I went out with Julian I ended up here, under much better circumstances." A smile.

"I love you, Todd."

Todd finished his tea and stood. Linc seemed ready to ask if he needed anything but Todd urged him to sit still. Linc waited while Todd went to the kitchen and returned with a pack of frozen peas and carrots. "We can spend the day taking care of each other."

"Oh? You're not training today?"

Linc fell back onto Todd's lap when he sat, then winced once the pack was against his eye. "I'm off the whole weekend," Todd explained. "Tomorrow I go down to Petersburg."

"So you're finally doing it? How are you getting there?"

"I'll pick up a car in the morning."

"For what? I'll take you. This is important to you. Let me."

"You only have one eye."

"And?"

"And I think I'm still mad at you."

"You should be."

Todd removed the pack so he could look down into both of Linc's eyes. "But I'm scared of what might happen while I'm down there. I might need somebody."

"I won't leave your side again," Linc said. "Not unless you want me to."

"I want it to feel as good as it did in the beginning. We still have a lot we need to figure out."

"But first . . ."

"But first Anthony."

thirty-five.

ON THE BACK PORCH of a newly-renovated Queen Anne rowhouse, three champagne glasses tapped one another. It was dusk, warm and breezy with the faint rustle of anticipation for the late night. But East Capitol Street's newest residents planned to stay in. From corner to corner the house radiated, awash in white and filled with restored antique pieces, original artwork and rustic accents. It was almost presidential. There was no way they were leaving it tonight.

"All this work," Cintra mused, "all the arguments we got into and this amazing, magazine-ready—no, *art book-ready*—result and we're toasting . . . outside?"

"It feels great out," Sidney said, back against the rail. They could admire the kitchen from their vantage, with its oversized French walnut farm table, distressed inset cabinets and gleaming steel appliances. "We have all the time in the world to walk through these rooms. Let's enjoy this weather before it's five-hundred degrees and humid next week."

"Cheers to *that*," William agreed.

"I just wanna say for the *final time*, William, that I'm really glad you did this." Cintra threw her arms around him. "You weren't taking on any new work and made an exception for us. I am eternally grateful."

"Light work," he chuckled as she pulled away. "But this is the last time. Don't recommend me to anyone saying I did you a favor."

"Me? *Never.*"

"I mean it, Cintra."

"You know," she went on, "this might get you on the AD100."

"Oh I know it will," he said confidently. "Get your friends from Conde Nast down here sometime this week. Preferably Wednesday at the Omni when I accept my award."

"I'm sure someone will already be at the banquet, but I'll put a bug in the right ear. You know what this party needs?"

"Steaks," Sidney offered. "On the grill."

"Yeah, too bad we don't have a grill yet and, while food is a fantastic idea, I was talking about music. I'll be right back." Cintra disappeared inside.

"There's carry-out menus in there somewhere," Sidney called after her. He looked at William once she was out of earshot. "I'm fucking starving."

"And neither one of you cooks. That's a damn shame."

"Now wait a minute, you get me behind a grill and I can burn a little bit."

"You and every other American male who can't tell the difference between a simmer and boil," William chuckled. "So what do you think?"

"About the house? I love it, I already told you. I haven't said it often enough but I really respect what you do, William. You deserve that award."

"I'm just making sure you still mean it when she's not around. And considering you don't plan on staying in it that long . . ."

"That conversation is nowhere near close to happening. You know that, right?"

"I don't *know* what I should know."

"I'm trying to figure out a strategy."

"A what? Sidney, this isn't a case. This is your marriage."

"It could become a case—a *murder* case—if I end up dead in a creek once I tell her. There's no scenario where either of us walks away from that conversation fully intact. I know it's insane to think there ever could be, but there has to be something else I can do, something else I can give her, to make it easier."

"There aren't enough things you can give her."

"And then there's you. I thought of our talk the other night, everything I wanted to say to you. I know there's some things you wanna say to me—"

"Your wife is inside—"

"I need you. I want you to kiss me. I need to feel your weight, your skin. I miss you and it's killing me."

William took a few steps back. He didn't want to give into it, couldn't risk it. It was love and that should have been all that mattered but it would hurt someone. He wasn't even sure he could call it love if it wasn't free, if it had consequences.

Sidney carefully set his glass on the rail and faced out into the alley. He didn't want William to see the pain etched across his face. "I almost didn't come back because of you. I *knew* this would happen, being in the same city as you. But I couldn't argue with both Cintra *and* Langley. When your father and your wife both agree on things, you go along with it. And of course you had to be involved with this house. I should've done something about this before we left New York. I should've done something the night I stumbled out of that fucking hotel room. I love her, I love you. But I don't want her and I *can't* have you. I even tried to figure out a way it could work, that maybe I stay with her just a little longer and somehow see you—"

"No," William told him. "You don't want to be one of those men. I love Cintra too and I'd never be a part of that."

"It only crossed my mind for a split second. I know it's foul. I couldn't."

"Tell her you want to end the marriage. Deep down she probably does too. You'll be doing her a favor. One day, when things are a lot more clear and safe, you can tell her the rest and I'll be there for you. Just stop wasting her time."

"And what about you, William?"

"I'll be patient. You set me straight on poker night, remember? You told me to back off."

"You still want me as much as I want you."

"Indeed."

Cintra returned with two small speakers. "This was all I could find for outside. What do we wanna hear? Oh, I know! Something old school, mellow. Ronnie Foster?"

"The *Two Headed Freap* album?" William asked. "Yes and yes."

Sidney shrugged. "EPMD would be nice too. Just sayin'."

Cintra connected the speakers to her phone, turned to him and squinted. "You know what? You've been so patient throughout all of this, you should be in charge of the playlist."

Sidney smiled, his love for Cintra so apparent William considered leaving early. "It's fine. Whatever you want, babe."

thirty-six.

THE CALL FROM CORRECTIONS came when they were halfway to Petersburg, in the middle of a thick, chilly silence once Todd realized this was maybe—*definitely*—the end of the road for him and Linc.

He was seized by anxiety from the moment he slid into the passenger seat, but the trip didn't start off so bad. Linc tried his best to put him at ease, giving Todd the opportunity to listen, rather than having him open up this time. "I have so many shots of DC no one has seen. I've been taking pictures of it for fifteen years." Linc's voice was comforting, sexy and assured. Todd loved hearing him talk. "It's beautiful. I mean, every city is beautiful in its own way. They all have their wildly contrasting neighborhoods and demographics. And it's always changing. You have to take pictures of it. You have to preserve the history, because someone with an agenda will pretend you never existed." Linc sighed, weary and bitter but filled with pride and love. "I'm fortunate to have been here most of my life. I'm glad I never left or had to."

"So what do you enjoy shooting more?" Todd ventured. "People or the city?"

Linc thought on it a bit. "I didn't start shooting people heavily, for myself, until this book. Been working on it for a few years now. I like shooting places more. It's easier for me, for one."

"Oh," Todd said, clearly confused. "I got the impression you preferred taking pictures of people. It comes across that way."

"It does, doesn't it? It's not as important to me, though. I think after this book I'll travel a bit, focus more on culture and texture. What I've become known for is kind of basic. And it happened so quickly. I'm a photographer, not an Instagram page, you know?"

Todd smiled. "I'm glad you realized that."

"And it doesn't get me into trouble."

"Don't do that."

"Do what?"

"No one's stopping you from shooting men, if that's what you want to do."

Linc squeezed his thigh. "I'm joking."

"Whatever," Todd mumbled. He tried to figure out what he'd say to Anthony while Linc turned up the music. He was on edge. Cranky. Exhausted with the prospect of facing this man for the first time in ten years. He dreaded it. He'd made it an obligation and couldn't wait to get it over with.

The rapport between Todd and Anthony deteriorated as Todd got older. When he was small and Renee brought him to the facility for family days, she couldn't pull him away from his father. Todd, cherub-cheeked and curly-haired, would crawl into Anthony's lap and lock his tiny arms around his neck. When it was time to leave, Todd wailed and his father would tell him not to cry. Todd remembered it as firm but tender. Anthony wasn't admonishing him or trying to toughen him up, he just couldn't bear to hear his young son's anguish.

The visits became less frequent over the years, replaced with phone calls a handful of times per year that never kicked past a perfunctory rapport. Todd detected a hint of devotion in Anthony's voice, a hopeful note suggesting his sentence would be cut short and he could reunite with his family. But on Todd's first visit as an adult ten years ago, the color drained from Anthony's face as Todd sat across from him. Todd wanted to believe it was because he'd just found out Renee had died. The more he considered it after, he couldn't shake the feeling it was something much worse.

"I'm sorry," Linc told him. "Maybe it's not the right time to be funny."

"I think I like everything you say between *I love you* and *I'm sorry,*" Todd said. "When you're not defending yourself or trying to convince me of your intentions, I believe you more."

"You're frustrated right now. I get it."

"I don't think you do."

Linc almost responded. His jaw clenched and he focused on the road ahead.

"I can't stop thinking about everything Mel said," Todd went on. "This thing with William, when did it happen?"

"I thought we could go a full day without bringing up those two."

"Mel is a part of you."

"It's been asked and answered, Todd."

"You wanna just skim through it because it's more convenient for you? We're wide open now, Linc."

"So you want the full details? Okay. It was back in December. William called me, sounding a mess. He said he needed something, I guess he meant something to smoke. That's not him. It didn't sound right. He was feeling bad. I'm not sure why. He called when I was in the middle of fighting with Mel. We were barely hanging on by then, couldn't stand the sight of each other. It was over petty shit, starting arguments just to prove something was still there. Mel has this thing about men like William, like *us*—the polish, the style. He wanted him."

"And you wanted him to go over there."

"I don't know what I wanted. I knew I needed to set him free some kinda way."

"Did they do anything?"

"Mel said no. I believe him. He could've said yes just to fuck with me. I don't know what William told him that night but it changed him. When he ended it, we didn't fight. It was the calmest, most adult, conversation we had in a while." Linc smiled a little. "And then I saw what it could be."

"What?" Todd asked.

"Baby, I'm sorry."

"Stop apologizing. Just tell me what happened."

"Knowing I'd lost him, seeing him so strong, it made it hard for me to let go. I kept going after him, begging him for another chance. He suddenly had all the cards. He looked good to me again. It's crazy how that happens."

"When did you stop chasing him?"

Linc turned to him briefly, his eyes long with regret. "Right up until I met you."

"So it was recent." Todd shook his head. "You didn't give yourself a moment to breathe."

They watched the road in silence. Linc didn't see the point in defending himself further. It was out there. Todd would do what he wanted with it.

He turned the music down once more when Todd's phone rang. Todd immediately knew it was the prison. The voice on the other end was efficient, clinical, female. "Mr. Mosley, you have a scheduled visitation today? You have been removed from the inmate's approved visitors list. Scheduled visitation has been cancelled."

Todd sat up in a panic. "What do you mean removed? By who?"

"It was at the request of the inmate, sir."

"But I'm on my way right now. I'm his son!"

"I'm sorry, Mr. Mosley—"

"Just tell him to call me or something, *please.* I'll put money on his books. Whatever he needs. Just try. I'm his son and I need to talk to him."

A pause. "I'll see what I can do."

Todd wanted to hurl his phone through the windshield. "Turn around," he told Linc, seething. "All of a sudden, he doesn't wanna see me. Right when I'm on my way. I didn't even know they could do that."

"Alright. I guess we're headed back to DC, then."

Todd gazed out the passenger side window as Linc turned off the exit. The thought he'd wasted his time had him boiling.

If he'd had the courage to visit Anthony sooner, if he hadn't gotten so swept up in Linc, maybe this would have turned out differently.

"I can't wait to get back to LA."

thirty-seven.

JULIAN HATED TIES. HE appreciated the opportunity to look dapper, to be invited to events where his attire mattered so much, but the feeling of a tie around his neck was a private Hell. He also hated the way his neck disappeared completely behind shirt collars. "Maybe you should lighten up on the shrugs," he told his reflection, then felt ridiculous. He realized he was making a fuss over himself because of William.

It fell so easily into place. Not a half hour after his fight with Linc, Julian found himself at Rafe's door, tempted by Amir's offer. He wasn't sure if he wanted the two of them, not the way Amir suggested, but he needed Rafe's healing hands, his calming presence. He needed the powerful bass of Amir's voice. As Rafe brought a cloth dabbed with antiseptic to the corner of Julian's bloodied mouth, the words tumbled free. "Amir reminds me of William a little. Maybe it's the voice or his posture. There's something about him."

Amir had just settled into bed, deciding any action was off the table after observing Julian's condition. "That's kind of funny, don't you think?" Rafe asked. "They're nothing alike."

"I mean, I'm not saying they're exactly the same. He's just . . . I don't know."

"Stable? Responsible? I love Amir, but that's not what makes him special. You're looking for William in every man you lay your eyes on. Maybe you *should* tell him."

"He's my friend."

"Then he'll understand."

"It could end our friendship."

"Either you open up to him or you move past it. Otherwise you'll keep going in circles, like you said."

Julian was ready to let it go. He'd convinced himself it wasn't worth the bullet or the potential heartache sure to follow. Then yesterday William called. His assistant James had come down with the flu and wouldn't be able to make the banquet. *Would you like his ticket?*

Presently, Julian took a step back from his mirror, noticing Todd standing in the doorway of his reflection. "How do I look?" he asked, turning. His head was freshly shaved and his suit was gray and lightweight, suitable for dinner but able to withstand the evening heat.

Romulus was at Todd's side, nuzzling against him for attention. He sensed his new friend would be gone soon. "Very clean," Todd remarked, scratching the boxer between the ears.

"You still haven't talked to William, have you?" Julian asked. "I'm gonna be with him all night and it won't feel right knowing what I know and not being able to say a word."

"You can tell him whatever you want," Todd said sharply. "I have nothing to say to William."

"You want me to be the one who tells him you bought a plane ticket? That you're leaving for LA tomorrow? Come on, man."

"Julian, I'm tired. I don't know what I thought I could get out of coming back here but everything has been a misfire. William's trying to control my life. My father gave up on me completely this time and Linc . . . I just need to go."

"What about working with me? Those clients love you, man. Plus I like having you around. And not just at the gym. You're a good dude. You should stay."

"There's so much you don't know, Julian. The ticket has already been bought."

Julian removed his suit jacket and sat on the bed. Romulus attempted to climb him but he gently pushed the dog away. "I have time."

"For what?"

"To understand."

"There are no CliffsNotes for any of this."

"I thought we were friends, man."

Todd smiled. "Maybe after you get back. Go have fun."

"You probably don't care but I think I'm telling William how I feel tonight."

"Good thing you're wearing a suit, maybe he'll take you seriously."

"Wow. When'd you get so sassy?"

"I'm sorry, I've been in a mood—"

"I like it!"

So that's it? We're done?

Todd got the text about an hour after Julian left, reminding him where William was accepting his award in case Todd changed his mind. He was stretched out across the sofa in the den, dozing off in front of *Sports Center* with Romulus luxuriating on the floor nearby. His thumbs moved quickly in response. *I'm leaving tomorrow. Coming here was a mistake. I enjoyed our time together but—*

He didn't have a chance to finish and send it. The phone rang in his hand. Todd thought of sending him to voicemail but answered it anyway. No matter how hard Todd tried, he was irresistible. "Hey, Linc."

"Where are you?"

"I'm at Julian's."

"I wanna see you."

Todd wanted to be firm but his voice softened. "I need to rest up. I leave in the morning."

"Wow. I didn't realize you already bought your ticket."

"I need to go back to the life I created for myself. The one I had before I met Deacon."

"So what time are you leaving?"

"Linc . . ."

"I'm not gonna tell you the same shit I told Mel when I was trying to get back with him. This isn't the same. With him, it was regret, it was guilt. It was me trying to have a do-over. But you and me just got started, Todd. Do you realize we've already addressed our baggage? Some people wait months, even years, into their relationships to do that. We don't have to go through this with a monkey on our backs." Todd didn't respond. Linc continued. "I know you're probably fed up right now. I can wait for you. Go back to California, do what you need to do. But tonight, before you get on that plane, I need you."

"If I see you, I might not have the strength to go, and *I need to go.*"

"I'm not trying to trick you into staying. I just need my baby tonight."

It was only days ago he was furious and exhausted with Linc. Sure, what Linc had done wasn't *that* bad, they were just the basic missteps of a man who didn't think things through in his relationships, who was so enamoured and distracted by physical rewards he never considered the complex emotions that came with them or the repercussions of his actions. It was frustrating. He thought Linc should have been smarter, *better* than other men.

Todd already missed him. His intoxicating scent, the cadence of his voice, the comfort of his sex. A distinct warmth and longing had Todd ready to give in.

Another call was coming through. The prison. Maybe salvation awaited on the other line.

"I need to call you back." Todd breathlessly answered the new call, accepted the charges. "Hello?"

"How much are you putting on my books?" Anthony asked him right away.

Todd sat up, his heart pounding. "It's up to you."

"So what do you want from me? And we need to make this quick."

There was activity in the background, the loud bang of

metal doors, the buzz alerting when a gate was being accessed, scattered conversations by the other inmates. Todd hated those sounds. "The last time I saw you—"

"Ten years ago."

Todd's voice cracked. "Yes, ten years ago. The way you looked at me . . . It was like you were looking at a stranger. It's followed me ever since."

"It's because of your face," Anthony told him.

He didn't spare Todd a single detail. He was so detached at this point, even the parts that should have been strained with anger were matter-of-fact.

As Todd listened his stomach turned. His blood ran cold. The phone slid from his hand and hit the floor before he could even say goodbye.

thirty-eight.

Yvonne Kendall was under no illusion Julian was anyone special. His embrace with William was brotherly, their conversation and dynamic no more affectionate than drinking buddies. And Julian so clearly wasn't William's type. He had a boyishness about him, a sophomoric quality that immediately exhausted Yvonne. It deflated her. She leaned over in the middle of the first course and whispered, "Who is this *child* you brought here tonight?"

"I told you. He's a good friend of mine."

"Do you know him from the gym?" she demanded, visibly irritated.

William immediately picked up on the subtext. Yvonne thought Julian wasn't in his league, not even as a platonic associate. "Come on, now."

"You couldn't give that ticket to anyone else?"

"My assistant is home with the flu."

"And what happened to *The One?*"

He could have explained that *The One* was married, to someone he considered a friend, no less. That *The One* had been under her nose for over twenty years. That he was, in fact, well within William's league, an equal and standard upon which William measured every date, hookup and short-term relationship. But his mother was already agitated. "And here I am thinking me winning an actual award was enough to make you proud." He grinned to let her know he wasn't seriously piling on the guilt, but it did the trick.

"You're right. This is about you and what you've accomplished this year. And, yes, I'm very proud of you, son."

William glanced around the Omni's Ambassador Ballroom, his design instincts firing away. Year after year, he reminded himself he wasn't at work, that he could allow the moment to breathe and not be consumed with aesthetic details.

He clapped along with everyone else when the society's Senior Strategic Advisor took the podium. "I hope you're not bored by any of this," he whispered to Julian. "Well, I know you *will* be but this is what they do."

"I've been to banquets before," Julian said. Julian likely had every right to be offended but wasn't. "Food's great. Portions are small, as usual. But I didn't come to get fed. I ate before I came anyway." He shrugged.

William chuckled warmly. "I should have known your context for this would be food-related. But I'm glad you're here."

"I'm glad you invited me. Sorry to hear about your assistant, though. That's rough, man. The flu in June?"

William cut right to it. "So there's something I've been meaning to ask you about. You remember Travis, right?"

"Who?"

"You know. The guy I was seeing for the past couple of months."

"I don't know who that is."

"You saw him at my surprise party and you *formally* met him about four years ago."

"Doesn't ring a bell," Julian said flatly.

"At any rate, you gave him the impression that you have feelings."

Julian almost choked on his dinner roll.

"At first I thought he was mistaken but you did seem different the last time I saw you. If it's not what Travis picked up on, then what was—"

"It's nothing," Julian told him, shaking his head. "Your boy read it wrong."

"Read *what* wrong? Do you know what I'm talking about? You have to identify it before you can deny it, Julian."

Julian reached for his wine glass and, upon finding it empty, sucked down the remainder of his water instead. "I think we're being rude," he managed, nodding towards the podium.

William let it rest and focused on the speech. Maybe Travis was right.

Once it was over Julian asked him to step into the hall outside of the ballroom. Julian took a breath to steady whatever was building inside of him. "It's complicated," Julian began, shoving his hands in his pockets to keep them from shaking. "I'm trying to figure out how necessary this even is, because if I do it, if I *say* it, it means I've owned up to this but . . . I don't want it to scare you."

"I'm listening."

Another deep breath. "You're the reason I haven't been able to be with anyone for long. I keep trying to find you in every man I end up with, and I dip before it gets serious because they *aren't* you. I had no idea what you were going through when I trained you but it seemed like you needed someone nearby. It was like, at any moment, you'd open up and tell me what was going on and what you needed. And I wanted to give it to you. William, I've never met another man like you and I still want you."

William stared at him with a mixture of worry and confusion, then he simply said, "No."

No to all of it, the suggestion he was solely responsible for Julian's relationships cratering. The thought that William, so long after their trainer-client relationship, could be considered more than a friend. The notion that there was any possibility of this bizarre, random, uncomfortable confession resulting in some kind of . . . William wasn't sure what Julian had in mind, but the answer to all of it was *No*.

"I don't know how I was expecting you to react to this." Julian looked away, mortified.

"I love our friendship, Julian. I don't think I'm what you need, not in that way. I'm certain of it."

"It's fine—"

"It's not you. You're great. There's someone else." Not the immediate reason but it wasn't exactly untrue.

"I think I'm gonna go," Julian told him.

"Why?"

"It doesn't make sense for me to be here."

"Of course it does. If you feel uncomfortable, I understand but I still want you here."

Julian gave it some thought. "This is me being more mature. Tonight is your night and I'm feeling very selfish right now so I need to go. I don't wanna spoil it for you. I just thought somehow . . . I thought maybe because I was somebody equal to you, we'd find our way there. Eventually. People like us can't constantly be around each other without at least considering it."

They were interrupted. A coordinator stuck his head out to remind William he was coming up next on the program. It was nearly time for him to accept his award.

"There's more to it than that, Julian."

"I'm realizing that."

"Consider this: we both chase some form of perfection because we think it's what we have to do as men. I keep rationalizing it. I always say we're here to improve on who we were the day before, otherwise what's the point of our time here? But I realized recently it's like selling your soul. The person standing in front of you paid a price. I've been paying it for a long time. There is no freedom in this."

"I'm not sure I follow."

"You don't want me anywhere near you if all you see is someone who's perfect. That can't be the basis of *any* friendship I have with you. It would be a lie." William looked towards the ballroom doors then faced Julian once more. "I have to get back in there. They're ready to announce me. Are you coming?"

thirty-nine.

TODD STRODE INTO THE office building at the corner of 18th and M Street, determined and oblivious, past the security desk and towards the elevator bank. "Sir!" The guard, heavy set and middle-aged, rushed to him, hand hovered on the radio at his hip. "May I ask where you think you're going?"

"I'm sorry," Todd told him. "I need to get up to the law firm. It's kind of an emergency."

"It's after six. I need to call up first. You can't get up without a fob. You need to wait." The guard's face was impassive and he seemed to delight in the opportunity to clock someone this evening. Todd stood at the elevators, arms folded as the guard sauntered back to his desk, lifted the receiver and dialed the law firm as slowly as possible. Once he connected he spoke low and slow. "I didn't get your name," he said to Todd.

Clenched teeth. "Todd Mosley."

The guard spoke again, then returned, slowly, to the elevator bank, swiped a card and sent Todd to the twelfth floor. "You have a good day, sir," he smirked as the doors slid closed.

Todd leaned against the wall as the car carried him up and realized how violently his hands shook. His ears burned. His throat was dry. He had no idea what he was getting into or what he wanted, or if he'd be able to keep himself from teetering over the edge.

When the elevator opened he faced the glass double-doors of Sweeney, Rothschild and Baptiste. Just on the other side was a tall and handsome Black man. Sharply dressed with a fresh cut and a five o'clock shadow neatly shaped. He held open the door for Todd. "Mr. Mosley?"

Todd swallowed and stepped towards him. They shook. "I was looking for Langley Baptiste."

"You just missed him. I was actually right behind him. Is this about a case?"

"Yes. An old one he worked on a long time ago."

The man observed him for a bit. He immediately picked up on Todd's desperation and was compelled to help. "I'm Sidney Baptiste. I'm an attorney here, too, along with my dad."

Todd's eyebrow arched. "You're Langley's son?"

"Yes. I have a few minutes if you wanna talk."

Minutes later Todd guzzled down a bottle of water in the firm's main conference room overlooking M Street. Sidney suspected he needed something stronger, but it was all he could offer. "You can start whenever you're ready."

"I'm sorry, I know you were leaving—"

"It's okay. This is what we do. If this is about a case, even if it's an old one, then I'm working for you."

Todd took a deep breath. "Almost thirty years ago, this firm defended Anthony 'Ant' Mosley. Back when it was just Sweeney and Rothschild."

"Ant Mosley," Sidney mused. "I think I might remember that. I was a kid but it was big news back in the day. You two related?"

"Doug Sweeney was the lead attorney but Langley was on the defense team," Todd went on. Sidney nodded, familiar with the background. "And he was the only Black attorney, which allowed him to, for lack of a better word, *endear* himself to Anthony's family, including all of his girlfriends and children. He was the only one, I'm told, who seemed invested in Anthony as a person and not just a case. Did you know that?"

"My father has mentioned in the past how he came to be valued here and why he became a partner and it's exactly that. He has the ability to relate in a way the rest of these guys can't."

Todd chuckled spitefully. "Relate."

"Is Anthony your father?"

Todd shook his head, the sting of tears in his eyes. "He's not. But that's what my mother told me. If she were still alive I'd be talking to her right now instead of you. I needed Anthony. I needed him to be my father. When you're a kid, your dad is everything. He's a hero, no matter what he did. And with each year that went by, he wanted me less and less. I've gone my entire life trying to reconcile this need I had for him to be in my life with the fact he was basically a kingpin. I felt guilty about it, I've avoided drugs my entire life because of it. Through it all I still wanted my dad. But it turns out Anthony's not my dad. My dad is actually a wealthy, successful criminal attorney."

Sidney sat back in his chair, regarding Todd carefully, trying not to react too strongly. If what Todd suggested was anywhere near true, surely the proof was physical.

"I'm starting to see the resemblance," Todd said. "Don't you?"

Certainly not in the eyes. Todd's eyes were steel, gray mixed with blue, not brown like Sidney's, and were differently shaped. But Todd's jawline was a Baptiste jawline. The shape of his nose, that strong, masculine nose, was similar to Sidney's. Not to mention his statuesque, athletic physique. His height. The shoulders. It was all enhanced by Todd's obvious weight training but Baptiste men had large, sturdy frames. Sidney's hand covered his mouth as he realized what this must have meant about Todd's mother. This man before him, this person who likely shared his DNA, was also likely biracial. Sidney couldn't be certain to what extent his mother would forgive an affair, but an affair with a white woman who also bore a child . . . The thought of how Monica would react if she knew nearly made him physically sick.

"No disrespect, but was your mother—"

"Yes. She was white," Todd told him. "Look, I didn't come here because I want anything from you or your family. I wanna look him in the eye so he can confirm it."

"WHAT I LOVE ABOUT us is, as people, we get to create ourselves. We don't have to let fate or genes or our circumstances tell us who we are. We create ourselves with how we dress, obviously, how we cut our hair. How we speak, the friends we choose. We also do it with our surroundings." William turned the award in his hand. It was a hollowed glass cube with a simple geometric shape cut from each side, balanced on one corner so it appeared to float against its small base. "Everyone isn't a photographer or a writer or artist so, for a lot of us, the way we outfit our spaces is our only creative outlet. That's why I do what I do. I believe each one of us should have the opportunity to create who we are."

William looked out across the ballroom. He hadn't written or practiced a speech but he'd jotted down talking points a few days ago. The words came easily. He only stumbled when he considered this had been set in motion ten years ago in another ballroom. Sidney and Cintra's wedding reception.

As the dutiful best man he'd maintained his composure for the entire ceremony. He presented the bride's ring on cue and held his peace when they were invited to offer objections to the union. He even offered Cintra an encouraging smile when their eyes met. "Marry him," he'd told her moments earlier in her bridal suite when she seemed unsure. "All he wants is to be with you."

He'd decided by then he was done with them, the entire Baptiste clan. It was time for him to move on with his own life, to try and create his own studio. He would smile through this wedding and reception before fading away afterwards, as much as he possibly could.

Then Langley cornered him. He joined William at a table, big, handsome and, at the time, fifty-five. A glass of gin hadn't left his hand from the start of the reception so he was drunk. Fully in control, never the kind to make a scene, but more relaxed and confident than usual. "Took him long enough, didn't it?" he remarked, gazing across the St. Regis Roof Ballroom. Sidney spun and dipped his new wife as the band played a rendition of Stevie Wonder's "As." Cintra was still in her full wedding gown and Sidney could have been a prince. They were breathtaking.

"Thirty is a fine age to get married," William offered. Defending Sidney was his natural instinct with Langley.

"Well, between you and me, I had my concerns. He spent an awful lot of time with you when you were younger. I always wondered, *where are the girlfriends?* I wonder the same about you sometimes, William." Before William could protest, Langley told him, "But you're not my son. So it doesn't really matter, does it?"

"I guess it doesn't."

The look Langley gave him was one of complete awareness if not approval. Nothing more needed to be said on the subject. "Be that as it may, I've considered you one, and you know I have a great admiration for your ambition. You've always been a focused young man."

"I really appreciate that, Langley."

"So I understand you want to set out on your own, to start your own firm."

William nodded, although he wasn't sure what Langley was getting at or if this was the proper time.

"Monica speaks highly of your talent and we both agree you should have your own space, your own imprint back in DC. I would like to make you an offer."

Langley allowed the words to hang dramatically. William shifted in his seat, wondering if it was a joke. Here he was, determined to get as far away from this family as possible and Langley, out of the blue, was offering to make his second most important dream come true. He swallowed. "What kind of offer?"

"I want to help you get started, invest in your idea."

William shook his head. "Langley, no, you don't have to do that. Your family has already done so much for me. I could never ask you—"

"You don't have to ask, William." Langley smiled. Upon

recollection, there was nothing comforting in that smile. His teeth were perfectly straight and white, his eyes slick with intoxication or something more sinister. "When you do what I do for a living, working on behalf of people many would consider scum, you try to find ways to give back. To help people who can't necessarily help themselves. It helps ease the conscience a bit."

"I have plenty of money saved up," William said, measuring his breathing so his heartbeat didn't shake his voice. He wanted that money, could practically taste it. But he had to decline as fiercely as he could. Langley's offer—his respect—could dissolve if he gave in too quickly. "This is something I have to do on my own."

"Having investors is perfectly normal."

"You're right, but I was waiting for the right time to put together a plan and present something to approach them myself."

"You don't need to do any of that." Langley took a swig of gin and retrieved his wallet from his inside jacket pocket. "When the time comes, you let me know how much you need. Whatever that number is, I'll give it to you. You want a huge space, a staff, marketing resources. You don't wanna keep operating as a one man show, do you? Of course you don't. You wanna compete like a boss. Monica and I are connected; imagine the business we can send you." He reached into his wallet and pulled out a small photo that he slid across the table to William. "But I need you to do something for me."

There it was. The Catch. William didn't recognize the guy in the photo. He was handsome and young with grayish-blue eyes, clearly biracial. "Who is this?"

"Some time ago, long before I became partner, I had a client. Major drug dealer in DC. Anthony Mosley. Such a big loss. He went in for life. That's his kid. Todd."

"What does this have to do with me?"

"His mother, the only parent he has, is dying. Non-Hodgkin lymphoma. I always felt I could've done more for Ant since we didn't win the case. I've been helping take care of the boy, sending money to his mother, helping with her treatments. But it looks like I can't save her either. Todd needs someone in his life to help him transition into adulthood. I can't have him lost in the world because of how I failed his father and, now, his mother. You understand?"

"Wait. You're trusting me to do this? Why me?"

"Why not? Did I not step in for you all these years when you needed a role model? A mentor? Why not pay it forward? Be an example for another young man who has his entire future before him. I'll pay for whatever he needs, whether it's school or a place to live. But I can't be a presence for him. I'm the man who couldn't keep his father out of prison. I can't have him looking at me as someone who destroyed his family. William, you do this for me and I promise you, you'll never want for another thing in your life."

It didn't feel right. It sounded so unselfish, so altruistic, but the undercurrent in Langley's voice, the look in his intoxicated eyes betrayed it all. William nearly handed the picture back over to him but Langley declined. "You keep it. I want the two of you to become friends. *Close* friends. I need him to trust you."

William made his decision that night. It would help him cope with the loss of Sidney, all of this new responsibility. He could throw himself into his work and create a friendship with this young man, Todd Mosley. He told himself it would be so easy. And it was. He observed Todd's routine from a distance, discovered he was sneaking into bars to drink and befriended him, steering him as much as possible away from the alcohol, teaching him how to shoot pool, offering advice and a shoulder when Renee finally succumbed to her illness.

Langley would soon suggest, then enforce, that Todd was better off going to school out of state. Langley didn't elaborate but it didn't take long for William to fill in the blanks. It made William sick. So much guilt followed, then the weight gain, the smoking . . .

Presently, William recovered and found his words again.

No one appeared to notice they had momentarily failed him. Yvonne was smiling. Julian watched him with a barely concealed longing. Everyone in the room was proud of him and impressed by him, but as William closed his speech and stepped away from the podium, he considered dropping the award in the nearest trash can.

"I'M GETTING ON A plane tomorrow. I was hoping to see him and find some kind of . . . I don't know. I just need some answers. Some peace. It's bigger than knowing who my father is," Todd explained to Sidney.

"I don't think you have motives but if we're gonna go down this road we can't just take Anthony's word for it."

"Then why not Langley's word? If I'm standing in front of him, right in his face, he can't deny me. If he defended Anthony he had the opportunity. And my mother . . ." Todd shook his head. "Anthony said the reason he didn't mention it before is because he didn't want to disrespect her. It was on the tip of his tongue the last time I saw him but he couldn't bring himself to say it. He knew how much she meant to me, that she was all I had. He's kept it to himself this entire time. You want me to take a DNA test, then I'll do it. But only after I've talked to Langley."

Sidney knew he was kidding himself. Of course Todd was Langley's. What other explanation could there be? "I am so sorry," he told him, coming over to Todd's side of the conference table, his mind racing with the possibility of having an actual brother. He calculated at least a ten year age difference between them. What if he'd been able to confide to Todd all the uncertainty he had growing up as Langley's son? He imagined, if Todd had also gone through it, it wouldn't have been as difficult.

Todd looked up at him, furious and defeated, unsure if he could trust him.

"I honestly had no idea," Sidney assured him, his own eyes

becoming moist. "But I'll do anything in my power to make this right for you."

Todd finally stood and took his hand. Sidney pulled him into a brief hug. Todd managed a smile before a darkness crossed his face. As he pulled back, Sidney followed his gaze to the portraits along the wall. They were oversized, so detailed they appeared to be photographs but the longer Todd stared the more he realized they were paintings. The men in each one sat erect, stately and grand like presidents. "Who is that?" he asked Sidney.

"Those are the partner portraits. The last one is Langley, of course. I assumed you knew—"

"I've been sitting here this entire time and it was staring me in the face." A dormant rage uncoiled from the pit of Todd's stomach and coursed through his body. "I've seen Langley before. I didn't meet him, but we were in the same room."

"Are you sure?"

"I'm positive. William had a surprise party—"

"William?"

"My friend William—"

"*William Kendall?*"

"Yes."

"William's a friend of the family," Sidney said carefully. "He's my best friend, actually. I've known him since I was seventeen." None of that mattered to Todd, who was fuming. "You don't think William is involved in this, do you?"

"He has to be. He came out of nowhere ten years ago, right when my mom was dying. It was like he dropped out of the sky, *right on time.* He's spent the last few years trying to convince me I didn't need to come back here, that I didn't need to visit Anthony. Coincidences like that just don't happen."

"Ten years ago?" Sidney asked. "Same year I got married."

"When I told William I was back he sounded like I'd inconvenienced him. He doesn't want me here. He knew I'd figure it out."

"Where have you been all this time?"

"LA. All William's idea, of course."

"And possibly my father's. You share the same last name with a DC legend and you resemble the lawyer who defended him in one of the biggest cases of the eighties. Of course he'd want you gone." Sidney was more furious with William than Langley. He returned to the same detail. "Ten years and he didn't say a word to me."

"Are the two of you close?" Todd asked him.

"You have no idea."

"Why would he lie to so many people? Langley, I understand. But what's in it for William?"

Sidney sat once more, putting his face in his hands. "I have my suspicions."

"Do you mind if I use your restroom?"

"To the right of reception," Sidney gestured, barely facing him now. He was too consumed with what he now knew about the two most important men in his life. He tried to recall a moment in the last ten years that could've prepared him for this. A clue, a slip of the tongue, a mysterious glance across a dinner party. But there was nothing. William had maintained a poker face this entire time, even as he claimed to be so entitled to Sidney's honesty.

It occurred to him William was more like Langley than he would ever be.

He wasn't sure how many minutes passed before he realized Todd was taking a while in the bathroom and after several more that Todd definitely wasn't returning.

Sidney went to grab his keys.

forty.

"THIS THING IS SHARP," Julian remarked, turning the award in his hands. "Clearly they aren't worried about it killing someone." He didn't mention it was also rather ugly, ironic considering the ideals it was meant to represent.

William gently took it from him and placed it in the center of the table. "I'll be sure to keep it away from the *zero* children who visit my home on a regular basis."

"Maybe you should adopt some," Yvonne remarked.

"I'll just send them to hang out with you anyway," William shot back.

"You promise?"

They both smiled at each other.

"So officially," Julian told him, "I need to jet."

"I was just about to let you go," William told him.

"Let me?"

"Well, I need to start working the room, you know how it is." A chuckle. "You must have been bored out of your mind. Maybe even a little pissed with me?"

"I stayed for the speech. And the cheesecake. And the mousse. And the sorbet flight."

"So we're okay?"

Julian stood, grabbing his jacket from the back of the chair. "We're gonna have to be."

William rose as well. "Julian, I asked you to come back inside because I needed a friend here. I appreciate you staying. But we haven't finished our conversation."

Julian was flippant. "So you can tell me everything you think is wrong with me? Do it now. I can take it."

"There isn't a thing wrong with you."

"So what makes this other dude so perfect?"

William placed a hand on Julian's shoulder. "Like I said, we can talk about it another time."

"Fine. I have questions." He glanced past him at Yvonne. "It was nice to finally meet you, Ms. Kendall."

She smiled as much as she could. "It was nice meeting you too, baby."

Julian made his way around the banquet tables and disappeared through the ballroom's double doors. Although their conversation didn't turn out the way Julian wanted, William was happy for him. It seemed like such a burden for Julian to carry for so long and William knew getting it off his chest would help him grow in all the ways he needed.

His phone vibrated in his pocket. He'd ignored calls all day, but now things were wrapping up and he could accept a few, especially this one. "Hey, Sidney—"

"Are you still at the Omni?"

"Yes, but I already gave my speech. If you're planning on being here it's too late."

"That's not why I'm calling you. I'm gonna ask you something and you better tell me the truth."

William realized Sidney was upset. "Okay, I will."

"Who is Todd Mosley to me?"

"Sidney . . ."

"Who is he?" When William didn't respond Sidney asked point-blank "Is he Langley's son?"

"There's so much you don't know."

"Answer my question!"

William ended the call and stuffed his phone back into his pocket, not because he was afraid to answer. Todd was now in the ballroom, barrelling towards him with Julian trailing behind trying to stop him.

Todd was larger in his rage. He usually managed to shrink himself—how he averted his eyes, his pronounced lack of confidence, how he nearly never raised his voice. Now the guests in the ballroom were silenced, those nearby immediately parting to make way for his mass. William held up his hands, ready to explain, but Todd grabbed a fistful of his shirt and tie and screamed in his face—"You knew Anthony wasn't my father!"

William couldn't hear Yvonne shouting for Todd to take his hands off her son, Julian begging Todd to release him or the scattered, nebulous comments to call security. All he heard was his own heart thudding in his ears. "Todd, listen—"

"You knew this entire time!" Todd roared. He didn't sound like himself. "Langley Baptiste is my father, isn't he? Say it!"

"Yes he is."

Todd let him go, tried to recover his breath. Julian grabbed his hand but he shook him off. "How long have you known? It was from the day you met me, wasn't it?"

William took a moment to glance around the ballroom, at the guests staring with their hands at their chests. Even without knowing the full context they had to know William wasn't exactly the victim here. He prepared himself for the stories that would circulate within his professional circles, how he would answer for being accused of something so unthinkable just after accepting an award he'd waited his entire career for.

"No, but I figured it out eventually. Todd, I didn't realize it would be like this—"

"Be like what?"

"That we'd become this close."

"You thought you and Langley were gonna ship me off to California and you wouldn't have to worry about me again. Is that it? You had so many opportunities to come clean but you didn't say a word. Not even when I was laid up in a hospital room with stitches and bandages all over my face after being pushed through a glass door! Did you feel any guilt then, William?"

"What is he talking about?" Yvonne demanded of her son.

"What is this about Langley?"

Todd's eyes burned. "You had Anthony take me off his list, didn't you? You didn't want me visiting him in prison because you didn't want me finding out—"

"Langley threatened me—"

"With what? What could he possibly threaten you with that was worth you lying to me for a decade? Our entire friendship is because of *him?* Do you realize how sick that is?"

"I know how this looks, but I wanted to tell you. So many times."

"You were the only person I had and you knew what I went through with my father, with Deacon. Don't you think I at least have a right to know who I am, William?"

"I didn't set this in motion, it was your controlling, philandering, homophobic father—"

Todd silenced him with a left hook, directly in the jaw. It sent William flying back into the table.

He slid across and landed on the other side, bringing the tablecloth and dinnerware along with a crash.

Todd stared at his hand, not believing what he'd done. It was as if he'd balled all of his power and anger in his fist before slamming it into William's face. He nearly collapsed from regret.

Julian rushed to William. As he helped him up, he seemed to be searching for something. He asked William repeatedly if he was okay, if he'd landed on it. "The trophy!"

Someone grabbed Todd from behind.

William massaged his jaw. He assured Julian he was fine. Yvonne held the trophy in her hands, her mouth agape.

"Come with me." It was Sidney, now in front of Todd, rushing him from the ballroom.

"I hit him."

"He'll be fine," Sidney offered with barely disguised contempt.

Outside Todd was shaking. They were at the taxi stand. Sidney insisted on getting him out of there. "I'll deal with William. You go home."

"Please make sure I didn't hurt him," Todd insisted.

Sidney observed him, ready to argue the point, then realized Todd wasn't the spiteful sort and nodded solemnly. "Fine."

Todd slid into the back of a waiting cab and Sidney handed him his card. "Call me as soon as you get to where you're staying. Call me anytime, for anything."

"Okay."

Sidney shut the door and watched the taxi pull off. He was sore for Todd and missed him instantly. He had questions. He wanted to know him.

He had a brother now.

forty-one.

LINC WAS AT WILLIAM'S door two weeks later. "I wanted to deliver this personally."

William let him in, taking the book from Linc's hands. William was in shorts and a t-shirt, damp from running on the treadmill in his building's fitness center. Linc thought he looked great, considering all that had happened. The swelling on his face from Todd's punch had completely healed.

"Thank you," William said, holding the book out in front of him. It was wide, a coffee table book. Todd was on the cover, facing the camera directly with romantic eyes and full lips. The title of the book was *Gorgeous*.

"I figured you might have questions about what I wrote about you," Linc began.

William placed the book on his breakfast bar, then grabbed two water bottles from the refrigerator. He took a healthy gulp from one while Linc sipped from the other. "I can't imagine it's at all flattering. Not after what Mel told me."

Linc opened it to William's page. *The Architect.* "Mel has his reasons, but motives aside, he's no fool. I picked up on something a while ago when it comes to you. You're manipulative. I know that because I am, too."

William didn't respond.

Linc read from his own caption. "'The Architect is a magician. He creates worlds from nothing, leads us down paths constructed from expensive materials. He surrounds you with beauty and comfort. You always feel at home with him.' There's more but you get the idea."

"It's not exactly a lie."

"I was so ready to get in your ass after I found out what you did to Todd. I still am but I don't have a leg to stand on. Have you talked to him?"

"I have. I just listened. There's no repairing that. I think he misses you, though. He asked about you."

"He asked *you* about *me?*"

"He already knew what he had to say to me. It was easy for him because he hates me now. He just hasn't sorted out his feelings for you. You frustrate him, but he loves you."

Linc considered this for a bit, then, "I don't deserve him."

"At least you have a chance." William flipped through the rest of the book. There was a photo of Mel at one of his shows, his hair full and big, microphone stand gripped firmly in two hands. *The Voice*. Mel, despite his methods, was right about so many things.

"He's in Atlanta, in case you were wondering," Linc offered. "I didn't find out until after he left. My girl Bree told me. He's working on an album."

"Good for him. It's about time."

"Not his own. He's writing, playing instruments. He doesn't want to be in the front. He's not ready for the scrutiny. But there's more than one way to be an artist, more than one way to tell your story. How are you?"

William took a stool at the bar, put his face in his hands. "In spite of everything I might still make the AD100. No one at Conde Nast cares about the so-called scandal or the part I played in it. But people here in DC, they have a lot to say about the Baptistes. Business-wise, we haven't suffered. Socially? Another story." William thought about the call he'd received from Travis. Chatter somehow made its way to him and he seemed all too satisfied to go on about how disappointed he was in William. *You kept Todd's paternity a secret William . . .*

Sidney's turn was the most painful but William accepted it.

There was so much Sidney needed to make sense of, telling William to go fuck himself seemed the most efficient way for him to sort everything else out. He had a divorce to worry about, the arrival of an adult sibling, a father who had lied to his mother for nearly thirty years.

Any chance of reuniting with Sidney was comedy at this point.

"But how are *you*, William? I'm not asking what everyone's saying about you or how it might have affected your clients. I want to know if it was worth it, if you regret anything."

"Of course I do."

"I've been thinking of Todd *a lot*. I haven't tried to call him, I don't think I'd be helping. I'm leaving him alone because it's what I need to do. That's what I learned."

"I was ambitious. I always overdo things," William said quietly. "And I fucked up. The minute I realized I cared about Todd I needed to tell him the truth." He didn't admit to Linc that it brought him, someone who never cried for any reason, to absolute tears. He wasn't sure it would go far enough to convince Linc that his sorrow gutted him. "Now I have to live with that."

forty-two.

TODD GOT THE CALL from Cole as summer winded down. He sat at the edge of a rooftop pool, his feet dangling in cool, pale blue water. A textbook and his laptop were nearby. Dusk gradually settled over Tribeca.

"Deacon knows the order ran out but he still doesn't think it's right to contact you himself," Cole said. "You want me to read what he has to say?"

Todd thought on it for a bit before responding with his typical leniency. "Go ahead."

"'Todd, I'm not asking for your forgiveness. I just hope you're doing okay. I hope you've found peace, that you can trust people again. Hurting you is my biggest regret. You're a good man. You're intelligent, you're sweet and you deserve to be loved by someone who respects you and has your back. You could have filed charges on me back then but you didn't. I'm grateful for that. I'm clean now and I've been seeing someone about my anger. There's nothing I can say to excuse what I did, but I understand what I had in you and I don't deserve the enormous pass you've given me. Take care.'"

Todd had been holding his breath the entire time and exhaled once Cole was done.

He hated himself after punching William. He thought he was more principled about violence, that if it wasn't to defend himself then it was just recklessness. Dr. Walker had warned him about this, that he'd be pushed and pushed until he broke, that it would be at the worst time and he'd act completely out of character. He just never imagined he'd hit someone. To Todd, it made him no better than Deacon, so he couldn't be entirely dismissive of his words. "I'm not sure what to say to that."

"You don't have to say anything. I wouldn't if I were you," Cole bristled. "He begged me to do this. When I found out what happened I wanted to kill him myself. But he's right, he's a piece of shit who deserves nothing from you. Other than that, how's school?"

"I'm getting back into the groove. It's tough but I like it."

"So you're good, right? You're finally in New York. I knew you'd end up there one way or another."

The loft inside was Sidney's. It was where he lived before returning to DC. Now he was back in New York and invited Todd to come with him. It was only fifteen minutes from NYU Steinhardt, where Todd pursued his Doctor of Physical Therapy degree. "I am," Todd assured Cole. "Everything is great."

"So no guys?"

It always came back to men with Cole. "They're a distraction," Todd said firmly, then laughed. It was his mantra now. "I have to finish school." Besides, he was getting to know Sidney. He realized Sidney was the root he'd needed all this time, someone who could represent a sense of home and family, things Todd had subconsciously sought in Linc.

He'd even explained it to Linc days earlier.

It was the first time they'd talked since DC. Todd was the one to make the call, his curiosity and longing getting the better of him. Linc mentioned he was headed to South Africa that week, living up to his promise to travel and immerse himself in culture. Before it was Costa Rica, a way for him to be close to Todd without seeing him. "I thought of you the entire time, boy." Todd could hear him smiling through the phone. "And I wasn't anywhere near San Rafael."

They nearly slipped into their playful, romantic rhythm but Todd changed the subject to Sidney and school. He explained things had settled into the kind of normal he needed since hiding from Deacon. Linc remarked on the lightness and enthusiasm in Todd's voice, he never sounded more confident. The call ended without Linc so much as suggesting they could see each other when he was back in the country. Todd resisted the urge as well. For now, he needed to focus.

He'd run into Linc soon enough.

It was Cintra who first suggested the separation, but it evolved into a divorce. She realized after Sidney's blow-up with William and Langley she'd never get him back, and she was content with that, right up until Sidney explained the real reasons the marriage had to end.

He left William out of it, not to spare him but only since he knew what he had to say so far would be an avalanche for her. He opened up about the parties, the hotel suite, feelings he'd suppressed during the marriage. She slapped him twice and ordered him out of the house.

They agreed to power through the divorce as quickly as the law permitted. All she wanted was the house. She wasn't interested in being a confidante or helping him reconcile his sexuality with the last ten years. She wanted it to be over, reiterating as often as possible that her time was wasted. Cintra wasn't spiteful, merely exhausted.

Presently, he made his way to the pool with a beer in hand as Todd finished his call with Cole.

"I don't wanna disturb you," Sidney began, "but I talked to Langley earlier. He's ready to sit down with you, if you're up to it."

Todd stared at him blankly before breaking into a smirk. "Are you kidding me?"

"My mother's making him do it. She's been breaking him down over the past few weeks. I can hear it in his voice. He's shook."

"He already confirmed I'm his son. What else is there for us to talk about?"

"My parents have been married for a long time and while she's not completely sure what she wants to do right now, she'll consider staying if he tries to build a relationship with you."

"But what if I don't want it?"

"She wants him to try."

"Are you asking *me* to try?"

Sidney shook his head. "I'm telling you what to expect. He will contact you. He might show up here. He knows he has very little time to become a completely different man and he's desperate."

"I'm not ready to forgive him, much less accept him into my life. Same goes for William."

"Consider this," Sidney offered, "I kept something from my wife, too."

"That's completely different, Sidney."

"It impacts them the same. One way or another, we were all dishonest here. There are things my wife *still* doesn't know. At some point I need to reckon with that when it comes to Langley. I can't stay on this high horse for long. I'm not asking you to try, but I'd be a hypocrite if I didn't at least suggest it."

"I hear you."

Sidney took a chair nearby and cracked the tab. "So what time does your friend get here?"

JULIAN WAS IN TOWN that weekend for his father's retirement party and Sidney's loft was his first stop. He frowned when Todd opened the door. "This again," he groaned, gesturing to Todd's hair, which again grew thick and curly. He also hadn't shaved his beard since being in DC.

"Who do I have to look cute for?" Todd asked as they embraced.

"*Yourself,*" Julian shot back. "Always do it for yourself."

Todd didn't want to admit he was a distraction in his classes for some folks, even instructors. He thought letting himself go a bit would mitigate it. It never did, really.

It also didn't help being on the cover of Linc's book. There was almost no chance anyone from school would make the connection but, every now and then on the subway or walking through Manhattan, he'd get that look from another guy who *must have* owned it or committed the image to memory.

"I'll keep that in mind," he told Julian. They made their way to the kitchen, where Julian unloaded wine and steaks from his bags. Sidney eventually joined them and Todd realized this was their first formal meeting. The incident in the Omni ballroom didn't allow for such pleasantries.

After dinner, Todd took Julian to the roof and reminded him of their agreement. "Men are a distraction."

"Your brother is fly, though," Julian countered. They'd hit it off immediately, especially when the conversation turned to music. Sidney and Julian were nearly in sync. Their enthusiasm for each other reached fever pitch when they realized they were both Alphas.

"He's going through a divorce," Todd explained. "He's not ready for any of this."

Julian chuckled. "I'm just checking him out, making a new friend. That's it. Besides, aren't you glad I'm over William?"

Todd shrugged. "It's your life."

Julian's face fell serious. "I get it. You're still upset with him and you should be. But I don't think he has anyone right now, Todd. I didn't realize William was so alone."

"I'm not feeling very forgiving yet."

"Except when it comes to Linc." Julian said. His tone indicated no chance of things getting better between them. "You've explained it so many times and I still don't get it."

Todd rested his elbows on the ledge and looked out over the city. It was dense and boisterous and glowing with activity. "I never said I forgave him, I just . . . God, I miss him. But I don't need him. I once thought I did. So, progress?"

Julian patted his back. In spite of Todd's lingering bitterness, he sounded free, which was all that mattered. Julian made his way inside while Todd stayed behind a bit longer. The smile hadn't left his face. He found that smiling came so much easier these days, even when he faced his own reflection. The scars hadn't haunted him for months. Nothing held him back now.

He rushed inside once he realized Julian was now alone with Sidney.

November 12, 2016 - 11:22am
January 31, 2025 - 10:51am

about the author

Renaldo Christopher is a native of Washington, DC. Although he has occasionally maintained a blog and freelanced for online publications, his main interest has always been stories chronicling love and friendship between Black Men. He has moonlighted as a bartender for seven years and makes a mean Sidecar.

www.ingramcontent.com/pod-product-compliance
Lightning Source LLC
Chambersburg PA
CBHW020132310726

48970CB00006B/1828